2004 Jasper G. and Minnie Stevens Literary Prize Winner

2005 Oregon Book Award Winner

2006 Women Writing the West Willa Literary Award Winner

2006 Western Writers of America Spur Award Finalist

2006 Washington Reads Spring List Selection

A Heart for Any Fate

A Heart for Any Fate

Westward to Oregon, 1845

Linda Crew

ISBN13: 978-1-932010-26-8

Second printing.

Ooligan Press
Department of English
Portland State University
P.O. Box 751
Portland, OR 97207-0751
www.ooliganpress.pdx.edu

Book design: Kari Smit
Cover design: Rachel S. Tobie

Set in ITC New Baskerville Std and Bodoni Std.

Printed in the United States of America.

For additional educational materials, see our website.

For Herb, with love and thanks:

For first suggesting the exploration of this particular story.

For driving the entire Oregon Trail with me.

For making an Eden of our home here at trail's end.

Let us then, be up and doing,

With a heart for any fate,

Still achieving, still pursuing,

Learn to labor and to wait.

From "A Psalm of Life," 1839
Henry Wadsworth Longfellow

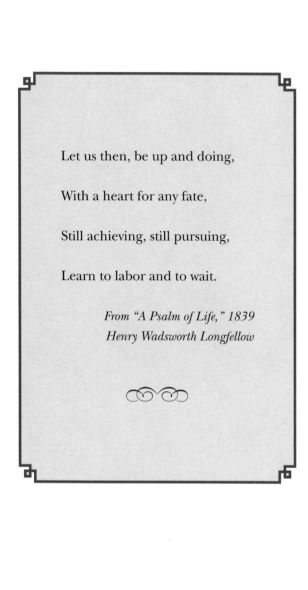

FOREWORD

WHO CAN DEFINITIVELY SAY WHY A NATION

does something? The actions and motivations of a nation are the thousands of actions and motivations of its individual people. There are a lot of actions and a lot of motivations when we're talking about a population of half a million.

That's the number of people, more or less, who traveled west on the Emigrant Trail in the 1840s, '50s, and '60s. Why these emigrants—families with grannies and infants in their wagons, groups of young single men hired on to help drive a team, folks starting out for the first time and folks starting over for the fifth time—braved more than two thousand miles of rough terrain is a complex question. Many of the pioneers would no doubt have given a straightforward answer: they sought good farmland and better opportunities.

But in many ways it was more subtle than that. At the time the pioneers started heading west, the Republic was fifty years old and experiencing some growing pains. The Trans-Mississippi territories were still largely unexplored (except by the Native Americans, of course). The continent of North America included British, Mexican, Texan, and Indian lands, as well as the United States of America; the staggering abundance of its gifts was just beginning to be recognized. The Monroe Doctrine had declared the interior of North America no longer open to European colonization, and as there was a growing sense among Americans that those lands should be one sovereign nation, the best way to enforce that doctrine was by settlement.

The paradox of settlement in the United States is that although settlements arose—and some grew to be mighty cities in short order—people didn't settle in one place for long. The American populace was in an almost constant state of relocation and redefinition, some families trying three, four, or more states and territories in succession. The continent had always boasted a frontier, even when the unsettled border lay well east of the Great Lakes. The frontier had forever been the dwelling place of the unknown, where real and imagined dangers lurked in the shadows, and new possibilities for success lay bathed in glory light. In America, people could start anew. It had always been that way. It seemed, somewhere deep in the American soul, that starting the whole world from scratch was not just a choice, but a God-given right—even a solemn duty. This shared sense of American pride, along with America's exceptional status, gave rise to the belief that the Mexican territory and Indian lands were occupied by people whose time was literally up.

On top of this sense of entitlement came a host of misfortunes both large and small in the States. Repeated floods on the un-levied and un-diked Missouri and Mississippi Rivers caused devastating farm losses. There were outbreaks of disease in the swelling eastern cities where industrial development and population growth outpaced the creation of sanitation services. Catastrophic bank failures in 1837 led to an economic depression that lasted into the 1840s. Growing tension over the expansion of slavery into new states prompted fiery debates in Congress and on the street corner. It was beginning to feel, well, crowded. To many people, it seemed as if there had to be something better just over the next rise, or at the end of the trail; they needed only to pull up stakes, head west, and start over, leaving all the mess behind. This was America: people believed it would always be possible to start over.

But was nation-building a motive on the individual level? Did families uproot themselves for something so abstract? Probably not. But it's quite possible that the pervasive atmosphere of nation-building made those personal upheavals seem more possible, if only subconsciously. And it certainly gilded personal ambitions with a glow of moral superiority. Starting over felt like the right thing to do, on so many levels.

How did they know what they would find at the end of the trail? How did they know, when they decided to start anew, that there was actually something good waiting for them? In the early nineteenth century, the plains and the Rocky Mountain West had been traveled by trappers and traders, the durable mountain men and buffalo hunters who scouted out trails and passes. Some explorers started on the West coast and worked their way inland, battling their way upriver like salmon. By traveling up the Columbia River from its outlet on the Pacific, explorers came to know the "Oregon Country." Before long, missionaries sent word back east of the fertile and tree-thick land where wheat could grow as tall as a man. There was a paradise of land: empty (except for the Native Americans), untouched (except by the Native Americans), just waiting for stout-hearted white American pioneers to claim it. Timber, farmland, abundant water, plentiful fish and game, a mild climate—if you could just get there, it was a new Garden of Eden.

The first wave of emigrants, approximately one thousand pioneers, left for Oregon in 1843. Who can say whether they were running away from hard luck or running toward a bright promise? Probably for most pioneers it was a combination of the two. Perhaps it was just as well that they had almost no practical idea of what their migration would cost them. Within a few years there would be emigrant guidebooks and trail narratives in plenty; some of these were filled with useful information, some riddled with errant nonsense; but the first waves of pioneers were setting out in almost complete ignorance of what the overland journey had in store for them.

It was never a single road—it was never really a road at all. Today's traveler pictures some old-timey version of an interstate highway, with all the wagons following one behind the other in an orderly line. In truth, it was far from that. Wagon teams spread out laterally like a buffalo herd on the move, grazing cattle on a wide front, following the contours of the land and roughly paralleling the courses of the rivers that led west—the Missouri, the Platte. It wasn't until the terrain grew more rugged and uncertain, and precision through the passes more critical, that the spread-out and multi-tracked wagon trains braided together into something like a single file. In some places where traffic followed the same wheel tracks day after day, month after month, year after year, the land was permanently scarred. Today, these scars are still visible in places such as the "Oregon Trail Ruts" near Guernsey, Wyoming, a site where the constant passage of iron-clad wheels eroded a ditch five feet deep into the limestone rock. There are many remnants of the trail, like faded ink drawing a line across the West.

Most of the wagons were pulled by teams of oxen, which were docile but slow—two miles per hour was their average speed. Some people preferred mules, which were a bit faster but cantankerous and much harder to manage. Whether powered by oxen or mules, the wagon trains seldom made more than fifteen miles a day. To complete a journey of two thousand miles that slowly, with livestock that needed water and grazing along the way, required careful timing. Start too soon in the spring and there wasn't enough grass; start too late and reach the hardest part of the journey—the mountains—as the snows were starting to fall. Often there were thousands of pioneers biding their time at the "jumping-off" towns: Independence or Saint Joseph, Missouri; Council Bluffs, Iowa; and Fort Smith, Arkansas. They were waiting for the time to be just right, until the wagon train captain judged the time had come. Then, amid the bellowing of cattle, the *yip-yip* and *gee-haw* of the ox handlers, the rumble of iron-rimmed wheels, the shrieking of children, and a few rambunctious and celebratory gunshots, the wagons would begin the slow surge westward.

In addition to careful timing, a journey that long required careful packing. Those covered wagons weren't filled with just *pioneers*. Far from it. The emigrant wagon was filled with everything those pioneers would need on the trail, and at the trail's end: flour, bacon, knitting and sewing needles, plow blades, baking soda, ammunition, a book or two (usually including a Bible), clothing, spare wagon wheels, dried beans, medicines, extra canvas, candles, fish hooks, buckets, rifles, spare oxen shoes, cooking pots, tents, saw blades, pillows, knives, matches, chamber pots, butter churns, family heirlooms, nails, tools, stoves, rope, bedding, seeds, blacksmithing equipment, a musical instrument or two—and in whatever inches of extra space were left rode the children too young to walk, the sick, or the otherwise infirm. Very few emigrants actually rode to Oregon Country—most of them walked. Until 1869, when the Transcontinental Railroad was completed, this was the movement of pioneers along the Emigrant Trail: half a million people, walking across the country.

No matter how carefully each family planned and packed, however, the Emigrant Trail was potholed with unforeseen troubles. Accidents could set a family back a day or more for repairs or doctoring; at worst, an accident could mean sudden death.

A child falling from a wagon could be crushed by wagon wheels in a heartbeat. A storm-swollen river might sweep a whole wagon away during a crossing. Lightning-strikes or hailstorms could extinguish a life on an otherwise dull and monotonous day. Inexperience with firearms or itchy trigger fingers led to countless gunshot wounds and deaths. Besides accidents there were diseases, chiefly cholera and typhoid fever, stalking the emigrants. Men who had once seemed invincible toppled with exhaustion. Women died in childbirth. Children were snuffed out by measles or whooping cough. Ten percent of the emigrants perished along the way, most of them buried without markers.

Daily life on the trail was utter monotony when it wasn't punctuated by the high dramas of life and death. Pioneers rose with the sun, made and ate breakfast, and prepared the midday meal. If the family had a milking cow, she would be milked and the cream set in the wagon to churn—a day's jostling over the rough terrain guaranteed butter by nightfall. Trail food consisted of beans and bacon, biscuits (until the flour or the baking powder ran out), and wild game, chiefly buffalo. It was an unvarying diet, and the landscape across the wide stretch of the prairie presented travelers with the same unvarying scenery day after day. Notable landmarks became cause for celebration, as proof that progress had actually been made. At the end of the day, wagons formed a circle as in an improvised corral for the livestock. There was water to be carried, and fuel to be found (wood if possible, and if not, dried buffalo dung). When dinner had been eaten (more beans, more bacon) there might be some storytelling or impromptu music. Song titles such as "Wait for the Wagon," "The Girl I Left Behind Me," "Bury Me Not on the Lone Prairie," and "My Old Kentucky Home" give a glimpse of the pioneers' preoccupations. The leaders of the expedition might sit up late, discussing the health of the party, or the state of the teams, or the conditions of the trail ahead. For most of the travelers, sleep came easily after fifteen miles of walking. For others, worrying about the future kept them staring at the stars.

This was travel across the prairie—but the trip didn't end at the feet of the Rocky Mountains. The much-dreaded barrier had to be crossed, and it was a sorry party of emigrants that rushed the trip. Hastening the time spent on the plains meant denying the livestock sufficient time to fatten up, which would cause them to falter on the climb. On the other hand, those who dawdled too long on the plains became trapped by winter. Of the many tragic tales of emigrants to the West, the Donner Party stands out—caught by early snows in the pass east of Lake Tahoe, they suffered starvation and worse. Indeed, very few wagon trains made it across the Rockies unscathed. The trip was simply too dangerous, the timing too tricky, the trails and passes too newly explored. How bitter it must have been to face the hardest part of the journey at the end, with everyone so tired, and the supplies starting to run out. Countless pioneers did not live to see the far side of the mountains.

And yet, despite the hardships, the emigrant wagon trains kept rolling west.

They didn't all end up in the same place, of course. The Emigrant Trail, or Overland Trail, was actually a number of different routes, converging and splitting apart like the tributaries of a river. It would be more accurate to speak of the Overland *Trails*. Some folks were heading for Oregon Country. Others, the Mormons, for example, were mostly headed for Utah. Still others, especially after the discovery of gold, were rushing to California to make their fortunes scraping money out of the ground. After the Mexican-American War and the annexation of Texas, pioneers also streamed into the Southwest. Depending on the destination, pioneers set out on the Oregon Trail, the California Trail, the Mormon Trail, or the Santa Fe Trail, even though jumping-off places and the paths were the same for hundreds of miles. There were numerous cut-offs as the years went on.

Trackers found shortcuts that shaved many miles and days off the journey—or mistaken cut-offs that led to disaster. The forts and trading posts along the way that served as way stations and resupply depots grew and spread, attracting settlers of their own. With each passing decade the way was made smoother, the chain of supply posts tighter and more closely linked. Increasingly, no matter the destination, the pioneers were traveling through a distinctly *American* landscape: the Native Americans were being boxed into smaller and smaller territories, the Mexicans shoved southward, the British elbowed north of the 49th parallel. Wagon by wagon, America was taking hold of the land and holding on tight.

The Overland Trail in this book leads us to the Oregon Country. *A Heart for Any Fate* is a fictionalized narrative of an actual emigrant family, the Kings, of Carroll County, Missouri. They set out in five covered wagons, a family of twenty-six, spanning three generations from the patriarch Nahum King to the youngest babies, Jimmy and Charles. In a wagon train made up of dozens of other families, they left St. Joseph, Missouri, a bustling boomtown "so new and raw it still had tree stumps in the streets." The company the Kings traveled in comprised sixty-six wagons, 453 oxen, 649 loose cattle, and 172 horses and mules, for the support of 273 men, women, and children. After two thousand miles, passing through what is now Kansas, Nebraska, Wyoming, and Idaho, the remnants of this wagon train reached the journey's end, with the King family settling in what became Kings Valley in the Coast Range of Oregon. Today, the state bears the Kings' footprints throughout, but especially in the Willamette Valley and the city of Portland—much of which was once King family land. They prospered in Oregon, which, said Anna Maria King in 1846, "is an easy place to make a living. You can raise as many cattle as you please and not cost you a cent, for the grass is green the whole winter…"

Their trek to reach this green valley, however, was marred by tragedy, as were so many of these voyages on the Overland Trail. The company the Kings rode with took a chance on an unproven cut-off; what was supposed to save many miles and days of travelling turned into a major disaster. In Fort Boise, near present-day Parma, Idaho, the travellers met up with Stephen Meek, a mountain man who offered to lead them by an old trappers' trail. There had been rumors of "Indian trouble" along the main trail, and the group decided to try their luck with the Meek Cut-off. (The rumors were greatly exaggerated; in fact, during the early years of the Overland Trail, the Native Americans encountered along the way were more likely to be helpful than anything else. Most "Indian trouble" existed only in the minds of the pioneers.)

True or not, the rumors were enough to persuade the party to take the untested cut-off. The eastern reaches of Oregon are rugged and dry, and the group soon found itself desperate for water as it struggled through the unbroken wilderness. Their livestock were failing; many members of the party perished of fevers, and to make a bad situation even worse, Meek was forced to admit that he was lost. While the main body of the wagon train made a miserable camp, men on horseback rode for miles in every direction, scouting for water and a clear trail. After six weeks of punishing travel—punishing even by the standards of the Overland Trail—the group finally made it to The Dalles, on the Columbia River. The wagon train lost at least twenty-three people on its shortcut, possibly more. And even though The Dalles was an important milestone, there were still the rapids of the Columbia to face. More members of the King family died on the river, almost within sight of their new home. But the survivors settled and flourished in the green valleys, told their stories to their kids and grandkids, and saw their names listed among the first families of Oregon.

So this is a true story—sort of. Oregon native and award-winning author Linda Crew studied the documents, diaries, letters, and personal reminiscences of many Kings, and selected seventeen-year-old Lovisa King as her narrator. Stubborn, hopeful, westward-looking Lovisa tells the story of the King family's journey as it might have been. Crew changes none of the facts, but invents the most likely narrative to support them. It makes for a compelling story, told with the excitement and misgivings of a teenager who is walking through the unknown toward a very uncertain future. She's a likable narrator, and readers will be happy to walk the trail with her as their guide.

Jennifer Armstrong

THE KING FAMILY

On the Trail to Oregon, 1845

Nahum, "Pa," 61 years old
Sarepta, "Ma," 53 years old

John, 32 years old, and wife,
Susan, 26 years old
  Luther, "Little Lute," 4 years old
  Electa, "Lexie," 3 years old
  Baby Charles

Hopestill, 30 years old, and husband,
Lucius Norton, 27 years old
  Isaac, 3 years old
  Wiley, 1 year old

Stephen, 27 years old, and wife,
Anna Maria, "Annie," 23 years old

Isaac, 25 years old
Amos, 23 years old

Sarah, "Sally," 21 years old, and husband,
Rowland Chambers, 32 years old
  Margaret, "Meggie," 3 years old
  Baby James, "Jimmy"

Lovisa, 17 years old
Abigail, "Abbie," 16 years old
Lydia, 14 years old
Solomon, "Sol," 12 years old
Rhoda Ann, 10 years old

In the spring of 1845, the King family of Carroll
County, Missouri, loaded five covered wagons and set
out for Oregon.

Historical records tell us the route they chose.
We know who lived to see the so-called Promised Land,
who did not, and which sweethearts married at trail's
end.

Beyond that we must do a good deal of imagining.

But perhaps the journey went something like this...

CHAPTER 1

WEST...

The sound of a wish in a single word.

That's how it sounded to me, anyway, and although a few of us were admittedly less than enthusiastic about having been enlisted in service to our father's dream, I myself was perfectly thrilled and willing to go along.

Pa's plan? To pack up all three generations of the King family and strike out for Oregon, there to claim good land and build new homes.

Splendid!

But as for the part about me riding in Rowland's wagon, I want to say right off that it wasn't my idea, nor was I pleased with the notion.

In fact, the minute my mother let on this was Pa's intention, I jumped up from my spinning wheel and left it whirling. I liked my older sister Sally fine, but the idea of her husband ordering me along every inch of our two-thousand mile trek…Well, I marched out to the tanning shed and got right to the point.

"Pa? Ma says you're having me ride with Sally and Rowland on the trip."

"That's right." Pa lowered a rack of cowhides into the stinking vat.

I felt conscious of my older brother Amos straddling a bench in the corner, hearing this, but pretending not to, as he worked the hair off a hide with a wooden scraper.

"Pa. I'm sorry to say it, but I don't get along with Rowland."

My father turned and leveled a look at me. "And I'm not sorry to say Rowland Chambers is about as fine a son-in-law as a man could ask." His neatly trimmed white beard was speckled with hickory-bark stain. "If you can't get along, missy, I have to wonder if maybe it's something about you."

I opened my fist and started pulling apart the wad of wool I'd still been clutching. "I didn't say anything bad about him. He's just… bossy, that's all."

Pa and Amos shared a smirk.

"Folks might say the same about you," Pa pointed out.

"Well then," I said, rising to it, "is it really such a good idea to put two bossy people in the same wagon all the way to Oregon?"

Wiping his hands on his leather apron, Pa crossed his arms over his chest and leaned back, studying me. "You can count, right? We'll have five wagons. We'll have twenty-two people, counting the new babies. Think on it—more than five of us Kings leaning to the headstrong side. See how that shakes out?"

I cut my eyes at Amos. Yes, I saw: Some wagons were bound to have people at odds. But it wasn't fair! In this match, I didn't stand a chance. Between a grown man and a seventeen-year-old girl, it was clear who'd forever have the final say.

"I'd rather have you bossing me," I said, pouting. My father I was used to. My father I knew how to get around.

"Look, honey, I've done all the figuring on it and tried to divide folks up the way I think's best. Sally's going to need your help with those babies." He turned back to the hides.

"But, Pa—"

"*Lovisa.*" He waited, making sure I wasn't going to talk back. "This is how I planned it and that's that."

Well, what Pa said, went. This we all knew. To him, careful planning fell somewhere between a fine art and a religious observance, and if me riding with my brother-in-law had already been set down as part of his sacred agenda, there was absolutely no use in me standing there suffering the stench of the tanning bath one more minute. I turned on my heel and flounced out.

Do mark how I had misgivings at the very beginning. It ought to be plain I didn't go into this with any designs. My only feelings as I left the tanning shed that day back in Carroll County, Missouri, were annoyance and resignation. I'd spoken my piece, now I'd have to do my duty, minding my father as any decent daughter would.

And that's all there was to it.

I was born in the middle of a long string of brothers and sisters, and at this time I was the oldest girl still at home on the farm. I'd been named for my father's little sister: Lovisa, not to be rhymed with Theresa. Lovisa doesn't rhyme with anything, really, but try to think… *horizon. Lovisa.* In the year of this great crossing, 1845, I was young, strong, and bursting with energy. The very word—*west*—set my toes to tapping.

And that other magical name: *Oregon!* Even whispered, it seemed to have an exclamation point permanently attached. Ever since folks first made it out there over the Rockies with wagons a couple of years back and the breathless descriptions began returning by dispatch, I'd been captivated by visions of those far-off green meadows, snow-capped mountains, and cold, clear rivers. Best of all, Oregon was said to boast the biggest, tallest trees anyone had ever seen, majestic firs pointing hundreds of feet right up to the sky.

No, I'd be shedding no tears to leave Missouri. We'd only been out here on the frontier three years—just long enough to have a fertile farm up and running and ready to be ruined when that old Big Muddy came flooding through. I was with Pa; who wanted to start over here? Maybe it was even in my blood. After all, "up and doing" had always been the Kings' motto; heading out to claim land in those far territories seemed like the biggest up-and-doing ever undertaken.

I couldn't wait to go. Couldn't wait to see that Golden West.

On April 22 we left Carroll County and two days later arrived in St. Joseph, our jumping-off place. Beside me on the wagon seat, my sister Sally sat clutching her baby, Jimmy, and I had three-year-old Meggie on my lap. As we pulled into the main street I craned forward, my head snapping from side to side as I tried to take it all in, this bustling boomtown, so new and raw it still had tree stumps in the streets. We rolled past stores and hotels and workshops of all trades—blacksmiths, wheelwrights, harness-makers. The place reeked of animals and industry. All this had sprung up over the past two years, we'd heard, just to sell traveling outfits to emigrants like us.

Sally seemed disconcerted by the uproar, but I found it thrilling. This was like the crossroads of the world itself! Men were loading bags and boxes of supplies into wagons; mothers called to their children above the din. Mountain men and trappers, Indians and hired hands. Big families like ours were spilling out of wagons, lots of them looking like they'd already been through much longer shakedown trips than what we'd had, having left homes in states farther east.

We camped that night near the ferry landing alongside hundreds of other travelers. The next day, while Pa and my brothers were off buying extra oxen and the last supplies, my younger sister Abigail and I sat on a stump and watched the different outfits edge into a line funneling toward the ferry.

"Can't say as I've seen any wagons nicer'n ours," I remarked with satisfaction, figuring I'd be forgiven for bragging on this to my own sister. They were her wagons too, after all. Pa had them specially commissioned, and although lots of folks were choosing blue with red trim, for the King family, the color would be green. Green for tool handles and buckets too, the better to keep them straight from some other family's things when we all found ourselves camped out here together like this. Pa'd even had a sailmaker in Independence sew up our wagons' canvas covers. Word was, lots of women were making their own, but Pa said we had plenty to sew without that, and in any case, he wanted an expert job done of it.

"My land," I said as one rickety contraption with "Oregon or Bust" on its canvas shuddered across the gangplank onto the ferry. "I'm glad we're not setting out with something like that."

Some of these poor conveyances had obviously already given years of service on someone's farm and only wanted putting out to pasture. Instead, the hapless owner had rigged a patched cover, painted a defiant motto on it, and optimistically pronounced it fit for the Overland Trail.

I had wondered if our wagons needed a hearty slogan, or at least, like so many, our name somewhere. But when I asked Pa why he hadn't arranged to have "Kings" emblazoned on the canvas or maybe even incorporated into the rich yellow trim of our paint scheme, he'd just said, "What for? We know who we are."

All around the landing camp, while the men did business in town, you could see the young mothers visiting from one campfire to the next, shyly spying on new acquaintances to see how they were making do, chatting and enjoying the thin spring sunshine.

Our littlest sisters, Lydia and Rhoda, had wasted no time joining a pigtailed pack of girls who were strolling through the camp, stopping here and there to plait each other's hair, demonstrate their favorite cat's cradle tricks, or show off their families' toddlers.

Our youngest bunch, the grandchildren, had some kind of a game going that involved pushing an old sewing basket through the mud. They were all of a size and a wild little set of tots, their daily presence a novelty to Abbie and me. To us, in the beginning, they weren't so much small people, I think, as they were a cunning collection of live playthings.

"I honestly think," Abbie said as we watched, "that our Lexie is the most beautiful child in this whole camp." This was the child of John, our eldest brother, and his wife, Susan. In Pa's meticulous orchestration of the expedition, Abbie had been assigned to their wagon, and now she already sounded as proprietary as if she fancied herself the proud mother of this child with the gorgeous golden curls, and not just her doting young aunt.

Personally, I found Sally's little Meggie, my own charge, with her ordinary, wispy brown hair, more to my liking. You just never knew what funny little thing she might say next.

"Meggie!" I called. "What's the game you're playing?"

She looked up. "It's 'Going to O'gen.'"

Now it made sense—the sewing-basket wagon, the wooden-block oxen, Lexie's four-year-old brother Luther barking orders as wagon master. Little Lute, the family called him, a child Ma was forever claiming had half the sense he ought and twice the sass.

The toy wagon had reached a small ditch crossing, an arduous endeavor that seemed to be taking a severe toll on the pinafores of Meggie and Lexie.

"Look out!" Lute yelled. "The wagon's going over! Cut the oxen loose!"

"Help!" Lexie cried in a high little voice suitable to the size of her peg people. "Oh, help us! We washing awaaaay…"

My smile fell. My neck prickled. Abbie and I glanced at each other uneasily.

"Somebody's got to be more careful," I said. "The stories that get told around these babies."

"Little Lute's heard it all from Susan, I'm sure. She's just full of death and disaster. Knows the details of every single person who's died so far trying to get to Oregon."

"Sally too."

Sally wasn't sorry to be going, though. Her worry had been that, without enough money for a traveling outfit, she and Rowland would be left behind, separated from the family. It was she who had persuaded Rowland to swallow his pride and accept Pa's offer of a loan. Still, she, too, fell prey to every frightening story and worried over warnings that she and my other sisters were about to sacrifice their precious babies to the ridiculous and far-fetched ambitions of their husbands.

"Pa says we have to think why folks like to tell such scary stories," I said to Abbie. "They're just jealous, see? They're too scared to go west themselves, and they can't stand seeing other people excited and hopeful. Bunch of wet blankets, you ask me. Some of them—well, it's not nice to say, but they'll probably be halfway disappointed when they hear we've made it to Oregon and all have fine, big farms."

"Works both ways, though."

"What do you mean?"

"I mean the fellows at the outfitting stores saying South Pass is just an easy-as-ever-you-please ramp over the Rockies. Susan says they just want to sell us wagonloads of stuff. No money in it for them if we turn tail."

"That's true, too," I conceded, but it didn't worry me. Pa knew what to believe and what to take with a grain of salt.

I watched a couple of smartly dressed men walking through the camp. At our parents' wagon they paused, one tapping the wheel spokes with his polished walking stick while his companion jotted notes on a pad.

"What do you suppose they're up to?" I wondered aloud.

"Law's sake, you two!"

I jumped. It was Susan.

"You just going to sit there, letting those children soak themselves in mud?"

Abbie and I exchanged a glance. What a shrew.

"What? Is that my sewing basket they've got?" Susan shoved her two-month-old baby into Abbie's arms. "Lute!" she yelled and then muttered, "That child!" She stomped down to the ditch. "Come on, all of you! Get up to the wagons!"

"Good land," I said. "I hope she doesn't think she's going to keep them spanking clean all the way to Oregon."

"I don't know what she thinks," Abbie said, patting baby Charlie, "except she doesn't want to be going at all and takes it out on me, like the whole trip is my fault."

We watched as Susan scolded Lute. As far as we were concerned, the scene might have been a little pantomime played out purely for our amusement.

"I guess I should have realized," Abbie said vaguely, "she wouldn't want her sewing basket out here." I shrugged and looked back toward our wagons. The men from town had moved on. Abbie elbowed me, drawing my attention to a girl our own age sitting on a wagon tongue a short distance along the slope, earnestly writing a letter. She had one leg crossed over the other, and the pointed toe of her boot poked primly from beneath her ribbon-banded skirt hem.

"I wish I had boots like that," Abbie said.

"Oh, don't be silly. She is going to be so sorry."

"I hate these clodhopping things Pa's making us wear."

I rolled my eyes.

"Don't do that!" she said. "Don't always be rolling your eyes at me."

Well, it was a two-way thing. Ever since Pa announced the trip, she'd been annoyed at me for getting so excited, and I'd been impatient with her for not being excited enough.

"That's the wrong kind of wagon her folks have, too," I said. "Pa says those big old Conestogas are never going to make it over the mountains. Oregon wagons ought to be lighter."

The letter-writing girl paused to think, lifting her head and gazing blankly at us for a moment. Her name was Mamie Brown, although, of course, we wouldn't find this out until later.

Now it's said we shouldn't make snap judgments about people, shouldn't rely too much on first impressions. There's wisdom in that, I suppose, and I like to think I'm capable of changing my opinion of a person if events warrant. That said, here's the plain truth: I didn't like Mamie Brown the first minute I laid eyes on her, and nothing that happened later ever moved me the slightest from that view.

"I'll bet she's writing to her sweetheart," Abbie said. "I'll bet anything."

Mamie sat with her back ramrod straight, like her mother no doubt advised. As she focused on us, her blank expression shifted to one of dainty disapproval. Then she sniffed and returned total concentration to penciling another line.

"Now to me, Abbie, that's just plain sad, to have so much happening right in front of you and not even be looking. When real life's so exciting, you ought to open your eyes and pay attention."

"Fine talk." Abbie jiggled the fussing baby and with one hand arranged her skirts over her knees. "Maybe you're just sore because you don't have a boy you're leaving behind."

She, of course, did, and was forever on the lookout for a likely opening to once again discuss her tragic situation.

"I'm not sore," I said. "And anyway, why on earth did you have to go get sweet on someone when you knew we were leaving?"

She tilted her face, eyelids lowered. "Maybe some of us just can't be as practical about love as you."

9

Oh, mercy. This courtship of Abbie's had consisted, so far as I could tell, of nothing but furtive glances across Sunday meetings, and I suspected she was rather enjoying the drama—young sweethearts separated by forces more powerful than themselves.

Maybe Rob Peters was even a bit proud of having caught the eye of one of us King girls. After all, we'd become almost famous in Carroll County. One day Abbie and I'd been examining bolts of muslin at the store in Richmond when we overheard another customer murmur the words "going to Oregon." We'd stopped, glanced over and then widened our eyes at each other. The woman was talking about us! Our family. The Kings.

Going to Oregon. People might say it with a certain awe or they might say it with skepticism or a hint of mockery. They might march up bold as brass and ask Pa didn't he know the whole idea of dragging women and children two thousand miles across the trackless wilderness was insanity? No, worse—suicide?

But whatever they said, no one could talk of Oregon and feign disinterest.

The day we left the farm, our yard had swarmed with the neighbors staying behind. Mercy. The weeping and wailing, the praying aloud and making of flowery speeches…Same thing all over again when we rolled through Richmond on the road to St. Joe—people pouring out of stores with sorrowful good-byes, grim advice.

We'd already had eight months of this. The papers were full of it too. I couldn't forget one chilling line directed to prospective emigrants: *Your bones,* the writer warned us, *will bleach with your story untold.*

Your story untold.

Well, *enough,* I wanted to tell these naysayers. *We've decided. We're going. This isn't a funeral; it's the adventure of our lives!*

"You have to admit," Abbie said now, "this isn't like any regular trip folks usually take. Once we make it out there, that's it. We're never coming back."

"That's not necessarily true. We might come visit sometime."

"Oh, Lovisa, really. You know Pa's just saying that to make it a little easier for Susan and Annie."

Annie was our other sister-in-law, married to our brother Stephen and no happier about the trip than Susan.

"It's hard for folks," Abbie said. "Saying it. Even thinking it. *We'll never ever see each other again.* Why, Rob said, when he thought of what we'd be facing out there…'Abbie,' he says, 'Abbie, I just can't say it. I can't say the word.'" Abbie swallowed hard, like she was right there with him again, holding his hands, looking into his eyes for the last time. "'I hate to say the word *farewell.*'"

I sighed. Did I envy my sister this? That tears were shed at her going? No, I did not. I was right glad I wasn't leaving anyone I loved behind. In fact, I was happy to be putting distance between myself and the man who'd recently been trying to marry me. Good old Mr. Collins, who kept claiming he hated having to inform us of certain things and then would launch, with relish, into terrible tales of Indian depredations—abductions and tortures at their savage hands. I'd overheard him at the blacksmith's telling Pa *he* certainly wouldn't want to be responsible for taking so many pretty daughters out there among those half-human natives.

"Lovisa! Abbie!" We turned. From the wagons, our younger brother Sol was waving us back. "Time to go!"

We jumped up. Time to get in line for the ferry. Time to hurry up and wait.

Wagons jostled for position in the huge fan of vehicles aiming toward the ferry's gangplank. The wooden craft could take only a few at a time, and it wasn't a fast trip across the muddy, spring-swollen river. I thought our turn would never come, but finally I was watching the roiling brown water in our wake as we floated out.

Susan and our brother Stephen's wife, Annie, I noticed, kept their eyes on the shore of Missouri as it fell away behind us. I, too, gave it a glance, but just a quick one. Then I faced forward, at the rail, and took a deep breath of the wind, imagining I could catch the scent of those far prairies.

"Oh, Abbie. The wide Missouri. Like in the song. '*Away! I'm bound away, 'cross the wide Missouri.*'"

Abbie tsked. "Lovisa, you've looked at the Missouri near every day the last three years."

I set my teeth. "Yes," I said, drawing the word out, "but I wasn't bound away across it then, was I?" Abbie was only a year younger, but sometimes I felt the gulf between us was much wider.

"Tell you what I think," she said. "I think you're just as foolish and romantic in your own way as you always say I am, only about different things."

I shaded my eyes against the lowering sun. Maybe so, but how could a person not be romantic about the prospect of going west?

West. If you said "east" it came out flat. No one ever said *east* the way they said *west*. West had magic in it. Mystery. All the wonder of not knowing what might be out there, the exhilaration of knowing you were about to go see for yourself.

West.

CHAPTER 2

FOUR.

That was the magic number. That was how many inches the new spring grass had to be up before we could go. Our own Amos had been elected superintendent of cattle—probably because we Kings had one of the larger herds—and he agreed we'd be fools to set out without this guarantee of decent grazing. Who'd be so short-sighted as to drive a herd including thirty-five of the finest Spanish Durhams out onto a pastureless prairie?

Four inches. We had to wait.

We'd been marking time in the rendezvous camp several days when the word finally went out: The blessed grass was up! Tomorrow morning, Monday, April 28, the St. Joseph Company of the Oregon Emigration Society would make a start.

My steps were springy as Abbie and I swung our wooden buckets through the sprawling camp—hundreds of wagons dotting the Missouri bottom here on the river's west bank, the beginning of Kansas

Territory, a temporary settlement that completely dwarfed St. Joe.

"My land, Abbie. So many folks here, makes you wonder if there'll be anybody left at all in the states when we roll out."

And truly, we'd not had the slightest notion it would be like this. When Pa and my brothers had been going to their Oregon Meetings all the past year, they'd figured most companies would still be jumping off from Independence. But why first veer south from our farm, Pa said, out of the way? Especially since this fellow Robidoux with the trading post in St. Joe was starting up outfitting stores every bit as complete as what they bragged of down in Independence.

So weren't we clever, going it this new route? Yessir, real ahead-of-the-times thinkers. Ha! Now we saw that thousands of people had got the very same brilliant idea.

"Did you hear about the girl who was running away?" Abbie said, ducking a line of laundry.

"No, what?"

"A girl who lived right here in St. Joe. A boy wanted to marry her, they say. Came round with an outfit all set to go to Oregon, but her folks said no. She couldn't bear to let him go alone, though, so she just ran off and figured her pa'd be chasing right behind. Found a preacher married them right on the ferry. Got over here, they were already mister and missus!"

"My land." Thrilling, I had to admit. So many people. So many stories—sweethearts parting, others quickly deciding to marry. The time had come; decisions had to be made. You could almost feel it, the way everyone's blood was pulsing faster. Life itself seemed to be speeding up. "So where'd you hear that story?"

"From the Hulls' hired boy."

"Abbie!" I acted shocked. "You talked to him? Oh, my. You know what Pa said." We'd been sternly admonished not to be forward with the young, single hired hands traveling with so many of the families.

"Don't tell," Abbie pleaded. "He's not really the rough type Pa's worried about."

I laughed. "Oh, for heaven's sake! I'm just teasing. Talk to anyone you want. I plan to."

We skirted a temporary chicken coop, nodded how-do to folks at a campfire. A man was showing off his clever new wagon jack to another man, that and the extra ox shoes he'd laid in. Everywhere women were trying out their new camp stoves, fanning smoke from their faces. And the children! Lord, they chased around pure crazy with excitement, the parents having long since given up trying to keep them damped down.

Guns fired off constantly. Men were out practicing, lots of them just now learning to shoot. We'd be heading out like some kind of an army, with even the youngest, most untried boys issued rifles of their own. They strutted among the wagons, chins stuck out, bragging on the buffalo they planned to bring down just the minute they got out onto the plains. Why, a boy a couple of camps over had already shot himself in the foot.

It was all new for the women and girls too—the cooking out-of-doors, the living in a wagon. Every little chore was a challenge, and all of us were in a constant stir, chattering away, seeing how others were making do, wondering if we were keeping up standards like we ought.

For me, the greatest novelty was simply being in the middle of such a great crowd. I was used to being stuck out there on our farm with none but family, after all. Now a short stroll to fetch water showed me more faces than I usually saw in a year.

"Just think, Abbie," I said now. "People *know* about this. People way back east. It's like all these folks heard the same message on the wind: *Come to St. Joe in the spring and we'll all head west!* Pa says it's even in the newspapers. He talked to a reporter himself."

This got her attention. "A real reporter?"

"Yes, for one of the local papers. Maybe one of those men we saw looking at our wagons at the landing camp. Says President Polk even mentioned us in his very first speech, told how thousands of people were out here, fixing to go help claim the Oregon Country. That has to tickle you at least a bit, Abbie. I mean, just to be part of it."

I looked back over the river in the direction of St. Joe, and it struck me right then that the very worst thing would be if for some reason we decided not to go after all. Why, I couldn't stand for it! I was wound tighter than a baby's top. Anybody pulled the string, I could have spun out and run right across that prairie all the way to the Pacific Ocean!

I'll wager no family ever rolled out on the road to Oregon better prepared than we Kings. Not only had we devoted the entire fall and winter to spinning, weaving, sewing, molding candles, and drying fruit, but Pa had made a science of researching and securing a complete set of the necessary items required for a top-notch traveling outfit.

Besides the basics, our wagons boasted every sort of clever convenience yet devised—neat sewing kits, washing outfits, the best Dutch oven for hooking over an open fire, a satchel of medicines, each remedy in its own glass vial.

Pa ordered a full line of rainproof tarps made from this brand-new stuff—India rubber. We even had scientific instruments such as a thermometer and something Rowland called an odometer. Grudging as I felt in ever giving my brother-in-law credit for anything, I had to admire how he'd studied on it and rigged wooden gears onto our wagon's back wheel to tick off and count each time it turned. A bit of arithmetic and we'd know exactly how many miles we'd traveled.

Still, to me, the most confidence-inspiring thing of all was not our modern devices but something more basic, a gesture on Pa's part that impressed me to no end. Back home, when we were working our way down the supply list, he'd brought a shoemaker with his bench and tools to the farm and had every last one of us measured for the best boots money could buy. And not just one pair, but two each, right down to four-year-old Lute, all cut from hides he and Amos had tanned just for this purpose, both upper and sole leathers. No silly ladies' boots, Pa had told the shoemaker. We girls'd be walking the same miles as the boys, maybe more. We'd be needing strong and sturdy footwear too.

And that's what we got. Abbie may have thought them cloddish, but I loved the surefooted feeling these boots gave me as I went striding along.

Whatever we took had to be practical. It had to be useful. I was pleased to hear Pa remarking on my spinning skills and saying of course my wheel would go. But things like the framed mirror went straight to the "sell" pile. Ma said we'd always need to spin, but we wouldn't need to know what we looked like. Annie had added that by the time we got to Oregon, we probably wouldn't *want* to know.

We intended to be smart about it and learn from the mistakes of folks who'd gone before, in '43 or '44. We weren't going to be one of those foolish families having to discard treasured possessions along the trail. Any lamenting about what we had to leave behind had already been done back before we had it all auctioned off right there in our yard.

Besides, we had new things, special, for the trip. Each of us girls had been fitted with a neat cold-weather dress of linsey-woolsey. Mine was maroon. We each had new bonnets and, packed away, freshly sewn calico wash dresses. Not that our folks thought we needed to be fine and fancy out on the trail. They just figured everything would get plenty of wear. No point taking clothes on the verge of shredding before we even started.

Along with items that could be ticked off a master list, we'd armed ourselves with something equally valuable: knowledge. Pa secured a guidebook someone had hurriedly printed up. He bought maps. Like he said, the road itself was nothing new. Trappers and Indians had been using it since way back. The new part was taking wagons over South Pass in the Rockies. This being the third year of large parties going over it, the wheel tracks would be easy to follow. The maps were mainly to show the best camp spots and such. After all, it wasn't as if we'd be in any danger out there of actually getting lost.

Finally, Pa had arranged for us to have one last important asset— trusted traveling companions. The Fuller family. Safety lay in numbers, Pa felt, even within the larger company.

We had known the Fullers forever, even back in Ohio, and more recently they'd farmed down in Lafayette County, across the Missouri from us. Travel being as difficult as it was, even short distances, we didn't get to see them near as much as we'd have liked. Now, though, we figured on one long social, all the way to Oregon!

They were a younger family, all the children unmarried. Price and Melinda, the oldest, were about my age, with Henry, the next one, a year behind me. Then they had a darling little girl named Tabitha. The rest was a swarm of younger boys whose names I never even tried to keep straight.

We'd been concerned, initially, when we couldn't find them in the camp, relieved when they at last appeared with their two wagons just in time, the day our departure was announced.

That night, the men of the two families—plus twelve-year-old tagalong Sol—went off to one last organizational meeting where they listened to many a rousing speech.

Sol was positively afire afterwards, jumping up in front of our gathered group, pressing one hand to his chest, throwing the other arm out dramatically.

"It is our right, gentlemen," he declared. "Nay, our *obligation*, to claim those lands of the Golden West." He thrust a finger heavenward.

"God Himself has ordained our country should spread from one ocean to the other!"

Delighted, we laughed and clapped at his canny imitation.

"Our finest, bravest citizens," he went on, "are even now massing here on the frontier borders, preparing to take their wives and children across the vast deserts to perfect that claim, that *divine* claim!"

"Is that what we're doing?" I said after the applause. "What'd you call it, Sol? A divine claim? I thought we were just going for the good land!"

"Well," Pa said, "folks do appreciate the chance to slap a high-minded name on what they want to do anyway."

People had a chuckle over that, and then Pa said, "Looks like Rowland here's gonna be too modest to announce it, so I'll have to tell you myself that he's been elected sheriff of the entire company."

Everyone rocked back in surprise and approval.

Rowland sat there grinning, letting my brothers shove his shoulders. John even managed a tousling of his thick dark hair before Rowland playfully batted him away.

"Sheriff?" Sally's brows pinched together. "What's that going to mean?"

Wouldn't you know? Leave it to Sally to see the worry in this instead of the honor.

"Oh, probably nothing much," Rowland said.

"He'll have to make sure everybody follows the rules," Sol said.

Rowland made a face, determined not to take it too seriously.

All right then, perhaps I shouldn't have been so hard on Sally for having mixed feelings about Rowland being elected. I confess to mixed feelings too. Sure, I felt proud like all the rest. A member of our own family—sheriff! But everybody celebrating him as such a splendid fellow, well—what did that make me then, complaining about him to Pa?

Sometimes I resented Rowland's confidence, I think. He acted like he was one of the King brothers and not a brother-in-law. And Pa treated him with the exact same respect he gave John, his own eldest son. Shouldn't Rowland be a bit more humble, seeing how he was only here thanks to Pa's goodwill and generosity in loaning him the money for his outfit?

Look at him sitting there, ruddy cheeks in the firelight. He knew he was good-looking. And half a head taller than any of my brothers to boot.

Not that people ever thought of my brothers as short, I'm sure. All the King boys, including Pa, carried themselves with a confidence that couldn't be measured in inches.

I looked up. The stars were coming out. This was to be our last evening at the rendezvous camp, so even when the sky blackened and the air chilled we lingered still, too excited to call it a night. And we weren't alone in this. The entire population of our temporary village seemed agitated, with evidence of every sort of activity heard from the hundreds of campfire circles dotting the Missouri bottom. One group was playing cards. Farther away, the minister in our company, Reverend Moore, led a group in an energetic hymn:

> *Thy praise shall sound from shore to shore*
> *'Til suns shall rise and set no more!*
> *Alleluia! Alleluia!*

From the Williams' camp nearby came music and bursts of laughter. They were a big family out of Tennessee who had everything from a brand-new baby to a boy who played the harmonica and an eighteen-year-old daughter who had already created a great sensation with her striking looks and charming southern accent. They also had a promising-looking boy a year or two older whom Sol had already obligingly reported was named Jonathan but who went by the nickname "Jont."

Now, as the Williams crowd started up with "The Girl I Left Behind Me," our boys joined in:

> *I'm lonesome since I crossed the hill*
> *And o'er the moor and valley*
> *Such heavy thoughts my heart do fill*
> *Since parting from my Sally.*

"That song," I pointed out when they stopped for breath, "has the saddest words for the cheerfullest tune."

"Nothing for us to be sad about," Sol said. "We Kings are taking all our girls along with us!"

"Don't forget the Fuller girls," eight-year-old Tabitha Fuller said, batting her eyes at Sol, making the rest of us groan knowingly and grin.

Bitsy, as we called her, was the sauciest thing, with black curls, rosy cheeks, and a beauty mark at the inner edge of her right eyebrow. And what a flirt! It was plain she'd already taken a shine to my younger brother.

"So, are we all set for tomorrow?" Pa asked. "How about a report on the sick ones. Arnold?"

Arnold Fuller took a deep breath, hesitated, then shook his head. His wife, mother of this large family, was lying sick in one of their wagons, eldest daughter Melinda looking after her. Her illness was the reason they'd delayed until the last possible day in leaving for St. Joe.

"I was hoping she'd be better by jumping-off day," Mr. Fuller said. "Hate to make her travel, but I don't see any choice. We've got to stay with the group. Wouldn't want to be lagging behind alone out there."

Pa nodded, gave it a moment, then turned to my sister Hopestill.

She shrugged. "Lucius is about like he always is, no worse anyways."

"All right, then," Pa said, not overly concerned. We were used to Lucius Norton being poorly, and so was Hope. Thirty, faded in looks, she seemed to accept as her due this invalid husband and never complained, as I probably would have.

Pa turned to Annie. "And Stephen?"

"The same."

Annie's reddish curls glowed so pretty in the firelight. I did feel sorry for her. She had left her own mother and brothers back in Ohio and come out to marry Stephen on Christmas Day the year before last. Then, in a winter windstorm, a stout tree branch cracked loose and whacked him in the chest. He still hadn't fully recovered and seemed forever plagued by one bout of ague after another. Poor Annie. When a girl promises devotion in sickness and in health, I doubt she's figuring the sickness will start right off.

"Well," Pa said, "I'll wager as soon as we get Stephen out on the plains, he'll come around."

Everybody except Annie nodded.

On her own she'd have been a lively thing, I think, but being Stephen's bride had dulled her spirit. I had the feeling that, unlike Hope, Annie *did* dare imagine how things might have gone better. She'd been fretful about trying to travel with a sick husband from the minute Pa announced last summer his intention to make the crossing. Who could blame her? I understood right well none of this would have looked like the same big adventure to me were I in her boots.

"Tell you what," Pa said. "There's a bunch from over there in Lafayette County, most *all* of 'em sick. It's the very reason they're going."

"It's true," Arnold Fuller said to Annie. "It's a well-known fact they don't have the fevers out west that we've got in these river valleys here."

Annie gave him a look of such sharp skepticism that Mr. Fuller rather took offense.

"Well, say now," he said to her. "You can be sure I wouldn't be getting ready to haul my poor wife two thousand miles in a wagon if I didn't believe that."

"There must be some truth in it," Hope said in that placid way of hers. "We've heard so many times that people don't get sick at all in Oregon."

"Of course," Annie said. "Everyone out there lives to be a hundred, right? And the wheat stalks march over and bind themselves into sheaves all by themselves?"

It fell so quiet around our circle, you could hear the pop and crackle of the fire. Some of the stories about Oregon did sound impossibly optimistic. Still, we wanted to believe. And if only part of them were true, it could still be a glorious place.

I half expected Pa to scold Annie for talking so pert; instead, his voice was almost tender. "Hate to see you look so worried, Annie." He stroked his beard. "Maybe I'll have to change my plans just a bit."

I blinked. Pa? Change his plans?

"Sol," he said, turning to my little brother, "much as your Ma and I enjoy having you with our wagon, I think you'd best go along with Annie here, help her out."

Sol sat up straighter and flashed his winsome grin. "At your service, Annie."

Annie dipped her head of red curls at him. "Much obliged, I'm sure." She couldn't help being cheered, Sol was so cute. "But that'll be *Miss* Annie to you, my young pup."

Sol squirmed, blushing deeply, pleased at the teasing. "At your service, *Miss* Annie."

And although it would be a long time before we all realized it, no truer words were ever spoken.

Finally Ma insisted on a hymn and a prayer and said that if the company was leaving in the morning, people had better get some rest.

23

No one moved, though. The very thought. Tomorrow the long-planned journey would finally begin.

"I just want to say," Pa said quietly, "how proud and glad I am to have you all with me on this. Arnold, it means a lot to me, your family joining ours. It'll be good to have a younger man along. I know some are calling me an old fool to try this—"

"You're not old, Pa," I cut in.

"Well, I never considered so," Pa said, "but I'll tell you, missy, I've heard enough times this past year that sixty-one is no age to be starting out on that Overland Trail."

The whole crowd of us cried humbug. Our pa may have had a joint or two that pained him from time to time, but he never complained or used it as an excuse to slack off work. I'd always figured my father, Nahum King, for a man who could do anything he set out to do.

"As you know," he said, "it's my aim to get you all to Oregon and see you set up with plenty of good land before I die. Good land that won't flood."

"Amen to that," Ma muttered.

And then, as if he were saying it for the first time and not the hundredth, "This family's got to stick together. And that's all there is to it."

I looked around the fire at my brothers and sisters, the husbands and wives, the little ones they held. The Fuller family too. I knew each had his or her own feelings about going west, but everyone, it seemed, trusted Pa. Looking back later, what I would remember most was our confidence. Our innocence, you might even say.

I would remember that campfire. There would be times ahead when I would think on that gathering and the ring of bright, beloved faces. Whatever our worries, on that chilly, star-spangled night, the future still looked perfect with promise. Everyone had faith that, as Pa said, we would *all* get to Oregon.

I would remember, and it would break my heart.

Finally, we turned away from the banked coals.

"Are you going to be all right out there?" Sally asked as I collected my bedroll from the little built-in wagon cupboard given over to me. "Because Rowland says he could sleep outside if you'd rather."

"Sally, I'm fine in the tent. I've told you." Each married couple had a wagon, each wagon had a bed for privacy. That was the plan, and I wasn't complaining. I jumped down.

"But don't you worry about snakes?"

I made a face in the dark. "No," I said. *Not until you mentioned it.*

"Well, as long as you're sure."

"I'm sure. Really." And I certainly hoped we wouldn't have to discuss this every night! I didn't need reminding of things I had no business thinking about—Sally and Rowland and their bed in the wagon.

I found Abbie in the little tent that had been set up for us. She was twisting her long brown hair into bits of rag for curling, a vanity I don't believe she'd undertaken since the night before she was to see her old sweetheart for the last time.

"Don't you think Price Fuller has gotten good-looking?" she asked as I crawled around, smoothing out my blankets. "He must have shot up or filled out or something."

I couldn't sleep; neither could Abbie. Sporadic laughter and the scratching of a fiddle continued from a nearby camp, and beyond that some fool kept firing his pistols. I don't know what was keeping Abbie's eyes staring into the darkness. For me it was a feverish imagining of the trip ahead, as if I could mentally cross every river and mountain ahead of time, as if I could spur the sun to rise so we could be on our way.

I awoke the next morning to an eerie quiet. Where was the bustle of a camp astir? For the briefest, half-awake instant, I thought the company had somehow left without me. Scrambling from the tent, I stood and came face to face with Abbie.

"We're not leaving," she said.

"What!"

She glanced around, lowered her voice. "Mrs. Fuller died. Just before dawn."

I drew a sharp breath.

"We can't leave until we bury her."

I let out a huge sigh, like all my pent-up energy for the trek had escaped at once. "So we're staying behind?"

"The whole company is. Nobody's going until after the funeral."

I dropped back into the tent and cast myself across the blankets, face down. What timing! And after all this buildup. Then, a flood of remorse. Sarah Fuller, a young woman, dead. Eight Fuller sons and daughters, motherless.

Abbie joined me and we lay there, all the spirit knocked right out of us.

"So, are they still going?" I asked after a moment. "The Fullers?"

"I don't know." Abbie hesitated. "I hope so."

Then, from outside the tent, we heard our own mother's voice, subdued in the presence of death perhaps, but still firm.

"Come on, girls," she said. "Let's be up and doing."

Abbie and I looked at each other. This is how it was going to be then. The King family had set its course. We were going to attempt this crossing. Even if someone died and our plans were delayed or rearranged, it didn't change this: Every morning we still had to be up and doing.

Two days later the entire company stood in a downpour to pay respects at Sarah Fuller's grave. Bible verses were read, hymns sung. The Fullers had decided that, as Melinda put it, if Oregon was a good idea before, it was still a good idea. They would continue. Everyone cast them sympathetic looks. This poor family, to be burdened with such an inauspicious start.

The rain beat down on us, but leaving the service prematurely wouldn't have felt right to anyone. No one moved. I looked at Abbie. The last of her curls were gone to wet strings.

When we finally departed, the mud sucked the boots right off the children's feet.

That was the first and last big funeral of the journey.

Not that we wouldn't lose more people. Far from it.

But never again—not on prairie, plain, or distant riverbank—would so many take so much time to acknowledge the passing of one solitary soul.

CHAPTER 3

"I AM NOT GOING TO BE ABLE TO STAND THIS
thing," I told Sally, peering through the curved brim of my sunbonnet
at the yoked oxen hitched ahead of us. We were sitting on our wagon
seat with the children. Waiting. Had been for some time. What on earth
was holding the men up? The wagons had formed the four columns
they'd decided on. Why couldn't we go?

"You won't want to spoil your complexion," Sally said, retying the
strings of Meggie's little blue bonnet. Poor child didn't look any
happier in hers than I was in mine.

"The sun's not even out," I said, lifting my face. "And I do kind
of appreciate being able to see where I'm going!"

The pattern for these specially recommended overland bonnets
had been brought home by Pa from one of his Oregon meetings
last fall. The brims were more exaggerated than what we were used
to wearing on the farm and called for thin wooden slats to hold

them out stiff. Trouble was, you ended up looking through such a narrow opening, you couldn't see but one little patch at a time of what lay ahead.

"Can you fold it back?" Sally asked.

"Not without snapping the slats." I took the bonnet off and started working the wood bits out, laying them on the edge of the wagon as I went. I looked around. Mercy, without the hat, blinders removed, there was a whole world around me. Little Lute, trying to climb out the back of their wagon, Susan hauling him back in. Sol daubing grease from a bucket onto Annie's wagon's axles. Ma sitting straight-backed, facing forward, ready, yet patient, knitting without looking at her work.

I put my bonnet on again, folding back the brim. "There. That's better."

"But the brim's the whole point," Sally said. "The light's on your face now."

"I don't care." Besides, I was having a hard time believing the prairie could possibly be as devoid of trees and shade as people were warning. "I can always put the slats back in."

Rowland stood, down by our teams, prod in hand. I had to admit, he did have an easy manner with the oxen, which was more than I could say for certain others. Trouble was, most of our men were used to mules. Since oxen were recommended as best for a trip like this, though, there was nothing for it but to become oxen-handlers. Thank goodness the necessary short, firm commands came so natural to Rowland. If I had to suffer close range the wheedling and cursing techniques of some of these fellows, I'm sure I'd be purely crazy before we'd made the first hundred miles.

I was watching him give the ox named Star a calming clap when a bugle sounded, jerking me to attention.

"That's it!" I grabbed Meggie onto my lap. "We're leaving!"

But again it was hurry up and wait. We were nowhere near the front of the caravan. Little did I know it was going to be like this or worse every single daily departure of the whole long trek. If somebody wasn't having trouble with his oxen or a broken wheel, it'd be some other bunch lazily sleeping late and simply not getting ready in time. Or the cattle would have run off or got mixed in with another company's drove. But that morning I was still fresh and unknowing and tight with tension, as if five minutes would make the difference in whether we reached Oregon on schedule or not.

Finally Rowland got the signal, prodded the oxen, and the wagon jerked forward so hard my bonnet slats went flipping off the wagon edge, clattering through the wheel spokes to the dirt below.

"Oh, dear," Sally said, seeing this. "Rowland, stop!"

"No, don't!" I whispered. "It doesn't matter." And when Rowland looked back questioningly, I called ahead, "Nothing, nothing. Never mind," and waved him forward. I wasn't going to be trouble right off, not now that we were finally rolling. I wasn't about to give him an excuse to grumble at me.

"Close up! Close up!" Lieutenant Waymire, our second in command, came riding back, looking half-panicked. "Why the devil can't you keep close together?"

Rowland frowned. "Hoy! Hoy!"

"The Indians could kill everyone in front before you'd know it," Waymire yelled, "then come back and scalp all of you at the end too!"

"Innians?" Meggie piped up.

"No, love," Sally said, eyes darting around. "He just wants us to make nice lines, that's all."

Daresay. Lord, he made it sound as if they were already lying in wait out there, just ready to jump us.

Rowland seemed to know instantly the effect this would have on Sally. "Now don't you girls worry," he said, coming back to her. "The Indians aren't going to bother us."

"See?" Meggie said, indignant. "He did say Innians."

Sally and I made eyes at each other. Not much got past this little one. We'd have to guard our tongues. Not that it seemed the moving wagon was going to be the best place for chitchat anyway, what with the creaking wheels, the cattle bawling, the bell on our milch cow Buttercup clanging, and the men all hoy-hoy-hoying. If there were any Indians out there at the moment, I wondered what on earth they'd think. Imagine hearing this cacophony rumbling across an expanse where before there'd been only birdsong and the shushing of wind in the grass.

I had begun to believe we'd never leave the rendezvous camp, and not just because of the funeral. Even after that the men had delayed departure three more days with one tedious debate after another—whether to ban the Vickers family with its case of measles (we didn't), Mamie Brown's family with their less-than-cooperative attitude about proper provisions (they would grudgingly be allowed to come), and the endless arguments about whether or not to travel on the Sabbath (we wouldn't).

Our long-awaited start now seemed anticlimactic. The overcast sky weighed down my spirit; the flat light dulled the look of the Kansas prairie. Worse, only two miles out I discovered the first disagreeable aspect of travel on the Overland Trail.

"Mercy, Sally, I feel like I could lose my breakfast. This infernal rocking!"

"Really? That's good to know. I thought it was just me. I was afraid—"

My head snapped around.

"No, see, if you feel bad too, then it's not likely that."

I sighed. Good. Sally was as hardy as any of us King girls, but nobody needed to be starting out with morning sickness and another baby on the way.

I wrapped my arms around my middle, squeezing hard. It wouldn't be polite, I decided, to point out that such close quarters with a baby in diapers—even a big-eyed, round-headed one as adorable as Jimmy—didn't help. Because what could Sally do about it? Jimmy was only seven months old. This is how it was going to be—and how it was going to smell in the wagon—all the way to Oregon.

"Maybe I'll just figure on walking some," I said, standing up, clambering over the bags and kegs through the wagon to the rear.

"Shall I ask Rowland to stop so you can get out?" she called back.

"Oh, you don't have to do that." I'd probably be getting in and out a lot. The oxen could be stubborn, and once Rowland had the teams in motion, I doubted he'd stand for stopping and starting up again all the live-long day.

I climbed over the tailgate, balanced briefly on the toolbox, then leapt. Mid-air, in the instant I expected the impact of feet to ground, I was instead jerked off balance as my skirt caught in the axle. I hit the dirt hard on one knee. Struggling to stand, tugging my dress down to cover my drawers, embarrassment shifted to panic as the huge rear wheel began dragging me, wanting to wind me up into it.

"Stop, Rowland!" I screamed as the rough edge of the metal rim grazed my shoulder. "Stop!"

"Whoa!" Rowland yelled, and the oxen obeyed.

Grasping the twist of linsey-woolsey in two hands, I gave a mighty yank and ripped myself free.

"What happened?" Rowland said, hurrying around the wagon. "Are you all right?"

Putting it all together, relieved to find me in one piece, he let loose.

"God Almighty, Lovisa! You could have been killed! Didn't we tell you girls not to be getting in and out of the wagons while we're moving?"

Finding my footing, I put my fists to my hips. "As if you'd have been happy to stop! I was trying not to bother you."

With a swish of my tattered skirt, I stalked off through the columns, out to the side of the caravan, hoping our little scene had been witnessed by as few people as possible.

No luck.

"What happened?" Abbie said, trotting out after me. "We heard you and Rowland yelling at each other."

"Wonderful." I rubbed my shoulder. It really hurt.

"And look at your dress!"

I grabbed up a fistful of my hem, glared at the great rent and flung it away. "Silly thing. Got in an argument with an axle."

"Looks like the axle won."

I smiled grimly. Why'd I have to be so clumsy? Abbie must have managed to jump clear of their wagon without asking John to stop.

"So," I said as my breath evened out, "how you faring back there?"

"Well, actually, I'm already in trouble! Susan can be so cross. Little Lute got into the crackers without permission, and she blamed me."

"Probably no wonder she's always ready to tear her hair," I said, glad to turn my focus to somebody else's troubles. "That rascal's a handful."

Abbie nodded. "Ma thinks she isn't strict enough with him. Started telling her so this morning too. The way Susan was slamming her fry pan around, I thought sure Ma would get the hint and button up, but oh, no, she kept going on until Susan looked ready to smack somebody. As soon as Ma left she turns on me and says, 'I don't care how many sons your ma birthed. She never had one like Lute and she just doesn't know!'"

Well, that much was probably true. I doubt any of my brothers were ever as trying as Lute.

"Ma's always rubbing it in about Sol too," Abbie said. "What a great kid he is, so helpful and everything. Like why can't Susan get Lute in hand and make him turn out like Sol."

I laughed.

"What," Abbie said. "What's funny?"

"Oh, I don't know," I said. "Us." The high drama of these little domestic disputes! My married brothers and sisters had been living on their own farms. This was new for them, too, trying to get along with the whole family all day, every day. I wasn't the only one who'd drawn a difficult lot.

I lifted my head. It was better out here to the side of the wagon columns. Much better. I liked seeing the wide sky, not just watching the back of the next wagon or the switching of the oxen tails. Patches of fresh blue were widening between the scattering clouds, shafts of sunlight lit the green of the prairie. Sighting on the horizon, I thought: I'll walk to that spot, and from there to the next horizon and on and on all the way to Oregon!

"I'm afraid Price Fuller already likes that Orlena Williams," Abbie said, plucking up a stem of rose mallow in passing.

"Well, they all do."

"Orlena Maria," Abbie repeated in a lofty tone. "Why couldn't I have a name like that instead of plain old Abbie?" She stuck the flower in her braid. "Do you think she's as pretty as everyone says?"

I shrugged, not the answer she wanted, but the kindest I could give. No denying it, Orlena Williams cut a splendid figure. Plus, she had those dark, darting eyes and an absolutely phenomenal way of teasing long, playful conversations out of boys who normally couldn't stand to string together three words.

"Better not let Ma hear you fretting on this," I warned my sister.

"I know, I know."

All of us King girls were short, tending to a robust roundness, with rosy faces and thick brown hair. We were all pretty enough,

Ma liked to say, that she wouldn't stand for us worrying on it. If we were interested in self-improvement, she said, we'd be better served looking to our spiritual sides.

Worthy advice, I suppose, but I hardly thought the boys were hanging on Orlena's every word because of her fine Christian spirit.

"It's hard to think Price would be ready to court anyone, Abbie," I said. "Don't you s'pose he's busy grieving his ma?"

"He didn't have to be visiting around to different campfires at the rendezvous camp like he was." She swooped up another flower. "Anyway, it already seems like way more than four days since we buried Mrs. Fuller, don't you think? Time just doesn't pass the regular way anymore since we left home."

I wouldn't argue. I'd noticed it too.

Now the three little girls came running after us.

"Look, isn't she pretty?" Rhoda said, showing off Bitsy, whose black curls were crowned with a wildflower wreath they'd woven— deep rose, yellow, and blue.

I gave over a moment to admiring the charming effect, then frowned sternly. "You really should have on your sunbonnet." Listen to me, I thought, picking up the pace again. I could hardly stand to wear my own, but all of a sudden I was issuing advice to this little girl about hers, sounding just like a mother! Well, maybe I was feeling conscious of her not having one anymore.

"Tell them, Bitsy," Lydia said. "Tell Lovisa and Abbie what you told us."

Bitsy showed her dimples in a smug little smile.

"Yes, tell," Rhoda urged.

"All right then." Bitsy stopped in her tracks to deliver the announcement. "I," she said, "am going to marry Sol!"

Abbie and I laughed with delight.

"Well, I am!" Bitsy said. "Someday, I mean. You just wait and see."

"Does Sol know?" I asked, amused.

"Not yet, but I aim to get his promise pretty soon."

"Tell you what, then—you better grow up right quick. Girls already have an eye for Sol."

"Who?" Bitsy demanded, face darkening as if ready to do battle with any potential rival.

I laughed. "I didn't mean anybody in particular. I just meant you're probably not going to be the only one with that idea." Then I added quickly, "But I'm sure you're the prettiest, pet, and we'd love having you for our little sis-in-law, wouldn't we?"

My sisters all nodded, and Bitsy looked pleased.

Watching her skip along, I thought she certainly didn't seem overly sad or preoccupied by the loss of her mother. Well, Sarah Fuller had apparently been poorly for quite some time. Maybe Bitsy had already grown accustomed to having only her big sister Melinda looking after her.

"Lovisa!" Lydia exclaimed, pointing at my skirt. "What did you do to your brand new dress?"

"Oh, it's just a little tear." I turned to the view ahead. "Look at that rise over there. Let's go out and climb to the top."

Abbie looked blank. "What for?"

"To see," I said, hurrying forward.

"See what?"

"Whatever there is to see!" I called back. "We won't know what it is until we see it, right?"

I left her muttering about already walking far enough without going out of our way, but shortly I heard Bitsy behind me, huffing hard, scampering to catch up.

Together, the two of us made our way to the top of the hill. Good thing I didn't know then how many times I'd be repeating this hopeful exercise in the months ahead, always thinking that surely at the summit there'd be a clear view all the way to...

37

Oh, this time the view was clear, yes, but of what? Just more of the same undulating prairie. Bitsy, however, didn't seem disappointed in the slightest at finding no particular feature to draw the eye. Her face tilted up with bright young eagerness. What a picture she herself made with her rosy cheeks, black hair, and bright flowers against the tender, new-sprung prairie green.

Now I looked back. Down the slope, Abbie drifted along with a certain dreaminess. Lydia and Rhoda bent over the flowers, brown braids swinging. Behind them, our wagon train came in slow procession. Four columns wide, some seventy white-topped wagons moved forward at a stately pace, the last of them still pulling up over the rise farthest back to the east. The oxen achieved no speed, yet, bless their stout hearts, neither did they flag. Something in my breast swelled. Maybe, I thought, this was something like it looked when Moses led the people out of Egypt in search of the Promised Land.

"They're finding the best firewood right up that way," Sol told us as we halted that first night on what was called the Wolf River. "And over there's the water hole they've set aside for dipping fresh buckets."

Sally and I just looked at each other. How did he know this already? Our little brother had an uncanny knack for instantly taking stock of things, and "Ask Sol" would soon become the answer to anything anyone wanted to know.

While Sally and the others started setting up camp, I hid in the wagon a few minutes, hastily mending my dress without taking it off. I didn't want Ma noticing. I didn't want any lectures.

That first evening meal on the road was a feast, I remember, complete with chicken, potatoes, and a tasty dried-tomato pie.

"You boys don't get too used to it," Ma warned. "This'll be it for chicken."

"Don't worry, Ma," Amos grinned. "Before long we'll have you frying up buffalo!"

"Ma, shouldn't you sit down and eat a bite yourself?" Sol asked, because Ma was already kneading dough for the next day's bread.

"I will, I will," she said, waving him off, trying to pretend she didn't enjoy his concern. "Just want to get a little head start on tomorrow, that's all."

No more lying awake for me, I thought as I pulled my blanket over my shoulder that night. Not after a full day of walking and such a hearty meal. Why had people tried to scare us about traveling the road to Oregon? This was nothing...I was already drifting off...This was fun...I could do it forever.

The days fell into a rhythm. Up before dawn to the bugle, get breakfast, and put up the noon meal. Pa would come around, asking was everyone fit to travel, and we learned real quick he wasn't interested in details. He didn't want to hear about baby Charlie's colic or that Annie had the sick headache again. Those were our problems, and wouldn't be his until somebody's illness threatened the company's all-important forward progress.

Every day's goal was the same—drag the cumbersome caravan fifteen miles or so farther along the road and find, at sunset, a campsite with three things—water, grass for the cattle, and wood to fuel the cook fires.

The men, especially Amos, put a priority on finding good pasture, but I soon determined that water was the most important thing to me. Good, clear water, which made the difference between being able to cook properly or having to dig out the hardtack and listen to everyone complain how the hard bread near to broke their teeth. It meant being able to wash the dust from your face and eat with clean hands. Most importantly, maybe, with baby Charlie, Jimmy, and Hope's one-year-old Wiley still in diapers, it meant being able to give those diapers a decent wash!

During the months we'd been making plans and laying in supplies for the trip, one of the biggest questions of debate had been this: Exactly how hard was it going to be to haul a wagon loaded with women and children such a terrible distance? Opinions ran the gamut. Some—folks who weren't going, of course—said we'd never a one of us live to see the Columbia River. Others predicted the whole trip would be one long picnic. These first days, and especially when we reached the beautiful valley of the Little Blue, it seemed like the ones expecting a jolly time of it had been closer to the truth.

Every evening, chores dispatched, we visited the neighboring families' campfires, everyone trading stories about where we were from, why we'd decided to go to Oregon, what we figured to do when we got there.

We Kings all told about getting flooded out of the Carroll County farm, how we'd barely escaped that night the Missouri rose so fast, drowning most of the cattle and every last one of the sheep.

Sol's version emphasized his role in riding through the thundering rain, warning the older brothers and sisters to leave their houses and get to high ground.

My brother Isaac bemoaned the loss of all Pa's fencing rails, probably because he'd been the one to split so many of them.

My brother Amos explained how the flood had simply been the last straw for him. He'd been running a ferry at the farm. The south shore landing opposite us was right on the beginning of the Santa Fe Trail, and he'd watched too many wagons heading west to escape a case of Oregon fever himself. By the time the flood floated away his equipment, he'd been more than ready to join the westward stream.

Ma's main theme was the mud we'd had to clean out of our log house when the water finally went down and how it being the richest soil God ever laid in a river valley hadn't made the mess smell any less nasty or the job one bit easier. She was sick to death of floods, this being her third. Same thing had happened to us in Ohio and also back in upstate New York, before she and Pa first started their westward moves. Looked like now we'd be going about as far west as we possibly could, and she was determined, she said, that the King family would never again settle any piece of ground that had the slightest chance of flooding.

Of course, we weren't the only ones who'd been spurred to leave by this disaster, which had turned out to be the biggest flood ever recorded so far on the Missouri. The whole valley had gone under. To hear Pa tell it, though, the flood of 1844 had actually been God's own answer to the personal questioning of Nahum King.

"I'd been thinking on bringing my whole crowd west," Pa would tell visitors to our wagons, his boot rocking a log at the edge of the fire. "Kept wondering, is it time yet?" He shook his head. "Woke up that morning, looked down and saw the old Big Muddy running over my whole farm. I thought, dang, there's a right plain answer for a man."

Like a small town on wheels, our wagon company was visited by every sort of life event.

One morning we had a funeral for two-month-old Mary Ellis at our camp by a limestone springs, and that evening, at the next campsite fifteen miles down the trail, a wedding. The day was so long, and the distance so far from the grievous event to the joyous, few seemed to find it inappropriate to finish the day in celebration after beginning with mourning.

"Oh, just look," Abbie whispered, standing back in the wedding crowd with me and Ma and our younger sisters, watching the couple trade vows. "Her flowers are so pretty!"

I gave her a look. As if a girl had to get married to justify a bouquet.

The gathering was large, and we were in back where we couldn't hear a word of the ceremony. Neither could anyone else, apparently, for all around us folks were carrying on their own conversations.

"And imagine," Abbie went on, "they say she's just thirteen!"

"Now that is a crying shame," Ma said under her breath.

Abbie lowered her lids and spoke sideways. "You were only fifteen when you married Pa."

"That's right, but your pa was twenty-four, remember. This fellow's forty."

Thirteen. That's the number I was stuck on. The bride was thirteen. Just the age I'd been when Rowland came courting Sally. I glanced over at Rowland, standing next to my father, holding Meggie up so she could see. Sally and I had five years between us, and I'd always looked up to her. She'd actually mothered me a good deal, Ma always being busy with so many of us, and when I remembered all those summers of fever, it was Sally's face over me that came to mind.

So I purely hated losing her to marriage. She must have understood how I felt that last awful summer, because she tried to raise my spirits by bestowing on me the honor of being her bridesmaid. No use, I stayed miserable. Such a cloud of gloom as I'd never felt before, and Sally said she wasn't surprised when it turned out right then I started my first monthlies. Poor Sally! Brides shouldn't have to deal with such things—temperamental little sisters—but she was always the picture of patience.

Thirteen. That was young. Just our Lydia's age. No, wait, Lydia'd now turned fourteen. Was that possible? Lord knows I still thought of her as a child. Tall as me, she was still stick-skinny and wore her brown hair in two thick little-girl braids down her back.

Probably how I looked when Rowland first came around.

And my first impression of him was this big grown-up man who stole my favorite sister. I guess I'd probably been holding that against him ever since.

"A man of forty has got no business," Ma said, "marrying a girl of thirteen."

I thought of Mr. Collins, who'd offered to marry me and make me mistress of his fine farm. I believe he was near to forty.

"That why you didn't care so much I turned down Mr. Collins?" I asked. I'd been a bit surprised my folks hadn't tried to change my thinking on that, him being so well fixed.

Ma frowned. "You didn't like him. You don't marry a man you don't like. Seems simple enough."

Well, yes, except that to me, none of this business of figuring out who you liked seemed simple at all. I kept expecting to be smitten with some fellow right off, the way Abbie had immediately taken to Price, or Bitsy to Sol.

Surely there was someone in our company for me. Pa said the official count was ninety-eight males over the age of sixteen. They couldn't all be married. Plus, there were just fifty-seven females over fourteen. The odds seemed to be in my favor. Unless, of course, as Abbie accused me, I was so picky it wouldn't matter if there were a thousand unmarried men...

They must have finished with the ceremony, because now we heard the fiddles starting up and my toes went right to tapping. Ma saw and waved us off.

The wedding dance was held on a patch of packed dirt. The aging groom appeared to have broken into his medicinal supply of spirits, and the little bride seemed quite bewildered. So much for the glory of it all. But, oh, the music! I loved a good dance. We couldn't have too many of them for me.

Right away my brother Amos got Melinda Fuller out there dancing the polka. If his old sweetheart could see him now! That Richmond girl had declared she would never in her life set foot the far side of the Missouri, to which Amos had replied he was sorry to leave her but he was bound for Oregon and that was that. Guess he made a smart choice, because here was Melinda with her cheeks glowing and her black curls bouncing, pretty as that other one and she wanted to go to Oregon. Plus, there wasn't a stronger or healthier-looking girl in the whole company. Even with her own mother left in that very first grave, you could see she was still full of spirit and looking ahead.

Pa and Arnold Fuller were watching the two of them together. I caught them trading a quick wink of approval. Then Arnold Fuller, that big bear of a man, leaned down to me.

"Oh, look at Price there. That boy of mine is so shy. Whyncha skip on over there, honey, see can you get him to dance."

I drew back, appalled, but my own father gave me a little shove. What a shock. They wanted us to pair up. For so long all Abbie and I had heard was to hold back, don't be too bold, hang onto our maidenly modesty. We were too young to even be thinking about such things, they were always saying. Now, all of a sudden, it was Here's your chance, boys and girls. Step up and choose your partners. And they didn't just mean for this one dance.

Oh, where was Abbie when I needed her? She was the one with eyes for Price. Well, I had to obey my father. And I did want to dance. I took a deep breath and started making my way through the crowd.

Now there are girls, I know, like Orlena Williams, who could manage this with some subtlety, flirt with a fellow so cleverly he'd not only end up asking her to dance, he'd do so convinced the invitation had been his own bold plan from the get-go.

Well, not me. Must have been behind the door when God handed out the talent for playing sweet and coy.

On the other side of the circle, I squeezed through to stand beside Price Fuller. I tilted my head toward him, smiling straight out at the dancing couples. "Your pa and my pa want us to dance together." Like I said, direct.

But he grinned and took me up on it. We were off and romping!

I was whirled around by a number of boys that night, and one who kept asking to be my partner again and again was a handsome, sandy-haired fellow name of John Noble.

"Splendid girls in this train," he shouted over the fiddles. "Plenty of pluck and pretty too." He winked to make sure I got the hint he counted me in this number. "My pa said I'd do fine," he declared, "to court any girl who could make a trip like this with her chin up."

I laughed, sashaying down the line with him. Every girl's chin was up! Why not? Dancing under the stars—we'd never had so much fun in our lives!

CHAPTER 4

"I DON'T KNOW WHY WE CAN'T SETTLE

right here," Susan said one day as we loaded things up after a nooning stop. "John says the soil seems as fertile as you please."

We all glanced around at each other. We were still in the valley of the Little Blue, with its rolling green hills and wildflowers, and nobody would argue it wasn't pretty. But something about Susan's self-consciously casual remark made me uneasy. Maybe it was the way she didn't meet anyone's eyes.

"It could use a few more trees," I offered, but the real argument against it, to my thinking, was plain: It wasn't west. At least not very far west. And that's what we had our hearts set on, right?

Her baby squalled from their wagon, and, as she hurried over and climbed in, Ma put a fist on her hip. "Suppose she's going to talk about settling every time we stop at a grassy patch?"

"Now, Ma," Hope said.

Ma's mouth was a thin line. Truth be told, she'd been hard on Susan from the first. Maybe she took it as an affront that our brother had deliberately chosen a fair, slight wife who ran so counter to the sturdiness of us King girls. A man needed a helpmate who could pull her own weight, Ma liked to say. Not a pretty burden. And when Lexie was born, Ma kept saying, "Electa? What kind of a name is that? What's wrong with one of our good family names?"

And most irrational of all, she seemed to regard Lexie's golden curls as some sort of extravagance Susan had conjured expressly to excuse the child from wearing the plain, no-nonsense haircut of all the other little girls—parted in the middle, neatly chopped at the chin. "Vanity, vanity," she would mutter, as if God Himself hadn't crowned Susan's daughter with this glorious halo.

"That girl," Ma said, "doesn't want to go one step farther from her folks than she has to."

"Well, neither would I, Ma," Sally chided gently, her voice low, glancing at Susan's wagon. It wouldn't help anything for Susan to hear Ma talking like this.

"Think how hard it must be for her," Sally went on. "For Annie too. Think how hard it would be for us if we had to go with our husband's families and be away from you."

"All right, all right," Ma conceded. "I might could be a bit more charitable."

It always amazed me how Ma softened to Sally's soothing. No one else could call her on something and get away with it.

Captain T'Vault came riding along with the command to commence travel. "All set?" he called. "Stretch out! Hep! Hep!"

With a cracking of whips and creaking of wheels, the wagons rolled again. From the corner of my eye, I watched my mother as she took up the march. Pretty spry for fifty-three, and my sisters and I naturally thought the world of her.

Sometimes you had to wonder, though, what she might seem like as a mother-in-law.

Folks hadn't been exaggerating about the lack of trees out here, I had to admit. What were we women supposed to do for privacy in heeding nature's call?

We took to forming a circle on the prairie, facing outwards, holding our skirts spread so that the one squatting in the center could take care of her business unobserved. Still an embarrassment, that the men passing would know what we were about, but what was the choice?

One time Abbie spotted Amos riding up opposite our group and urged Melinda, in the middle, to finish up.

"Well, I hope to shout," Melinda said, not to be hurried. "Your brother knows women have to do this business, too, doesn't he?"

"Well, sure," Abbie said, flustered, "but...it's so unladylike!"

"Our days as delicate ladies are long gone." Melinda stood, flounced out her skirts and grinned. "Not that I ever qualified."

I laughed and stepped into the middle for my quick turn. This was one of the things I would always remember about those days on the prairie: being inside the ring of wind-whipped skirts, clouds scudding overhead, my sisters joking about the sacrifice of their modesty, worrying aloud for the plight of any poor woman traveling without female companions.

One night I needed privacy after somehow missing the nightly group outing before bed. I slipped between the wagons, walked out fifty yards beyond the light, and ducked behind some willow bushes. Crouching there, I kept my eyes on the cluster of wagons, the glow of firelight on faces and the shadow show of figures moving inside the lantern-lit canvas covers.

Standing, I rearranged my skirts.

"Who's out there?" a voice demanded. "We hear you!"

Startled, embarrassed, I hesitated. Just as I drew breath to answer, right past my ear, a bullet zinged.

"Hey, don't shoot!" I yelled.

I heard some mutter of surprise and then, "For cryin' out loud, who is that?"

"It's just me." Weak-kneed with the near miss, I stumbled toward the wagons.

"Lovisa King!" It was Price Fuller, gun lowered. "Girl, you almost got yourself shot dead!"

"Got myself—?" Quick anger boiled. "You pulled the trigger, not me!"

"Well, what in blazes are you doing out there?"

"What do you think?" Oh, my cheeks were hot. Good thing it was dark.

Folks gathered. Sounded like a gunshot. It was! That King girl shot off her pa's rifle? No, no, she's the one got shot at! In a big hubbub everyone tried to explain to each other what had happened. My oldest brother, John, was yelling at me while Price's sister Melinda was giving Price a good jawing.

Red-faced and flustered, sputtering his defenses, Price turned and leveled a look at me. "Just never do that again, you hear?"

I looked him right back. "No, you never do that again."

Shocked, his mouth fell open. The rest watching seemed startled too.

"Now look here," he said. "We're just trying to protect you gals."

"Ha!" I tossed my hair. "Big, brave boy, just can't wait to shoot your gun off, can you? Shoot anything that moves without even seeing what it is!"

"You think it's fun, standing watch all night? You should be thanking us."

"Oh, sorry, I forgot. Yes, thanks, Price. Thanks for being such a poor shot!"

I felt Rowland's firm hand clamp around my upper arm. I looked up. With Rowland, this was farther up than it would have been with Pa or one of my brothers. His jaw was set. He looked mad. As he steered me back to our wagon, I heard more arguing among the folks left behind and then, clear as day, from one of the men I heard the words "bossy little thing," followed by laughing agreement.

I jerked back, wanting to thump someone.

"Oh, no, you don't." Rowland held tight. The man had an amazing grip. And a long stride. I was stumbling to keep up.

"You let me go," I said, struggling. "None of your business, anyway!"

He smiled grimly. " 'Fraid it is. Anything happens to you, I'll be answering to your pa." I realized he was dragging me the long way, avoiding my folks' wagon.

As we reached ours, Sally poked her head out from under the canvas flap to see what was up. This time, when I pulled away from Rowland, he released me.

"Now let this be a lesson."

I spun and climbed up over the buckboard. A lesson? And what would that lesson be? Don't do your private business in a willow thicket? Watch out for trigger-happy idiots with firearms?

"What on earth happened?" Sally asked.

"Oh, nothing. Price Fuller tried to shoot me dead, that's all."

"What!"

"So of course I'm the one in trouble." Still breathing hard, I summed up the story as I helped Meggie into her nightdress. "I'm telling you, Sally, it's a wonder there aren't a dozen dead already the way they've given a gun to every boy in long pants. And they won't so much as step away from their wagons without cocking them."

"I know, it's a worry, all right. Did you hear about Little Lute? Abbie caught him playing with one of John's pistols."

"Oh, my land!"

"But don't tell anyone. Susan doesn't want it getting back to Ma."

"That child needs two or three people riding herd on him." I turned to little Meggie. "Not like you"—and here I switched to baby talk—"You are such a little lovey, aren't you? Yes, you are a smart little woman, and you would never do a silly thing like play with guns."

"I heard that big bang," Meggie said. "Did you hear that?"

I nodded solemnly. "Yes, I did."

"Oh, dear," Sally said. "Too bad this had to happen with Price."

I cut her a look.

Sally winced.

"I just meant…well, I know Pa thought…Price being nineteen and you seventeen…" Sally lifted her shoulders and smiled as if this weren't the worst idea in the world. "Folks were saying you two looked fine together at the wedding dance."

I glowered, pleased and annoyed at the same time.

"You did complain Mr. Collins was too old."

"Well, I never said I wanted some wet-behind-the-ears boy, either. Anyway, Abbie already has her eye on Price."

"Oh. My, she doesn't waste any time, does she?"

I shook my head miserably. Was there something wrong with me that I seemed to be dragging my heels about this pairing-up business?

"Goodness sake. You all just met up again. She can't be promised to him yet! You've got just as much right to like him as she does."

I shrugged. What did it matter, now that I'd fouled it all up? I sighed, took up my bedroll and climbed out of the wagon. I spread my tarp and blankets next to Abbie, who was apparently so exhausted she'd slept through the whole incident.

We'd stopped bothering with the tent when the sky was clear, so

now I could stare at the stars while I brooded. The pure indigni-
ty of the whole thing! Honestly, half the camp must have seen me
come squawking out of the bushes with my skirts hiked up around
my knees! And the other half, I thought glumly, will have heard of
it by morning.

After awhile I heard Rowland's voice in the wagon. He was laughing. Well, not loudly, but it sounded like he and Sally were having
a good chuckle together. Probably laughing at me. I glanced over
there. I could see their silhouettes against the canvas cover, head
to head. I hated that. I rolled over, pulled my blanket up over my
shoulder and shut my eyes tight.

CHAPTER 5

"I AM DESPERATE FOR A HILL," I SAID

to Abbie one hot afternoon as we trudged along the outermost rut of the dozens that made up this section. "Even a little old puny one. Is that so much to ask? Just something up ahead to look at?" We'd been out here a month now. This dead-level stretch they called the Great Platte River Road was hundreds of miles long, and apparently every single one of them was going to look exactly the same.

"Pa warned us," Abbie reminded me.

"I s'pose." But hearing something as a fact—that the flat, treeless plains would make up a full quarter of the journey—was a far cry from walking it step after monotonous step, eyes straining ahead, positively aching to see something new.

It seemed we were forever sleepwalking our way toward, but never reaching, a waving wall of hot, shimmering air. Sometimes in the distance we'd see evidence of one of those fearsome Platte River Valley storms we'd heard so much about—curtains of slanting black rain, flashes of lightning. But always the curtains seemed to part for us. Our journey, in that respect, seemed charmed as we passed peaceably on. So peaceably, in fact, that the daily trudges put us to sleep.

I could see Amos now, riding out by the cattle, slumped in his saddle. Likewise Sally nodded off on the wagon seat, Jimmy lying across her lap, Meggie's bonneted head bumping rhythmically against her shoulder.

Oh, the dullness of this country! One evening as the wagons were halted and Meggie was awakened and lifted to the ground, she took one look at the campsite and burst into tears.

"What is it, honey?" My eyes followed Meggie's for the cause, found none.

"It's the same!" Meggie cried. "We can never get to O'gen 'cause every night we camp in the same place!"

"Oh, sweetie." I struggled to keep a straight face. "It just looks the same. Honestly, we're getting to Oregon. Every day we're a little bit closer."

If the days were drearisome, though, the nights, at least, could be pleasant. An arch of blank sky at noon, after all, made the most magnificent canvas for the painting of a prairie sunset come evening. Out here you didn't so much watch a sunset as stand and let yourself be surrounded by it. The entire sky, horizon to horizon, would be flung with a tracery of puffed clouds, then lit to gold and deep rose.

I loved the mornings, too, when fires were stirred and sweet smoke spiraled into the brisk air. Lacing my boots, I would marvel at this miracle of daily renewal. No matter how spent I'd felt crawling into my bedroll the night before, a good night's sleep always let me awaken with new energy and optimism. Downing my first cup of coffee, it didn't seem so impossible that perhaps today would be the glorious day when something new would finally appear up ahead!

I'd be milking Buttercup when the sun would rise in one fast flash over that lowest of horizons behind us, instantly flooding the world with light and warmth. Birds warbled musically in the river's willows, and the children called to each other from wagon to wagon.

"Here, Auntie Lovisa!" our littlest ones chirped, holding up their bowls of porridge for a splash of Buttercup's fresh milk.

They were all looking so bright and healthy. I guess it was true what they said about the clean air of the plains. People were positively thriving. You couldn't walk fifteen miles a day, after all, without building some stamina. Personally, I'd never felt healthier or stronger in my life.

Little Lexie, pale and spindly back home, was now round and rosy and insisting on walking some each day, marching along with "the big girls."

Even brother Stephen and Hope's husband, Lucius Norton, seemed some better, actually getting out of their wagons in the evenings, looking almost cheerful as they sharpened an ax or spliced a bit of trail rope.

Everyone had such hearty appetites. Food had never tasted better than it did out here in the open air. I got used to eating standing up myself, and many an evening found my slab of bacon between pieces of bread the most delicious thing I'd ever tasted. My brothers cheerfully gobbled whatever we cooked and never complained about the grit that invariably made its way into the beans, or the mosquitoes that occasionally flecked the biscuits. Any day now, they promised each other, we'd all be dining on big, thick buffalo steaks!

"I don't think you're going to want to be starting in on a washing," Rowland warned me one evening as I emerged from the wagon with an armful of laundry. He was shaving in front of a sliver of mirror propped on the wagon seat.

"I most certainly do. Sol says it's a good little stream here."

"Won't be here long enough to get things dry, though."

"I don't care," I said, jumping from the wagon, eyes averted. Things were different out here, true, but it still didn't seem quite right to see him doing something so personal, his galluses down and all. "I'm dying for clean clothes." Clean underthings, I was thinking as I flounced off, but I wasn't about to say that to him.

Quite a few of the girls had the same idea, and in short order we were lining the creek bank, dunking our camisoles and split-legged pantalets.

"So," I whispered to Abbie, who knelt beside me, "I see we still have the Browns with us." Across the swale, up in camp, I could see Mamie Brown sitting on an ox yoke, writing. Our company had divided into two smaller groups, and I would have been just as glad if the Browns had gone with the other.

Abbie refused to echo my derisive tone. She was still rather impressed with Mamie, partly, perhaps, because we'd learned she actually had three different dresses to alternate. One, Mamie had enjoyed pointing out to us, featured sleeves cut in the very latest French fashion.

"Did you know she's keeping a journal of the whole trip?" Abbie asked.

"You don't say. Why?"

"Well, I imagine because she wants to remember all this, of course."

"Abbie! As if we could ever possibly forget."

"She probably writes her thoughts," Abbie said. "Maybe she wants to express the secrets of her innermost heart. Or maybe she's even writing about us."

"Daresay! Complaining what a low lot we are, how terribly her circumstances have been reduced seeing as how she has to travel with such common folk!" And then I thought of something else. "You suppose she'll put down the truth about what a perfect blockhead her pa is?" Mr. Brown had stirred things up before we'd even left the rendezvous camp by stubbornly refusing to adequately stock his wagon. Pa said he argued over every last item during his official inspection. It wasn't a question of not having the money, either. No, he was just determined to get to Oregon with more cash than the rest of us and be ahead. As Mamie had pointed out to us, her pa wasn't "just a farmer." He intended to set up some kind of business. I guess that made him think he didn't have to stick to the same rules as others. He'd even hired two young men to drive his oxen. He wasn't going to walk along yelling Gee! and Haw!

"Maybe," Abbie said dreamily, "Mamie sets down which boy danced with which girl when they got out the fiddles." A topic far from boring as far as she was concerned, obviously. "I hope she noticed me dancing with Price Fuller."

"Don't worry," Bitsy Fuller said, skipping up from behind. "Everybody did."

"Bitsy!" Abbie said, flinging around. "Where did you come from?"

"Back there," the little girl said. "Now, I have it all planned out, see." Her tone was low and confidential, her expression serious. "Amos and my sister Melinda like each other, right? I'm gonna marry Sol, and Abbie, I just know Price likes you."

Abbie sucked in her breath. "Did he say that, Bitsy?"

"Abbie." Bitsy admonished her with a you-should-know-better look. "Boys don't actually say those things, do they? But anyone can see it!"

Delighted, Abbie went back to scrubbing her linens with renewed vigor.

"I'm not sure about you, Lovisa," Bitsy said, and then added with an attempt at charity, "I guess you could marry Henry."

"Henry! Bitsy, I like your brother Henry fine, but he's a little sixteen-year-old boy!"

"Well, I just wanted you to have a sweetheart matchup too, and I didn't know who else to say."

I laughed, but partly as a cover. Good Lord, even the children were worried about me becoming an old maid!

It was a bit embarrassing, having to prop our wet underthings on sticks by the fire to dry, but worth it to see the look of shock on Mamie's face when she came over to our campfire and spotted the indecency. Horrified, she spun on her heel and went right back to her own wagon.

I grinned at Abbie. "Shall we do this every night?"

I wasn't grinning in the morning, though, when we had to put our underthings back on, cold and damp. All the forenoon, those of us who'd been tempted by thoughts of cleanliness traded grimaces with each other. What a novel discovery—wet clothes were worse than dirty!

Later, when I'd remember this incident, I couldn't imagine what we'd been thinking. Why hadn't we just gone without underthings for awhile? Who would have even known? But that was back when we still had our standards to keep up. The pure foolishness of enduring such discomfort for propriety's sake never occurred to us. We were too busy seeing ourselves as bravely bringing civilization into the wilderness.

I felt sorry for the boys.

How long the hours must have seemed to them without the distraction of chatter that helped pass time for us girls. You could see them sitting stolidly on their horses or trudging beside the oxen, nary a sound from them but the occasional grunt at one of the stubborn beasts.

Abbie and I could talk endlessly, we found. Mostly we argued, and beyond that we could recount the past, analyze the present, and speculate about the future, all stories told with an unspoken agreement that repetition would be permitted when necessary.

Sometimes we compared the nieces and nephews in our charge. Abbie envied me my good-natured Jimmy while she had fuss-face baby Charlie. But when it came to the little girls, Abbie clearly thought Lexie superior.

"We have to keep special watch on her," I remember her remarking once. "Indians get a look at that hair of hers, they'll just go crazy. Steal her in a flash."

I gave her a sideways glance. "You really think so?"

"Yes! Everyone says!"

It's true, people couldn't keep their hands away from Lexie's spun-gold curls. Still, all we'd seen of Indians so far were a few Pawnees watching us from a distance and a party or two that had come closer to trade. They hardly seemed the threat anticipated when we formed such a huge company for protection's sake. Now our men had agreed that, at least for the present, having too many cattle trying to graze the same patch of grass was a much more immediate concern than Indian attack, and that's why they'd split the company.

Abbie and I eagerly awaited the gossip our scouts brought back from groups ahead of us on the trail. Measles had broken out, they would report. A girl had fallen out of a wagon, and the front wheel ran right over her. Luckily it happened in a mirey spot, though, so she wasn't badly injured. A man from Texas in one of the California-bound groups was making everyone nervous, bragging he aimed to catch himself an Indian slave first chance he got. He was such a brute, no one had the nerve to even speak up to him, much less kick him out like they wished they could.

These tales passed back through our family's wagons as fast as we could tell them. Sometimes we'd dart ahead in line to hear some new bit of gossip, walk and talk and get the details, then slow our pace, allowing our own wagons to catch up with us again.

"They had a wedding in the train ahead," Mamie Brown lingered to tell me one day when I happened to be walking alone.

"Another one?" People seemed to be pairing up at an amazing rate.

"Yes, and a baby born. The whole train had to lay by half a day for that birthing. People weren't too happy."

"Well, honestly! The poor woman couldn't help it."

"My mother says she could. Says it's pure foolishness for women to be in that way on a journey like this. People ought to consider things beyond their own appetites."

I gave her a sideways glance, not wanting to let on I wasn't quite sure if she meant what I thought she meant. Too bad Abbie was having to ride with Lexie and Lute at the moment. I needed her here to help think of smart answers!

Now Mamie stopped and aimed the barrel of her bonnet right at mine, the better to see my face. "How many brothers and sisters did you say you have?"

"Don't know as I did say."

"So, how many?"

I glanced over to our wagon. "Well, eleven of us, going west."

"My goodness," Mamie said, askance. "That's a lot of babies to have."

My cheeks went hot, and I wasn't even sure why. Maybe it was the scandalized tone of Mamie's voice, as if she were morally superior somehow, for having just one pasty-faced little brother. For a moment I watched Sally swaying on the wagon seat, Jimmy in her arms. I wasn't about to mention our older married sisters back east who hadn't come, or the ones who'd died as children. If Mamie thought eleven babies excessive, what would she say to Ma having delivered, altogether, sixteen?

"Well," Mamie said, "I certainly hope our company won't have to stop for any of that business. It's so unfair to the rest."

"Look, Mamie, with three thousand people on the road, there's bound to be babies born. Life's not going to stop, just because we've all pulled up stakes and headed west."

Even as I was trying mightily to sound like I knew what was what, though, a quick mental count of the young wives in our family—Sally, Hope, Susan, and Annie—made me realize we had no one in that expectant condition right now. No one had started a baby since Pa announced we were making the trek. So how had my older sisters managed that? Was this just another phase of the planning that had gone into the overland journey, one no one had needed to discuss with me?

"That new baby up ahead?" Mamie said. "They named her Missouri."

"Now that," I said, relieved for a topic on which I had a confident opinion, "is something that qualifies as pure foolishness to me. I mean, if that's how they feel about it, why didn't they stay home? If I had a baby out here, I'd name her something hopeful and for-ward-looking. Like Oregon. Or Columbia. Or...West."

"If you had a baby out here," Mamie said darkly, "you would be in deep, deep trouble."

Gossiping about folks in other wagons did help pass the miles, but what we really longed for were stories about what to expect on the road far ahead. These could only come from the handful of travel-ers working their way back east. Once, we heard a wagon was com-ing our way, but when the turn-back family got closer, they pulled away and skirted the train entirely.

"Now why did they have to go and do that?" I complained to Pa, watching the turn-backs' cloud of dust in the distance as they steered clear. "Don't they know we all want to hear what's ahead?"

"Know it all too well," Pa said, prodding his lead ox. "Know if they stopped and told their story to everyone who wanted to hear it, they'd never get anywhere."

"I suppose."

"Besides, you want to be careful about listening to anyone heading back."

"What do you mean?"

"Well, they'll lie. Say whatever makes them feel better about what they already decided. There was a turn-back wagon a few days ago, told Captain T'Vault they'd been attacked by Indians."

"I never heard that!"

"That's right, because we didn't want to worry you girls. Turned out it wasn't true anyway. Remember that outfit we passed yesterday? They said no such thing happened. The turn-back wagon had been with them and the people just lost heart, that's all. Got scared."

I watched the lone wagon in the distance.

"Pretty low-down," I said. "Blaming it on the Indians."

"Easier than the truth," Pa said.

"Right." I smirked. "Howdedo, there! We're the Cowards! Yep! Got scared, headin' on home!"

Pa laughed. "Like I've always said, missy—think why folks say what they say. It's not that they're mean-spirited, most of them. Just that they naturally have their own interests at heart. Far as this trip, it's up to us to hear everybody out, take what they got to say with a grain of salt, and make our own decisions."

Walking along beside him in these fine boots he'd had made for me, I wasn't worried. My father was a wise man. I was confident he'd make the right decisions.

We'd never be those turn-back types, telling low-down lies to save our pride.

Not the Kings.

CHAPTER 6

I PRIED UP ANOTHER HARDENED DISK OF buffalo manure, ripping it free from the whitened-out grass beneath. Bugs scattered in panic, their world disrupted. I watched the crawlers a moment, then tossed the big chip into our basket. At first this whole business had disgusted me. Pick up manure with our bare hands? Didn't take long to start seeing the droppings as the blessings they were, though. What else were we to burn in this treeless expanse? When our noon stop found us at a place with lots of dried droppings, as today, we weren't above toting a few in the wagon against the possibility of not finding enough later to get the evening meal cooked.

As I bent for another of the flat, round piles, something hit me in the rear.

"Hey!" I snapped up, whipped around. "Lute! You little—" Picking up buffalo chips I'd consent to; being pelted with buffalo chips I wouldn't.

"Watch this!" Little Lute curled his arm and flung out a disk, sending it hurling.

"Lutey, stop it!" Susan ordered, marching from their wagon with a washtub for collecting the fuel. "That's a fine trick but it won't do the cooks a lick of good. And now look."

The little ones, Meggie and Lexie, Hope's Isaac and the smallest Fuller boy, had usually been good for collecting a chip or two. Now they were trying to throw theirs, which gave the bigger girls an excuse to stop and laugh and play audience instead of doing their share of the gathering.

"Come on, you all," I said. "Many hands make light work." The sun was blazing, but I folded back my bonnet brim anyway. A person had to be able to see.

"Whoa!" Little Lute cried. "Looky here, a snake!"

"Don't, Lutey," Susan said mildly. "I won't have your teasing."

"It's an old rattler," Lute went on.

Still no one looked. Little Lute fibbed so much, we were used to ignoring him.

"Let's see if we can't fill this tub," Susan said, dropping in another chip.

"Here he is!" Lute cried.

I glanced up. Gasped.

On a forked stick, Lute displayed a rattlesnake.

"Looky this, Lexie!" He swung the writhing serpent toward his sister.

Our golden-haired girl stared, transfixed.

Susan sprang to action. Dumping her chips, she moved smoothly, calmly toward the little group.

"Lute! Drop it!"

He obeyed.

In one fluid motion, Susan scooped up Lexie and threw the wash tub over the snake. Then, while the rest of us let loose a hysterical torrent of advice at each other about what to do next, she darted back the few steps to the wagon, deposited Lexie, pulled the ax from the wagon rack and returned.

"You flip up the tub when I give the word," she told me. "One chance. Kids—stand back."

Terrified, completely in the power of Susan's firm command, I moved to the appointed position.

"Now!"

I took a breath, reached over the far side of the tub to catch the handle, flipped it back toward myself and sprang away. I never saw that snake alive. Never saw if it was coiled or laid out. By the time I turned around, Susan was standing there with a gory ax, gaping at her own handiwork.

The children stared too. Then they cheered. Attracted by the commotion, others from camp came running.

"Susan!" I pressed my hand over my pounding heart. "Oh, my God!"

Susan's eyes met mine, and only then, it seemed, did the drama register. The blood drained from her face and she crumpled to the ground.

Well! This was a story. This was worth repeating. It shot through the train. Every witness, down to the tiniest, told it his own way, and nobody embroidered it more elaborately than the folks who hadn't been there at all.

"I can't believe I did that," Susan kept saying later, claiming it was like hearing a story of someone else's daring deed. If I hadn't seen her in action, I might not have believed it myself, for she was the last of all of us I'd have credited with the grit for such heroics.

Now we were all looking at Susan in a new light.

"Did you hear about our Susan?" Ma would be heard bragging for a good time to come. "Killed a rattler, saved our little grand-daughter. The goldy-haired one."

"When are we gonna see those buffalo?" Sol wondered aloud every evening, and often he'd wander among the other camps, asking about sightings. And he meant the real thing, the big shaggy-headed beasts themselves, not just the fresher, thicker concentrations of their droppings we'd recently been encountering.

Finally one day at what we thought would be our nooning spot, he came riding back from the lead wagons, flushed and excited.

"They're up ahead," he announced. "Buffalo!"

Amos and Isaac and Price jumped up.

"We're ordered to stop and camp right here tonight," Sol said. "Come on, boys! We're goin' on a buffalo hunt!"

With an eruption of whoops, the would-be hunters grabbed their guns, adjusted their saddles, and stuffed down the rest of their bread and bacon as they rode off.

They say no one who crossed the plains in those years would ever forget the buffalo. I believe it, especially anyone who was a privileged witness, as Jimmy and I were that afternoon, to the interminable passing of an entire herd.

Hiking ahead with the baby on my hip, standing on a rise, I gazed west as the earth itself seemed to come alive with brown movement, mile after mile of the animals thundering north, plowing, bellowing, pounding the ground to powder, plunging right across the river.

"Look at that," I crooned, holding the baby up, his soft cheek to mine. "What is that?"

Does a baby really see? His astonished eyes told me yes. But can a baby remember? At least hold on to a deeply implanted feeling of awe? For a once-in-a-lifetime spectacle like this, it seemed only right to give him the chance.

How many animals could that possibly be, I wondered, when it took hours and hours for them to pass? I couldn't take my own eyes away, and if Jimmy hadn't eventually started fussing for his mother, who knows how long I might have stood captivated by the panorama.

That night when my brothers returned, Sol bounced down off his horse like he'd conquered the world.

"Four! We got four of 'em," he cried and then launched into a dramatic recounting of the hunt, how they'd picked them off in ambush from a bluff. "You wouldn't believe how many of 'em. Ran so thick, you couldn't miss!"

Ma surveyed the slabs of meat they'd unloaded. "This is four buffalo?"

The boys laughed. Ma was so foolish!

"You know how big those things are, close up?" Isaac asked.

Ma squinted at him. "I'm not stupid, son. I know they're big. So where's the rest of the meat?"

"Well, we couldn't bring it all," Amos said.

"So what did you do with it?"

The boys looked at each other uneasily.

"Left it there," Isaac said. "What'd you think we were going to do with it?"

Ma frowned. "Well, that seems kind of a shame, doesn't it? Wasting it like that?"

"Ma," Sol said. "You didn't see the size of the herd. We're telling the truth—there's thousands and thousands of them!"

"Hmm." That's all Ma would say.

The boys hunched their shoulders, not appreciating her implication one bit. Why'd she have to go spoil such a splendid hunt? I heard Isaac mumble that he bet the Indian women didn't complain when the men brought home the dinner.

Rowland had rigged up some racks, and we were busy hanging the meat for jerking when Captain Barlow rode into camp. His company was occupying a grassy swale nearby.

"Looks like you boys did pretty well out there," he said.

My brothers swelled. This was more like it. They ought to be congratulated! Sol looked like he was gearing up to tell the entire story of the hunt again, but Captain Barlow cut him off.

"We can't have you killing more than you can use, though," he said. "Indians are already complaining that's what happened with the group ahead of us."

Isaac flung his hat to the dirt. "Oh, for Pete's sake!"

"Remember now, this is their country," Captain Barlow said. "We're just passing through."

"You know how long we've been looking forward to this?" Amos demanded.

"I know, I know." Captain Barlow held up his hands. "But I'm not just picking on you. We're making this announcement at all the campfires. We've got to bear in mind that the less attention we attract out here, the better, and leaving the plains littered with buffalo carcasses definitely won't win us any friends with the Sioux. We have to think about the welfare of every single emigrant on the road. And that includes the folks bound to come next year too."

Isaac and Amos hung their heads, trading dark looks with each other.

"If there were rules," Sol said, speaking up rather boldly for a twelve-year-old, "I think somebody should have laid 'em out before."

"Well, son," Captain Barlow said, "that's the thing about doing something brand new like overland travel. We have to figure out the rules as we go. And the first rule's got to be that we all use some common sense. You boys didn't even skin those carcasses! You know those hides are worth eight dollars each?"

"All right, all right," Amos said, weary of the lecture, and finally Captain Barlow moved on to the next camp.

The meat was delicious, and I determined to enjoy it in spite

70

of being forced to dine to the accompaniment of the boys' grumbling.

"What do you think, Rowland?" Isaac said finally. "The man's not even our captain. Has he got any right to come over here and treat us like a bunch of naughty schoolboys?"

"Well," Rowland said, "you don't want to hear it, but I think Barlow makes a lot of sense."

My brothers regarded him in surprised silence a moment, then shut up once and for all and ate.

Now, how did Rowland get away with this? Ma could say the same thing, and they'd hardly pay her any mind. But if Rowland so much as hinted they'd been wasteful, they seemed instantly to declare themselves guilty as charged.

I watched Rowland forking up his buffalo steak and wondered: Did I admire him for this or resent it?

CHAPTER 7

"INDIANS!"

My God. I dropped the pot of beans I'd been stirring.

"Get in the wagons!"

I scooped up Meggie and made a dash. All around me the other women did the same—snatching a screaming child here, a silent, petrified one there.

The men seemed panicked, running every which way.

I heaved Meggie over the tailgate, hoisted myself up and tumbled in after.

"Get down," I ordered Sally, who was braced against a wagon bow, dozing, nursing Jimmy. Unaware of the alarm, she looked annoyed for an instant.

"Lovisa. Honestly, I don't know why you—"

A gun cracked. Her eyes flew wide.

"Sally!" I could hardly breathe. Nightmarishly, words wouldn't come. "Get down!" I finally managed. "Just. Get. Down!"

Drained pale, she obeyed.

I wedged the whimpering Meggie down among the boxes and lay over her. My heart pounded like to burst. Outside, the men yelled, the fear in their voices my undoing.

This was it! The Indians would scalp us all! Oh, we never should have relaxed our guard. Never should have mocked the men for keeping their guns so close at hand when we started out. Now we'd pay. It all came back—a hundred horrid images, every awful story of girls carried off by savages that Mr. Collins used to enjoy telling; Captain Waymire warning that the Indians would scalp us, every one; terrifying scenes Mamie liked to recount from certain forbidden novels. Now I saw they were right about the Indians. We never should have come out here! Nothing in Oregon could be worth it. Why hadn't we listened to the warnings?

"Oh, my God," Sally panted. "Oh, my God."

And then, from outside the wagon, a man yelled, "Wait! Hold your fire!" and another muttered, "Well, I'll be."

After a moment, Rowland appeared at the wagon flap.

"It's all right," he said. "False alarm."

I sat up. "What?"

He peered right past me to his wife and babies. "Are you all right, Sally? Meggie?"

"What's happening?" I asked, faint and shaky.

"It's just the cavalry."

Sally burst into tears, clutching and rocking Jimmy.

"Colonel Kearny's men," Rowland said. "I guess Brown didn't get the word they'd be coming along behind us, so he just assumed, when he saw that big cloud of dust and men on horseback…"

"Rowland," Sally whispered. "Oh, Rowland."

"Oh, for land sake!" I sputtered, as Rowland and I traded places and he gathered the others in his arms. I pushed past him, out to the wagon seat.

Children swarmed from the other wagons, laughing in thrilled relief. Lydia let herself down from Pa's wagon and staggered, reeling. Annie hurried to poor Stephen, standing there with his rifle. He'd risen to the occasion but now leaned against the big rear wheel as if he might pass out.

The rest of the men looked sheepish.

I climbed down and marched back to the cook fire. Fine thing. The beans were burned. Were we supposed to start cooking all over? Disgusted, I started dishing up plates. Let 'em eat burnt supper, then. They ought to be more careful, scaring everybody like that. So much for all parties knowing what to do in an emergency. We'd every one of us been racing around crazier than bugs under a ripped-up cow chip! And Sally—well, this would set her back a good fortnight. This made her fears seem reasonable. She'd be able to think of nothing but the bad things that might happen in the days ahead.

As for the soldiers themselves, when they rode up, resplendent in their red and blue uniforms, I'll be blamed if I didn't catch something of smugness in their smiles. Why, they thought it was funny! They thought our panic just showed how pathetic we were, how grateful we ought to be for their disciplined military presence.

The worst part of all was the way Abbie and Lydia fawned over them. So relieved they weren't Indians, they greeted the soldiers as if they had, in fact, daringly rescued us all from the horrible savages we'd been imagining! Instead of merely scaring the daylights out of everyone.

Plopping out burned beans, I glanced back at our own wagon. Rowland was still in there, comforting Sally.

After supper, Abbie combed out Lydia's braids and pinned her hair up into a chignon. Then the two of them ran off to the Williams' campfire, where the soldiers had come back to visit after setting up camp nearby.

From several fires away I could hear the convivial conversation and pictured the soldiers walking about with puffed chests, trying to look bold and manly for Orlena. Her little brother was playing a jaunty tune on his harmonica. "The Girl I Left Behind Me."

I sat by our own fire, bouncing Jimmy on my knee. Funny, every time a burst of laughter escaped the Williams' camp, his eyes would go wide and he'd twist around, trying to figure it out. Annie came and sat with me a moment, crocheting the length of lace she'd been working on ever since St. Joe, but before long she rose to return to her wagon.

"Stephen gets lonesome when he hears everybody off at another campfire. I can't let him think I've gone over there."

I nodded. There was something hard about hearing fun being had when you weren't in on it. Now and then I'd catch the trilling notes of Orlena's musical voice, followed by another round of appreciative laughter. Obviously, all the young men found her far and away the wittiest thing ever to swish a petticoat.

"Don't you want to go over there with the others?"

I jumped. Rowland was standing at my shoulder.

"You scared me."

"Sorry."

"Figured it was my job to stay here," I said, recovering myself. "Look after this little feller. I imagine Sally's still rather poorly."

"She'll be all right." He looked toward the Williams' camp. "Sounds like they're having a good time. You ought to go."

"So I can flirt with soldiers?" I cut my eyes at him. "No, thanks."

He looked back at the wagon. "Suit yourself. But Sally wants the baby in now anyway." He scooped Jimmy away from me and headed off.

Oh, dear. Rowland was just trying to be nice. Why'd I have to act so insulted? Now I was completely alone and disconsolate. Without Jimmy, I didn't even have an excuse for not going over to the Williams'. Nobody needed me here. Nobody cared a snap what I did.

I sat staring into the fire, grudging audience to the distant ripples of merriment on the night air. Around me shadow stories were being enacted on the canvas covers of each wagon as my older sisters tucked in their children.

Here I was, in the middle of this huge family, yet I felt as lonely as some poor orphan girl.

I stood up. I couldn't sit here like this. If Ma saw me, she'd come out and give me a job, put some bit of work into my idle hands. I moved between the wagons and out into the darkness. Everybody else had a place, a purpose. But not me. Not really.

I threw my head back and stared at the sky, white with stars. Wasn't this the same sky I'd thought made such a pretty dance canopy before? But somehow, if you're having a good mope, that wide prairie sky is the very thing to make you feel all the smaller and more insignificant.

I wrapped my shawl tighter, wishing somebody would miss me and come out here looking for me. I wished somebody would ask what was wrong so I could say how lonely I felt. I wished I had the faintest clue who I wanted that someone to be.

Now the reedy notes of a mouth organ pierced the night with the plaintive strains of "Shenandoah."

That song! Swelling anticipation. Love and longing. Unutterable sorrow. It was all there, tightening my throat, making tears sting my eyes. Away! I'm bound away, 'cross the wide Missouri…I swear, hearing it was like having someone reach out and squeeze your heart, make you weep for every sad thing ever happened, then weep for all the sad things sure to come.

The South Platte River was wide and shallow and sandy, treeless except for the scrubby willows on the islands, the only shrubbery to somehow escape the relentless grazing of the vast buffalo herds and the prairie fires folks said the Indians set.

Every night I dipped up buckets of the thickest, muddiest water you've ever seen. Week after week we followed this stretch of the river, and I hardly knew which was more tiresome, the horrid water itself or the oft-repeated joke about the Platte being too thick to drink, too thin to plow.

You'd think the cloudy water would settle sometime, but the scouts who knew said it was the buffalo herds ahead that never gave it a chance. Stood to reason. If a girl's foot made brown clouds billow in the water, what would the churning hooves of a great buffalo herd do?

Each evening as I waded out to break willow branches from the islands for cook-fire fuel, my bare feet would sink deep into that softest of sand, liquid powder. Miring to my calves, I'd worry—how on earth could heavy wagons and oxen pull through this muck?

I wasn't the only one dreading the upcoming crossing. Mrs. Brown, Mamie's mother, was doing her best to make sure everyone stayed nervous about it, reminding any who'd listen of how many wagons had been lost at the South Platte crossing last year. And what about '43, when the river flooded a mile wide and one company spent six whole days getting across? Several wagons never made it. River swept them from the end of the chained-together line, it was said, and tumbled them under the current.

What a pleasant surprise for our company, then, to find, at the fording spot, the river running closer to a half mile wide and not deep at all. We doubled the oxen on half the wagons and brought the first batch across. Then the men splashed the teams back, rehitched them and drove over the rest of the wagons. Keep 'em moving, was the word. Don't let 'em stop and sink in the quicksand bottom. The tremendous noise is what I'll always remember, I think—the alarming roar of the sand-laden Platte River rushing through the wheels' wooden spokes. In the end, though, the whole business required only two hours, and we didn't lose a single wagon or animal.

Spirits were high in camp that night. A milestone to celebrate! We'd made it through this tedious stretch and successfully completed the crossing—a challenge we'd been dreading, I reckon, more than most of us had cared to admit. Now we'd done it! The relief was like corks popping off bottled fizz drink.

Fiddles made a jolly time of it, and we danced 'til the dust flew and our hands smarted from clapping. You never saw such bright eyes, such lively stepping. What an enterprising outfit we were! Best darned company on the trail, truth be told. We had men who could bring down buffalo! Brave young mothers who could chop the heads off rattlesnakes! Lively girls who could walk all day and cut capers all night! Common sense, that's all it took. Good planning and a pinch of grit. God Himself was on our side, and we were going to Oregon!

Everybody paired up—Amos and Melinda, Abbie and Price. Little Bitsy got Sol to whirl her around, and Lydia went after Orlena's older brother Jont Williams. Those who didn't dance watched and clapped. Even the captains. Even Rowland.

That boy, John Noble, came straight for me, and, as the music played on, I began to think him rather attractive. Maybe soon I'd be pairing up like the rest of the girls!

I had never danced so long or so hard, and I remember thinking, This is it—we are having the time of our lives! My heart pounded, my cheeks were hot, my lungs pumped that good air of the plains. We all acted a regular parcel of fools, and when John Noble pulled me into the shadows, I even let him kiss me.

To be honest, I kissed him right back.

Judging from the giggling in the dark all around us, we weren't the only ones.

Funny. I'd always imagined a moment like this would mostly be about the boy I was kissing. Instead, it seemed to have more to do with a blazing-star sky and the heady thrill of making it over the South Platte River alive.

But that's the way it seemed to go out there on the plains. Loneliness felt lonelier, excitement more exciting. Just being alive was so much more intense, and everything was different—even first kisses.

CHAPTER 8

"FOLKS ARE TALKING, YOU KNOW," MAMIE
Brown whispered over my shoulder.

I pulled my toothbrush out of my mouth and spit. Then I turned, regarding her warily.

"About the dance last night. About you. And your sisters. How you went off in the dark with the boys."

I blushed red-hot. "Is that so?"

"My ma says you better be careful. She says you keep this up, she wouldn't be one bit surprised if you all get to Oregon with your aprons riding high."

My mouth fell open.

"I'm only telling you for your own good."

And before I could think of a snappy reply, she was gone.

Well.

Abbie and I got a full two miles out of Mamie's saying this, furiously recounting our outrage as we walked. The audacity of the girl! Lydia joined us, thrilled to learn she'd been included in the insults.

"Are you sure Mamie meant me too?" Lydia asked again.

"Well, she said sisters. Who else could she mean?" Suddenly I stopped and really looked at her. "Lyddie! Who were you off in the dark with?"

She blushed furiously, happily. "Jont Williams."

Oh, mercy. When did our Lydia stop being a little girl? I guess she wasn't looking so bony anymore, now that I truly paid attention.

"Tell me again," Abbie demanded, clearly having given up any remaining feelings of admiration she'd harbored for Mamie. "Tell me exactly what she said."

Honestly, we didn't shut up until that long, miserable hill at last required the full measure of our energy and attention.

"This is all your fault," Abbie huffed and then mimicked me in singsong. " 'Just show me a hill!' "

"I never said…" I stopped for breath, "…I necessarily wanted to climb it!" Anyway, at least hills showed we were getting somewhere. If we were climbing, we might actually be able to see farther ahead at the crest.

But when the weary oxen had snorted and bellowed and struggled to the summit, I scanned a full circle and…couldn't see a thing. It was like we were on top of the world. So close was the horizon, the land just seemed to drop away into the sky's blue oblivion.

This pull over the ridge between the South Fork of the Platte and the North was proving as difficult as anything we'd yet encountered. To make it worse, the pilots led us the wrong way, forcing us to double back and march late into the night. After a miserable, waterless camp, we faced, at daylight, the descent of an incline so steep we had to rough-cock the wheels and rig ropes to ease the wagons down.

But then we were rewarded with arrival at Ash Hollow. Clean, burbling spring water! Trees big enough to cast shade. Wildflowers.

Sprung free of the wagons, we ran around like a giddy, bouquet-picking pack of lunatics.

Too bad John Noble had to spoil it.

"I feel bad about what happened," he said, cornering me in the meadow. "You know, after the dance."

"Don't worry about it," I said lightly, plucking a yellow flower, wondering whether it would make a decent wool dye. I looked up at John and smiled. "I forgive you." In this pleasant place, the sunlight itself felt like a kiss, not the usual daily punishment, and put me in a benevolent mood. Who cared what people were saying? It was probably just Mamie and her mother anyway.

"But, Lovisa." He hesitated. "The thing is, you kissed me back."

I stood up straight, blushed.

"My pa says...well, good girls don't do that."

"Oh, for Pete's sake! You ran and told him?" I whirled and started away as fast as skirts dragging in deep grass allowed, then stopped and turned back. "Go kiss Mamie Brown, why doncha? If you're looking to get slapped, I'm sure she'd be happy to oblige!"

I stomped off fuming, and although some might call me over-hasty with my decisions, that was it for me right there regarding John Noble. I didn't care if he was my only hope for a sweetheart. A boy mad I'd kissed him! And was he mad at himself, pray tell? Not so's you'd notice.

Something twisted about that, to my mind. Something dark.

We could have happily rested at Ash Hollow a whole week, but as Pa pointed out, a good campsite here in June wouldn't do a thing to stall off those early snows in the Blue Mountains.

Hurry. We always had to hurry. We had to keep moving.

More days of dreary monotony as the North Platte we now followed looked pretty much like the South. Was it possible the tales of magnificent scenery on the road to Oregon were pure humbug?

And then the terrain began to change.

Finally, those castles. Those ancient citadels of which we'd heard tell. I found myself completely enchanted by the tawny bluffs and rocky crags rising up along the road. I was a girl, after all, who'd never before laid eyes on a geographic feature more dramatic than a hill. I walked many an extra mile with those who chose to climb, just to claim the view ahead.

One of those was John Noble, and although for the life of me I couldn't understand why, it was no time at all before he was once again following me around.

"You better watch out," I told him. "Don't want your pa seeing you going off with a bad girl!"

He reddened as if baffled by his own contradictory feelings, then went right on dogging my steps like I had him on some kind of halter.

"Couldn't we just forget I said that?" he pleaded.

"Oh, no, it's a serious matter, your spiritual welfare. I couldn't bear to have your downfall on my conscience."

Maybe this pert talk was just me trying to cover my own uneasiness, though. Could he possibly be right? Was I a bad girl? Once, I brought it up to Sally.

"Can I ask you something?" I said.

"Well, of course."

"But it's kind of…personal."

"Lovisa, you're my sister."

"All right, then. Um, when Rowland kisses you, do you kiss him back?"

"Lovisa!" Her face went beet red.

"What?" I said, instantly mortified. "You told me I could—"

"I didn't know you meant a question like that!"

Well. So, maybe I was bad. You can bet that was the last time I sought anyone else's opinion on the subject!

As we moved westward, I reveled in the way new scenes unfolded daily. Every night we camped amid the most romantic and fantastically shaped bluffs.

"Sally, you've got to come out and look at the sunset," I told my sister one evening, lifting up the canvas at the side of the wagon.

"Too tired."

"But it's glorious! Come on, it'll make you feel better."

Sally wasn't budging, poor thing.

So I watched with Meggie as the slanting rays transformed the bluffs into the coppery domes of ancient cities, and in great majesty the red sun sank.

"See, Meggie? It's like a beacon. Like the sun is saying, Yes, this way. Keep coming this way. West."

And then that one particularly memorable day. It was hot and glaring, and I had just climbed to the wagon seat to trade places taking care of the children and let Sally walk awhile. As the wagon hauled up onto a rise affording a view across miles of plains, I saw it and—mercy—tears sprang to my eyes. Wordlessly, I seized Sally's forearm. There, against a band of outcroppings at the horizon rose that most celebrated rock spire some trappers had named the chimney, a singular formation pointing hundreds of feet into the heavens, glowing a pale gold.

"Lovisa, what is it?" Sally said, seeing me so moved, looking to Chimney Rock herself to see what significance she must have missed.

I shook my head, just staring at the landmark. For a moment, I honestly couldn't speak.

"What's wrong?" Meggie whispered.

Her grave concern broke the spell and I laughed, lifting the corner of my apron to dab at my eyes. "Nothing, sweetheart. Truly! It's just that…they told us Chimney Rock was out here and…well, there it is!"

Sally smiled quizzically. "You were worried it wouldn't be?"

All right, I wouldn't try to explain. But to hear of a thing, something everyone talks about, and then to finally see it with your own eyes...

Rowland had halted with the oxen, and I saw in his stance that he, too, had been overtaken by this same unexpected thrill.

Sally was trying to free a lock of her hair from Jimmy's fist when Rowland looked back, so mine were the eyes his met.

It was unsettling somehow. Lord knows I didn't want to be in agreement with him on anything, almost didn't feel I should. Like it wasn't quite right that he and I should feel the same about a thing while Sally wasn't even paying attention. But there was no denying we were struck by the same notion, that this was somehow an important moment. The ruts of a thousand wheels had constantly been confirming we were on the right road. Still, this formation, appearing as promised, was reassuring in a way that's hard to explain. The sight of Chimney Rock seemed to offer visible proof that everything was going to be all right, and we would reach Oregon in due course, just as we planned.

Meggie was staring up at me, far more intrigued by my reaction than by Chimney Rock itself. No wonder. I probably did look a bit simpleminded, weeping over a rock!

Now Sally climbed down to walk beside Rowland.

"Gee up!" he cried, and the wagon rolled forward. As we went into a dip and the spire sank below the horizon in that odd way things distant will, Meggie straightened in alarm.

"It's gone!"

"Oh, no," I said. "It's still there. Just because you can't see something, doesn't mean it's not there. Just wait. You'll see."

For two full days Chimney Rock would remain tantalizingly in sight and yet continually distant, as if some unseen hand were pulling it away at our approach. Finally we began to grasp how the faithful oxen had indeed been pulling the wagons gradually higher in elevation each day, for up here the atmosphere was thin and disorienting. At one point we nervously kept watch on a band of Indians ahead, only to have them spread wings and rise into that deceptively clear air. Turned out to be a flock of crows!

A day past Chimney Rock we arrived at the most massive formation yet, Scott's Bluff. A lay-by day was planned, and at dawn, a small band of us began its ascent. Amos and Melinda led the way. Behind me came Sol, Price, Lydia, Jont Williams, and John Noble.

Climbing that steep, eastside trail, the sun warming my back, I had never felt so alive. Pausing to glance over my shoulder, I realized how spectacularly high we were going to be. Why, from the top a person would probably be able to see all the way west! My heart pounded, my lungs pumped with exhilaration. For some reason, I found myself remembering folks back in Missouri who called us foolish for heading out on this trip. What would they think to see us now? Look at me, I was thinking. I, Lovisa King, am actually climbing this mountain.

I felt lucky to be getting away with it. Rowland had worried Sally would be needing my help that day, and Sally herself feared I'd fall and hurt myself. Ma said it seemed like a waste of energy, but Pa stuck up for me. "Lovisa's got feet like those mountain goats they talk of," he said. "She's not going to fall. And if they're willing to climb for the view, let 'em. Just the sort of thing young folks ought to do, and I'd say now's their chance. I sure don't expect to be hauling them this way again."

Amos and Melinda reached the top first.

"What can you see?" I called ahead.

Any answer given was lost on the wind that rattled the scrubby pines clinging to the rocky bluff crest, and in a moment I had scrambled out onto the opening on the summit myself. Lord, we were way up in the sky!

Breathing hard, I turned west.

I squinted.

Nothing.

I rubbed my eyes, scanned the whole horizon. Miles and miles I could see, more of the earth than I'd ever in my life taken in at one time. But it was all so depressingly flat. I sighed, sagging with sudden fatigue.

"Are you all right?" John asked.

I nodded, slowly regaining my breath.

"Amazing view," he said. "Water?" He offered me his canteen.

I took a swallow, gave it back.

"Lovisa! What the devil's the matter?"

"I don't know," I said. "I guess I just thought, getting up this high, we'd see the Rockies. Or something. I thought we'd see we were getting somewhere."

I noticed Jont Williams taking Lydia's hand, and I quick tucked my own hands under my arms in case John tried the same.

Sol pointed. "Look over there. Isn't that a mountain?"

"Laramie Peak," Amos confirmed.

I squinted, making out a faint triangle in the farthest distance.

Together we all stood there, silently contemplating the vast expanse over which our wagons would soon be rolling. The wind sighed forlornly in the needles of the twisted pines.

I can't say what the others were thinking. I suppose it's not impossible they felt some sense of triumph for having climbed so high.

But for myself, reaching the top had only shown me just how small we really were. I felt defeated by the distance before us. I was thinking that the West was a whole lot bigger than I had ever imagined.

And that we still had a dismayingly long way to go.

CHAPTER 9

"A DOLLAR A YARD!" ABBIE WHISPERED
in disgust, shoving the dusty bolt of blue calico back onto the trading post shelf. "And poor stuff, too."

Fort Laramie's adobe compound had been a thrilling sight to eyes that hadn't seen the straight lines of a man-made building in six long weeks. But Pa had been right in warning us we'd likely be disappointed by the trade goods offered. Not to mention the prices.

"Look here," I said, indignant. "Sugar's a dollar a pound! Coffee, too."

"You're not buying any, are you?"

"Well." The coffee smelled so good. "Rowland did give me two dollars to get some. I expect he thought it would go further, though."

"Rowland gave you money to spend? Mercy, John wouldn't trust me with a nickel."

I suppose it was nice of Rowland, saying if some sugar and coffee would perk us up, he didn't begrudge the money. On the other hand, it was my own Pa's money on loan to him. Why should I have to feel beholden?

I paid for my purchase and Abbie and I left.

Outside, broken-down wagons were heaped like so many skeletal carcasses against one of the fort's corner towers. Lots of folks like the Browns who'd insisted on starting out from St. Joe with heavy wagons now sought to trade for lighter ones. Mr. Brown complained to Pa about the small amount they'd been offered, insisting that, as one of our leaders, Pa ought to make the fort people pay fair. But Pa told him the price was fair. Here at Fort Laramie, the value of a Conestoga that couldn't make it over the mountains was just about equal to the price of so much firewood.

I guess if you're the only trading post for hundreds of miles, you can charge what you want and pay what you want, too.

All around us the grounds stirred with the comings and goings of emigrants, trappers, and Indians. Hundreds of wagons of various companies were clustered in camps on the bottomland lining the Laramie River. On the fort's side, the Sioux had erected villages of paint-decorated tipis. I veered toward them to look at the trade goods they'd spread out in front.

Abbie hesitated. "You're going over there?"

"I want to make a trade."

"You're sure it's all right?"

"Pa said I could. Said just be smart about it, and don't be expecting something for nothing. These Sioux are sharp."

I found them also the handsomest Natives we'd yet seen. I much admired their proud bearing and elegantly fashioned deerskin clothes. As we passed among them, the raven-haired women smiled and beckoned shyly to us, perfectly friendly and eager to do business.

"These are what I'm going to need," I told Abbie, picking up a pair of beaded buckskin moccasins. "Look at this." I hiked my skirt to show the sad state of what had started out as the sturdiest footwear on the Missouri frontier. "I don't understand. How can we be only a third of the way to Oregon if my first pair of boots is already shot?"

"Well, mine are too." Abbie stuck her battered boot out for comparison.

"But Pa figured two pair each. Shouldn't we be halfway?" And I wasn't saying this in jest! Oh, looking back, I would never believe how trusting I'd been. I never saw my own innocence, how perfect and unshakable had been my faith in my father's planning.

"I'm not sure about these, though," Abbie said, examining the moccasins. "Are they thick enough? They don't really have proper hard soles."

"Well, it's what they wear. You don't see them limping around with blisters like our folks, do you? I reckon they know what works best out here."

Now I took from my bag the muslin shirt I'd made back in Missouri for this very purpose. One of Pa's overland travel pamphlets had suggested shirts as a likely trade item. I remembered sitting by the fire one winter night, sewing on the last buttons, wondering where I'd be when I went to trade it and what I'd be trying to buy. Now here I was at Fort Laramie, facing a sparkling-eyed young Indian mother with leather-banded braids.

I could tell she was impressed with my needlework, but like Pa said, they were sharp traders. A show of enthusiasm wouldn't do. It didn't help her cause, though, when the other Indian women nearby noticed my shirt and started motioning Abbie and me to look at their goods. I particularly admired this girl's moccasins, though. In the end, with little common language for bartering, she and I simply made it a straight trade and were both pleased, I think, to leave it at that.

"Did you notice her papoose?" Abbie said as soon as we were out of the girl's hearing. "It had blue eyes."

I nodded.

"Well, that means she must have a white husband. One of the trappers."

"I believe that's common, Abbie. You needn't looked so shocked."

"But, didn't it startle you? Those eyes?"

"I suppose," I admitted. It made me think of that line in the Shenandoah song about the white man loving the Indian maiden. It wasn't hard to see why. Some of the Indian girls were quite comely. And they seemed so calm. This was their country. They knew how to do for their husbands and children out here. They didn't have that tense, half-frantic look you saw on the faces of so many of our women. The Sioux probably weren't always worried and asking themselves would there be enough food? Would there be enough water? Would the patched-together wagon wheel break again today?

"Look at this needlework," I said, showing the moccasins to Sally when I got back to the wagon. Such neat, tight stitching, such care taken in the intricate pattern of beads. Surely these flowers were as cleverly executed as any white woman's embroidery. "Makes you wonder, doesn't it?" I said. "How folks call them savages?"

But my sister wasn't listening at all. Only now did I notice I'd interrupted her Bible reading.

"Sally." I set the moccasins aside. "What's wrong? What's happened?"

She sighed. "The Vickers girls."

I caught my breath. Ill for weeks, these little ones had been the concern of the entire company.

"Did they—?"

Sally nodded. "In the middle of the night."

I looked off to the low hills ringing us. "Not all of them...?"

"Well, Ellen will live, they think, they hope, but Katie and the baby..."

I darted a fearful glance at Meggie, who was squatting with Hope's little Isaac, scratching the dust with a stick.

"I checked her," Sally said, patting Jimmy. "No sign. Poor thing, she's so tired of me looking for measles every other minute. Oh, I must seem like a crazy woman to you, Lovisa. But you can't imagine how it feels. Once you have these little ones, the thought of anything happening to them...You feel you'd die yourself."

I nodded. She was right. I didn't know how it felt. Not the way a person knows a thing when it's happening to her. But I'd become attached enough to Meggie and Jimmy now that I could begin to imagine.

"Did you know it was measles James died of?" Sally said. "Back when I was just four or five?"

James was the brother who'd have been between us in age, the one after whom Sally named her own Jimmy. I knew only that he'd been taken by a sickness of some sort.

"I remember him dying as plain as anything," Sally said. "That's how I know the little ones like Meggie understand a lot more of what's happening than most folks give them credit for. That's why we have to be brave in front of them."

I nodded.

"I just feel so helpless," she went on, her voice suddenly close to breaking. "I feel like all I can do is pray."

I stood there a moment, feeling helpless myself. Then, awkwardly, I patted her hand. You pray, I thought. I'll do the laundry. Sally's prayers had a better chance than mine of reaching God's ear anyway. He certainly heard from her more often.

At the river, Abbie was already bare-armed, working on a pile of dirty duds from John and Susan's wagon. She, too, had just heard about the Vickers girls.

"I couldn't stand it if that happened to Lexie," she said.

93

I nodded, rolling up my sleeves. I pulled out one of Rowland's shirts and slapped it on my washboard.

The Laramie really was the nicest little river, the first water running right down from the mountains, and a much-appreciated change from the Platte. The sun warmed our backs. Above the river's soft gurgle, the twittering of birds, and the muffled bits of chitchat from the other women scrubbing their things upstream, we could hear the noise from the blacksmith shop. Our company had rented the facility for the entire day, and the ring of hammer on anvil would not be stopping. Many of the oxen needed new shoes.

"Did you hear what Sol was saying?" Abbie asked. "That some trappers are offering to take letters back east?"

I nodded. I'd seen Annie perched on her wagon tongue, working a pencil to a nub. "You writing to Rob?"

Abbie rocked back on her haunches.

"Rob?" I said, needling her a bit. "Rob who couldn't bear to say farewell?"

"Oh, stop it. How was I supposed to know how it would be with Price?"

"So you're not writing?"

"I thought about it, but how could I begin to explain everything that's happened? And anything I write today might not even be true by the time he reads it. That's what happened to Susan. She's got a whole packet of letters for her mother, but now she doesn't want to send the first ones. Says they sound too sad. She's writing a new one to say how well Lexie's doing, how John calls her his little Girl of the Golden West."

I stood and braced my hands against my back. "Lucky for me, I don't have to worry about it. Nobody back there's waiting to hear from me in the first place. Although there's a few I'd like to write and say, 'Too bad for you, we're not dead yet!' "

"Lovisa!"

I bent back to my task. Grateful as I was for a nice laundry spot, washing clothes remained an odious chore, even though we'd long ago given up any thought of heating water, bleaching, starching, or, heaven forbid, getting out the flatirons. Still, although this was just a partial effort, this quick rinse in the river, it dismayed me, understanding now how fast our work would be undone.

"Remember that day at the St. Joe landing," I said, "when Lexie and Meggie had on those brand-new clean pinafores and we were just sitting there watching them splash around in the mud?"

Abbie nodded sheepishly.

I shook my head. "I don't know why Susan didn't smack us!"

"Say," Abbie said. "See that girl in the brown bonnet? The one down there on the flat rock with the washtub? When I came to get water this morning, she was here and she started telling Susan's snake story like it happened in her company."

"No! Really?"

"Yes, only it was two snakes, and one was already wrapped around the little girl's leg."

"You mean Lexie?"

"Well, yes, but she didn't say Lexie, of course. But the rest of the details were so close—the mother chopping the snake and all—I just knew it was the same story so I said, 'Wait, this happened in your company? You saw it?' And then, of course, she admits it was another company but swears her good friend saw the whole thing!"

I shook my head. People sure do love passing on a good story. True or not, they don't care. By the time this one came around again, it wouldn't surprise me to hear tell of three snakes and Lexie as a golden-haired beauty of sixteen. And of course there'd be some who couldn't tell it at all without working in a way to blame the whole thing on the Indians!

That evening we had company at our campfire, a grizzled old trapper Pa invited to share supper. Phew! I'll bet this fellow hadn't sat himself in a tin tub since about the time he let his long hair and beard start growing uncut. And his skin was just a wonder, like tough, deep-tanned leather. I met his stained-toothed grin with a smile as I spooned out his share of buffalo stew, but I declare, I was holding my breath while I did it.

Everyone was telling tales of trading with the Sioux and comparing the deals they'd made. The cleverest, to my thinking, was Susan's purchase of a fine little beaded purse to send home to her mother. The price? One tiny sewing needle, which weighed nothing and took up no space. We should have brought packets and packets.

"We heard the Sioux'll trade ponies for girls," Sol said, straight-faced, and then added with a wink. "We were thinking of trading Lovisa."

"Very funny, young man," I said, swishing past him. "No extra helpings for you."

"Not Lovisa, though!" Amos said. "God Almighty! We'd have the whole Sioux nation trailing us, trying to trade her back!"

My cheeks blazed as all my brothers had a great laugh. The old trapper too.

"Fine bunch of gentleman," Mr. Fuller said, grinning. "What a way to treat your sister."

"Nothing but the truth here," Amos said. "Trying to marry this one off has purely been a trial. Right, Pa?"

"Well," my father said, "she does have a habit of making me turn away her suitors."

"Only two!" I protested. Besides Mr. Collins there'd been that preacher man. As if I'd make any kind of a preacher's wife! Honestly, it was just beyond me how a man could spot a girl slopping hogs and from one look take up the notion of marrying her. As if hair the right chestnut shade or a waist that nipped in just so was all that mattered.

"Pa always tells 'em he's not a man can stand having a mule returned," Amos went on, "likewise a stubborn daughter!"

My mouth fell open. I lifted the ladle as if to strike, hardly knowing whether to laugh with them or be mad.

"Oh, we're just joshing, honey," Pa said.

"Sure," Amos said. "And don't worry. Pa'd never take you back!"

Blushing furiously, I kept ladling the stew. The banter did feel affectionate somehow, though, and when I glanced at Abbie, I'd have sworn she looked like she wished she were the one being teased.

When word got out we were entertaining this buckskin-clad authority on the territory ahead, folks from other wagons started drifting over to get in on his stories. Even Mamie Brown came mincing along behind her folks.

Indians. That's what everyone wanted to hear about. What could we expect? Had there been reports of attacks on wagon trains ahead?

The trapper waved away these concerns. "More boys gettin' shot by their own guns than killed by Indians. Indians won't give you any trouble."

"You don't call it trouble," Mr. Brown said, "stealing our horses?"

The trapper laughed, maybe partly in surprise. Mr. Brown had an oddly high voice for such a big man. I sometimes wondered if he made a point of talking tough just to try countering the effect.

"Go steal 'em back," the trapper said. "Just a game to them. They don't mean no harm."

Mr. Brown bristled, and even Pa didn't look like he felt terribly forgiving toward the Indians. It had been annoying, this recent thievery. And they were just so good at it. Why, John Noble'd had his horse tethered to his own wrist while he slept, and a young brave had managed to loose it without even waking him. Far too much time had been spent chasing after the missing livestock; far too much had been paid to Indians in "finder's fees."

"No denying Indians can be pesky," the trapper went on. "But stealing's not the same thing to them. It's not a sin, it's a skill. Shows who's cleverest. Fellow that's holding the horses right this minute is the owner, simple as that."

"Stealing's stealing," Mr. Brown said.

"It is one of the Commandments," his wife added.

Ma pursed her lips. Like the rest of us didn't know our Bible.

"Yeah?" said the trapper. "Well, there's other ways to look at it. Let me ask you folks this. Indians ever bring you anything?"

"Gave us some buffalo steaks," Sol offered.

"Anything else?" He looked at Mr. Brown. "You?"

Mr. Brown shrugged. "Some antelope meat. Just extra they didn't need."

"More than once? How many times?"

Mr. Brown looked annoyed. "I can't keep track of stuff like that."

"You can't? Well, dang, that's funny, because you seem to know every last head of livestock that's gone missing."

And none of it was even his, I felt like saying. It seemed he just didn't want to miss a chance to be mad. His face had gone dead red now.

"See, whites just don't understand the Indian ways," the trapper said. "Folks are supposed to trade gifts. They give you something, you're supposed to give something back. When you don't, they feel justified to take it."

"But they're begging food off us all the time," Mrs. Brown said indignantly. "And it's not like we're hauling a lot of extra."

"We do have to be careful how much we give them," Arnold Fuller said. "I'm concerned they'll just keep wanting more. Folks coming after us won't know what hit 'em when the Sioux expect to be fed all the time like this."

"Well, that's gonna be true whatever you do, good or bad," the trapper said. "Waste a lot of buffalo, for instance, they'll expect the same from the next company. Can't blame 'em for getting grouchy when they see another batch of wagons coming."

"Say, you're quite the Indian lover, aren't you?" Mr. Brown said, bellying up close. "I'll bet you got a squaw of your own tucked out in a tipi somewhere, huh?"

"What if I do?" the buckskin-clad man asked mildly, making a point, it seemed to me, of not standing to a fight.

"All right now," Pa said to Mr. Brown. "Let's keep this a friendly campfire."

Mr. Brown backed off, looked around for support. Seeing none, he started to leave. Then he stopped and turned back with a high-pitched bark at his wife. "Martha! Come!"

Sticking their noses in the air, she and Mamie followed him into the shadows beyond the fire ring.

"Don't mind him," Rowland said to the trapper. "He's just sore things aren't going like he planned. Looking for somebody to blame. His hired boys quit on him today. Helped themselves to a couple of his horses and lit out ahead."

"Lemme guess," the trapper said. "These'd be his lily-white hired boys, right?"

"That's right," Rowland said, with that wry grin of his.

"Dang. Ain't folks funny?"

When our guest let it be known he'd recently been as far as the Willamette Valley, people perked up with more questions. Or rather, the same question with fresh intensity.

Indians. What was the situation in the Willamette Valley?

"Ain't no Indian situation." The trapper wiped bread through the last of his stew. "They're gone."

We looked at each other, uncertain.

"You never heard that?"

"Well," Rowland said, "we've understood the Indians in that part of the country weren't troublesome."

"Ha! Got that right. Hard to be troublesome when you're dead."

"Dead?"

The trapper nodded. "Ten, fifteen years back the place was full of villages. Then the first whites showed up and those Indians just couldn't stand up to the fevers that came along. Laid down and died, pretty near all of them."

No one spoke. What could we say?

"Pitiful business," the trapper added, "running into one of them abandoned villages. Nobody left to even bury the dead."

The fire crackled. I glanced around, wondering if anyone else felt like I did, a bit responsible somehow. Not personally, of course. Ten years ago I was a child back in Ohio. Still, I was white. Whites brought the diseases. Even now our own train was carrying the measles a little farther west each day. We'd known the Vickers family had it when we left St. Joe, and it hadn't stopped us. I couldn't feel good about that. And yet, to be honest, I was relieved to think that once we got to Oregon, we could stop worrying about the possibility of being abducted by Indians.

"Oh, there's still a handful of Kalapooias and such out there," the trapper went on, "but what the hell—just the number you got on the road this one season you'll pretty much outnumber 'em, least along the Willamette. Naw, your problem ain't gonna be Indians. Gonna be this dang drought."

Drought? I looked around. First I'd heard of it. I saw Rowland frown, like maybe he had heard the rumor but wasn't pleased to have it confirmed.

"Grass never was much from here to Fort Hall," the trapper said, "but this year's the worst ever. Just haven't had the rain. It's parched out, dry as dust from the pass on."

"No grass at all?" Amos asked, quietly alarmed.

"Well, you're always going to find some. But only around the waterways. And you got a lot of wagons and herds out there ahead of you. Not as many as behind, that's true. But still…"

Pa and Amos traded a dark look. Others muttered. I thought of all our planning. How could you plan for this? Who could have known back when we started that the West would have an unusually dry spring?

Sally cleared her throat. "Maybe," she said tentatively, "maybe we should think about going back."

Startled, everyone turned. Stared.

"Because beyond this we can't turn back." My sister took a deep breath. "I heard a woman saying Laramie's the point of no return."

"Sally," Rowland said, obviously disturbed.

The group members fell to mumbling among themselves.

The point of no return—that sounded so frightening. Yet my heart sank at the notion of giving up after having come so far. What, travel back? And what would we do in Missouri? Wait and try again next year? Forget our dreams of the West and take up another mosquito-infested, flood-washed farm? I glanced around at the others. Surely no one would even consider it.

"Now, Sally," Pa said. "You don't need to be worrying about the cattle. You just let us take care of it, all right?"

Sally hung her head. I don't think it was really the cattle that concerned her.

"Not to discount your reports," Pa said to the trapper. "Appreciate 'em. But I'm sure we're all agreed we've got too much invested in this to turn back now." Only after making this statement did he look to the others for support, which every man gave him by way of a quick, deliberate nod. "We never set out with guarantees, after all. And plenty of things we were told to worry on haven't come to pass. Rivers weren't as bad as folks said. We dodged the big storms. Haven't lost anybody to the Indians yet."

People nodded, glad to be reminded, in the middle of all the worrying, of the ways we'd been blessed.

Now Amos spoke up.

"You all know I've made the getting of this herd to Oregon my main goal. But if we don't, we don't. We can still get ourselves there and claim our land. They've already got some herds up there from California. We might could buy some of those and start that way. But for now, I'm not near ready to give up with the ones we've got this far."

In the wagon later, Sally sat weeping. "Everybody's mad at me for saying that, Lovisa, but I couldn't help it."

I reckon she expected me to reassure her nobody was mad, but frankly, I think folks were, a little. At least as mad as we could be at a sweet, helpless person everybody adored. But it did seem like she'd broken some kind of unspoken rule, something about not discouraging other folks by putting fears into words.

"I just have this awful feeling," she said, breaking the rule again, this time for my benefit alone. "I have this terrible feeling that somehow we're not going to make it."

Next morning before we pulled out, Abbie, Lydia, and I represented the Kings at the burial of the Vickers girls in the fort graveyard. Someone had painted the children's names with axle grease on a barrel stave for the double tombstone. As the light of the rising sun flooded the hills and hollows around us, Reverend Moore read Bible passages about lambs and angels and little children entering the Kingdom of Heaven. The hymn began, but I was hardly hearing the words. Babies dying anywhere would tear at your heart, but out here…Oh, it was just a horror for their mother, having to leave their graves behind. Poor Ann Vickers could hardly stand up. Her husband kept shifting to support her weight. As we sang, you could see she just wanted to lie right down in the dirt with those children and never go one step farther.

The service concluded, I glanced down the slope to the wagons, which were lined up, ready to start. The oxen were newly shod, supplies restocked, the wagons straightened and cleaned. People stood watching, shifting impatiently, waiting for us to come and take our places.

The funeral had already held us up. We had to keep moving.

The minister gave a slight nod and we turned away. Behind me, Ann Vickers let out a blood-chilling wail. Her husband and the minister were having to drag the poor woman from the graves.

She knew, you see. No matter what they said to comfort her, no matter how they lied, she knew. She would never be able to come back to this place again.

CHAPTER 10

THE METAL-RIMMED WOODEN WHEELS

ground the pale rocky road to fine sand that the wind drove into our eyes. In the narrow passages, the heavy wagons were wearing the ruts into trenches. Had we really thought that first hill past the crossing of the South Platte so difficult? It seemed nothing now, compared to this miserable region where the track was interrupted by one ravine after another, each of which we had to skirt. Through the dark, cedar-studded hills, many a twisted mile was traveled without our caravan actually progressing any farther west.

Up ahead, I could hear Mr. Brown struggling with his oxen.

"I cannot bear that man's voice," I complained to Sally. Ditched by his hired boys, he was now compelled to drive his teams himself, employing a technique that relied heavily on whipping and whining.

"He'll kill them," Sally said. "You watch."

Oxen were starting to die. The poor beasts would give their all, but once they finally went down, no cruelty of whip or kindness of water from a bucket could make them rise again.

In one horrible spot, Sally and I had to press our dusty aprons to our faces to block the stench of the rotting carcasses we passed. Just beyond were the remains of the wagon rendered useless by the lack of living beasts to pull it. Here we began to witness the whole-sale abandonment of every imaginable item of equipment, stark evidence of the failures and loss of spirit of those who'd passed before. The first items thrown out seemed to be the heaviest—clever cook ovens women had so proudly demonstrated back at the jumping-off camp, cast-iron wash kettles, plows, anvils.

Rowland paused to examine a discarded millstone. He glanced at our own wagon. He couldn't possibly be considering claiming and carting the stone himself, could he? If so, he rejected the idea, instead picking up a book, which he set on the wagon seat.

"So many of these things look perfectly fine," Sally said, eyeing a plumed hat tossed on what looked to be a sack of bacon. "It's just a shame."

"People were warned," I said. "It's their own fault if they didn't pay any attention. Honestly, a hat like that? Pa never would have let us get away with it. Everything was supposed to be useful."

Sally sighed. "Won't you be glad, though, when this is over and we don't have to hear that all the time? Things can just be pretty for the sake of pretty? Anyway, a lot of these things are useful. A man needs a plow."

I didn't appreciate having this pointed out. To see all the tools needed to build a home and farm cast off this way was disturbing— silent testimony to a desperation I didn't care to contemplate. I wanted to simply assume these people had been frivolous or had made bad decisions. Our family wouldn't be making such mistakes, I figured, and I clung to the reassurance of believing that bad things could happen only to people who did.

Hundreds of miles we'd followed the Platte and now, farewell. To leave this river and take up another, we must ford it one last time and then strike out across a mean and foreboding stretch of territory. More ways for water to be difficult—rivulets that simply sank into the sand, out of sight, out of the reach of a wooden bucket. Worse were the treacherous alkali pools, fast becoming ringed by the rotting carcasses of cattle whose owners hadn't been half-careful enough, I thought, in keeping them away from the poison.

How could we appreciate the flat parts of the road when it meant miles of walking in clouds of churned-up alkali dust? We had become a plodding ghost caravan—wagons, animals, and people alike, all dusted white. Our eyes burned, our lips cracked. The dry air sucked every bit of moisture from our skin so that my face felt tight to bursting and began to blister. The ointment in the medicine kit was quickly used up in vain attempts to soothe the red eyes of the whimpering children, and we girls resorted to smearing our own mouths with axle grease.

One afternoon when time and distance had compressed to nothing and there was only the hellish present, the wagon rattled suddenly and lurched to a halt.

"Goddamnit!"

Now I'd heard my share of cursing. It wasn't as if I'd never seen a man get kicked by a mule and mutter a crude word or two. But I'd never seen Rowland get so mad he forgot to keep things nice in front of Sally, and the explosion of angry epithets he unleashed now was loud enough I'm sure she heard every awful word, even inside the wagon.

The other wagons divided around us in passing, billowing up even more dust.

Skirting ours, I saw the left rear canting backwards. Sally stuck her head out to see what had happened.

"Tire popped off the wheel," I told her. "The metal part."

"God damn it to hell!" Rowland wiped his whiskered face with a bandanna, squinting ahead, then behind, as if somebody might come riding along with a clue about what to do.

Sally and I glanced at each other, not daring a word.

"You'll have to get out," Rowland told Sally.

"Here?"

"Here's where we broke down, isn't it? Hard enough to jack the damn thing up without you and the kids in it."

Sally swallowed hard.

"Let's go, Meggie," I said, reaching for my little niece.

"Don't wanna! Out there hurts my eyes."

"I know, sweetie, but we have to."

"Why?"

"So your daddy can fix the wheel."

"Why?"

"Because it broke, that's why!"

I never pictured this, I thought, hunkering down in the dirt, trying to shelter Meggie's face against my chest. Sitting in the blazing sun without a scrap of shade, hot wind blasting sand hard enough to take the paint off the wagon, the skin off your face.

Sally whispered what a bad omen it was, having broken down out here on the Fourth of July when everybody knew that by Independence Day we were supposed to be at Independence Rock.

I watched Rowland crank up the jack. I wanted to ask him how far behind we were running, see if he knew when we'd reach the landmark, but now wasn't the time. I'd learned that. You didn't talk to men when they had a problem to work out. You waited patiently, letting them think. You'd better, because say one little word and they'd jump at the chance to yell at you like the broken wheel or whatever was your fault.

I hoped we weren't too far behind schedule. I sure did prefer running ahead. How smug we'd felt that time back at the ford of the Big Blue, finding a date carved on a tree by someone in a company that had crossed the previous year. Our company had been ahead of theirs by a full month! Nothing to feel smug about now.

Rowland had the wheel off and was tacking a narrow strip of wood around the rim, trying to increase the circumference so the metal tire would fit tight again. He was just about to try resetting it when Sol came riding up.

"We're stopping," he told us. "Everybody. We got tires popping off right and left."

Rowland nodded, suddenly looking not quite so frustrated. Maybe he felt better finding out this wasn't something he'd personally done wrong. No moral failing, no lack of planning. Just a technical problem plaguing everyone.

"Must be the air's too hot and dry," Rowland said. "Wood just shrinks up. Metal comes lose."

"Pa's wagon's lost two," Sol said.

"I've just about got this," Rowland said to Sally. "You can get back inside in a minute." He looked up at Sol. "Tell your pa I'll be up there pretty quick. I think this'll work, how I fixed it. I'll come show him."

Thank God we finally struck the Sweetwater a few days later. Just beyond Independence Rock it flowed right through the most amazing cleft between cliffs three hundred feet high. Why they called this Devil's Gate was beyond me. Should have been the Gates of Eden. That perfect little river turned the day from miserable to heavenly in the time it took to bring the wagons around the short pass and park them on its banks.

I jumped down from the wagon, ran to the gravelly shore, and threw myself fully dressed into one of its pools. It was shallow, no more than a creek really, and just the right temperature. I lay back and let the cool water rush past me, caressing my limbs like a blessing. For just a little while I wanted to escape the hollering of the children, the bawling of cattle, and the sharp voice of Mrs. Brown, bickering with people over whose wagon should be staked where. I tipped my ears back into the rushing stream. Wasn't this God's own reviving miracle, to find a thing like this out here in this otherwise parched country?

"I hope Pa's claim has a stream like this," I said when Abbie came to join me. "Don't you?"

She sank into the water with a blissful expression. "I don't think much about Pa's claim."

"You don't?" I sat up, blinking water from my eyes. "What do you think we're doing this for?"

She smiled mysteriously. "I don't think about Pa's claim, because I'm thinking about Price's claim."

Oh. Of course. How foolish of me. I kept forgetting. This wasn't just about finding our place in Oregon, our land. Every step, every day, folks were sorting out who they'd be sharing that place with.

Abbie whipped back her wet hair. "Has John Noble told you where he hopes to take up his claim?"

"No," I said flatly. "Why would he?"

"Oh, Lovisa, don't be that way. What do you think it means when someone carves your name with his on that cliff like he did? He's a perfectly nice boy. And he likes you. Do you want to be an old maid?"

I dunked under the water, shutting her out. Did I have to pair up with the first suitable young man who came along imagining he liked me? Seemed smitten with me even if he didn't quite approve of me? When I came up for air, Abbie was still at me.

"Look at little Lydia, for heaven's sake," she said. "Getting herself courted by Jonathan Williams. And he's nineteen! Lovisa, you could have gone after him!"

"Leave off, will you? Why are you so set on pairing me up? I am not that old. Look at Hope. She didn't get married until she was twenty-four."

"Yes," Abbie said, "and you see how that turned out."

Abbie was right; Hope wasn't the most fortunate of examples. None of us had ever envied this sister her husband, who was three years younger than Hope and, actually, our cousin. Not terribly romantic, not to mention we couldn't remember a time when he wasn't sick. I wasn't unselfish and patient like Hope. I could never be happy with a marriage like hers.

Oh, what was I going to do? What if we got to Oregon and I still hadn't paired up with anyone?

Well, I could stay with Pa and Ma. Ma always said it would be fine with her if one of her daughters never married and stayed to help her. But then she'd forever be the boss of the house, the boss of me. I did like the idea of having my own place, running things my own way.

"Lovisa!"

I looked toward the wagons. Rowland was standing there holding Meggie, waving me back. I stood, water streaming from me, wet skirts clinging to my thighs.

"Lovisa," Abbie said, staring pointedly at my skirts. "You don't have all your petticoats on, do you?"

"Oh, for heaven's sake." I plucked the fabric away from my legs. "Isn't one more than enough?" I dragged out and went to fetch Meggie.

"Come along," I said, scooping the dusty little girl from her father's arms and trotting back toward the creek. "I'm going to wash you and wash you and wash you!"

She squealed with laughter as I tossed her in the air, caught her and swung her down for a dunking.

Sleep was sweet that night, and in the hopefulness of a new morning, with the women and girls having had our much longed-for baths, the men all freshly shaved, and the babies in clean diapers, we were a cheerful company that left Devil's Gate receding in the distance.

Ahead, the morning light flooded a fair prospect, a rising plateau of open country promising good traveling, the ridges beyond hinting at progress into the Rockies.

We were to follow the wonderful Sweetwater all the way to the South Pass.

On July 25, Pa turned sixty-two, Sally twenty-two. Because we had reached the verdant Bear River Valley, we were able to put together a halfway decent celebration meal. Susan roasted a nice mess of sage hens John and Isaac brought in, and I made wild-currant pies from the children's pickings. Ma managed a cake of sorts, which we might have enjoyed more if she could have stopped saying how it lacked for eggs and we shouldn't expect her to be able to keep to her usual standards.

"We know, Ma," I said as my brothers and sisters and I all suppressed smiles at each other. By now everybody understood how hard it was keeping to any kind of standards out here. You didn't see me making apologies for the tartness of my pie on account of scant sugar, after all. Everybody understood. Nobody would dare complain.

"Little Sally here was the best birthday present I ever got," Pa remarked as he did every year, something of a tradition. "But what do you say, girl?" He gave my sister a fond wink. "Personally I feel about ten years older than I did on my last birthday!"

Sally nodded, smiling, and we all joined in the gentle laughter acknowledging how beaten down we were feeling, for we had come through some difficult days.

South Pass itself had been nothing, just as the guidebooks promised, a ramp over the divide so wide and flat we'd hardly have known we were rolling over it if Sol hadn't got word from the guides and told everyone.

But other stretches we'd never worried over proved more challenging. A few days into the actual Oregon Country, Pa informed us we'd be bypassing Fort Bridger in order to try a shortcut known as the Greenwood Cutoff. In taking this chance, we ultimately saved a number of traveling days, but the twenty-four-hour forced march across a barren, forty-mile tract of wormwood took its toll.

And it wasn't the physical exhaustion alone. At the Green River camp, a child in a nearby company died. It was awful, that keening wail from the little boy's mother, and the way Meggie's eyes went wide as she looked to me saying, "What's that?" And then the wolves taking up the howl. Lord. Sitting at the campfire that night as darkness fell over the wilderness, I did not feel one bit the stouthearted girl I liked to think myself.

The traveling itself never seemed to get any easier. What we gained in practice and experience was countered by the constant breakdown of wagons and the increasing difficulty of the terrain. In the last two days we had struggled to pull the wagons up yet another particularly miserable hill, and I had come to believe the devil himself had laid out the road's course to Oregon, with every new twist of geography more formidable than the last.

Now I watched Sally standing by the fire, Jimmy on her hip, her small frame slumped with his weight. Twenty-two. She had always seemed so much older than I, a lovely woman when I was still a skinny girl. Now I had grown, and the contrast wasn't nearly so great.

Oh, dear. She looked so terribly tired. Was she actually faring worse than the rest of us—we were all pretty well pegged out—or was it just that I loved her especially and felt responsible?

She looked up, but before she could see all this on my face, I put on a quick smile. Knowing how I worried for her wouldn't do her any good at all.

Pa couldn't get us past Fort Hall fast enough, even if there was good grazing and nice trout to be had from this stretch of the Snake River. He said the Hudson's Bay Company's prices were outrageous and the fort was full of half-drunken mountain men arguing with the emigrants. Our company would delay departure for only one morning so that people could make their necessary trades, then we'd be on our way. Pa wouldn't even let us girls visit the trading post.

I tried, though. That morning I started marching toward the adobe fort, ignoring the whooping young Indian braves who swooped by on their sleek ponies, cutting right in front of me. They didn't scare me. I was used to Indians now. And these were just like white boys, showing off. I had almost reached the big wooden gates when Rowland rode up alongside me, reached down, and grabbed me by my upper arm.

"Ow! Rowland! Lemme go!"

"Sorry. Your pa's orders."

He pulled me up in front of him and honestly, I could have died of embarrassment, having to ride back with his arms around me like that.

"I'm sick and tired of being kept out of things!" I raged. "And I don't see why it's any business of yours!"

"This fort's no place for girls," he said. "Too many rough types."

"Well, maybe I'd like to see those rough types for myself!"

He laughed.

"Don't laugh at me! I mean it, Rowland. You have to make this up to me. If you go in there, you have to promise to tell me all the gossip you hear."

That afternoon as we pulled out, I dogged Rowland's heels, making good on my threat to pester him for reports from the fort.

"All right, if you want to know," Rowland said, "the big debate was whether folks should stay the course for the Willamette Valley or turn off for California. Up here at Raft River's what they call the Parting of the Ways, so anybody changing their mind, now's the time. And the folks at the fort want to steer as many to California as they can. Got an old mountain man in there talks a fine stream of scare stories—the Blue Mountains, the Indians ahead, the rapids of the Columbia. Probably in the pay of Hudson's Bay. They don't want Americans settling in Oregon at all, see? How can they hold it for the British if we take up all the land?"

I remembered Pa talking about that too. And how you have to think why people say the things they say.

"And then the folks down there at Sutter's Fort send up word how easy that route is," Rowland went on. "Want us all to come down California way. Get more Americans in, help hold that territory."

"But who's going to settle for California when the whole idea in the first place is taking up land in Oregon?"

"Quite a few families, looks like. People getting worn out. I s'pose whatever sounds easier at this point, sounds better."

"Well, that's just wrong-headed," I said. "What's the use of easier if it only gets you somewhere you didn't want to go in the first place?"

Rowland flashed a quick grin at me. "I like the way you put that."

Well.

Good to know we agreed on this, anyway. For us Kings, California was never a possibility, not for one minute.

We were for Oregon, and that was that.

CHAPTER 11

"**DO STOP SCRATCHING, MARGARET**," **SALLY**
said to Meggie. "Look, Lovisa, she's made all her mosquito bites
bleed. It's dreadful."

I lifted Meggie down from the wagon and loosened the tie of
her dirty calico smock.

"Itchy," she said. "And my mouth hurts."

"You poor little puddin'." Her tummy was covered with bloody
sores. I started to cinch up the drawstring, then stopped, picking
a crawly thing from her armpit and squinting at it. "Ick." I flicked
it away.

Sally turned. "What?"

I wrinkled my nose at her over Meggie's head and mouthed the
loathsome word: Lice.

"Oh, Lord," Sally said. "I never! Well. She's just got to have a
bath, that's all." Her voice went trembly, like she suddenly wanted

a good cry. "Really, I can't stand this, the children so filthy day after day and not being able to do a thing about it."

I looked around. There was no stream. There would be no baths. Here we were—another hard day's travel to reach another dirty, comfortless place to sleep the night. Lord, I hated making dry camp. Nothing to do but scrape the babies' soiled diapers and lay them to dry, still stained.

Looking around at my exhausted sisters as they lifted boxes and barrels from the wagons, runny-nosed toddlers squalling at them, I suspected Sally wasn't the only one ready to call this whole expedition a big mistake. To me, remembering how we'd started out, it didn't even seem like the same trip.

We hadn't had music in weeks. There'd be no dancing tonight or sharing of Oregon plans. Nobody would be standing up to deliver patriotic speeches about beating the British out of the Northwest. All that seemed a very long time ago. This stretch of sagebrush barrens was the rockiest, most miserable we'd yet traversed. And the Snake River! God's cruel joke, you ask me, the way it mostly ran along in a canyon hundreds of feet deep. You couldn't even get to it. All you could do was stare down at those glittering green pools and white rapids, wishing you could be next to it instead of up in the hot, pitiless sun.

"Oh, my Lord," Sally said. She had her hand on Meggie's forehead. "She's burning up. Lovisa, come here! She's really sick!"

"Haircut time!" I announced, waving the King family's one treasured set of scissors. "All children, report to our wagon."

Susan, Melinda, and Lydia started sitting the youngsters one by one on the wagon tongue so I could clip their dirty curls to the dust.

"You really think this'll help?" Lydia asked, trying to help Susan hold Lute still.

"It's something to try," I said, trimming around Lute's ear. "If we can't bathe them, at least it makes a little less to keep clean."

"Body lice," Susan muttered in disgust. "What next?" But still she couldn't bear to let me take more than a token snip of Lexie's glorious gold floss. "I'll cut it all, I promise," she told me apologetically, "the very first time I see any."

"No, no, not me either," Bitsy said, as Melinda tried to position her on our makeshift barber chair.

"Now come on, Bits," Melinda said, "don't make this hard."

"You're not cutting your hair," Bitsy pointed out. "I'm not one of these babies, remember. I'm one of the big girls and I want to be pretty too!"

Melinda and I traded a weary look. Three months ago we'd have been charmed by such talk; now Bitsy's feistiness just wore us out.

"All right, then," Melinda said resignedly. "I reckon the crawly critters can just have you."

I know she didn't mean that, but I'll bet it bothered her later. If she remembered.

"You know what I miss?" I said to Abbie and Lydia as we began the next morning's trudging.

"Water?" Abbie said. "Clean clothes? Hot baths?"

"Something to eat besides beans?" Lydia guessed.

I rubbed my already encrusted eyes. "Colors. I miss colors. Remember when a dress could be blue? Or red?"

Our whole world was dun-colored now, coated in dust. Even if the sky above us was blue, we could rarely see it, walking along in this choking cloud, dust puffing around our ankles like hot ashes.

When we stopped for nooning, Isaac announced that the thermometer in Pa's wagon read 104 degrees.

"Oh, be still with that," I snapped. "What's the use of knowing?"

I glanced at our wagon. I didn't want Sally hearing. She had a child burning with fever in there already. Why put a number on the misery?

All these modern scientific tools of ours—useless, you ask me. Look at the Indians—they got along without them just fine. To us, this was hell. To them it was home. Because they had something more valuable. They were the ones who knew the places to get down to that river and catch the pink-fleshed salmon leaping at the falls.

One evening two Shoshones came into our camp, crying, "Swap! Swap!" and traded us some fish.

"They're so ragged and dirty," Abbie complained later as we were eating supper.

I just stared. Her hair, like all of ours, was a greasy braid, coated in dirt, her dress hadn't been washed in weeks, and her face was smudged with dirt.

"Abbie," I said. "Look at us."

"What." She looked down at herself, looked around at the rest of our family. Then she caught on. "Oh. Well. That's different."

I shook my head, too tired to argue. Didn't seem right, though, her saying such things about the Indians with her mouth full of their good salmon.

One hot evening, when the precious odometer indicated we had accomplished for the day only eight miles, the order went out: Lighten the loads.

"But not us, Pa," I said. "Right?"

"Well, of course, us. You think we're something special? Our oxen are as bony and worn out as everybody else's."

"But, Pa, we thought of this ahead. We already planned it all out so this wouldn't happen."

"Can't be helped." He looked around at everyone and spoke up. "I know it's hard, girls, but think of it this way—if we can't get something all the way there, why drag it one mile farther?"

"Couldn't we at least wait until morning?" I said. "We're all so tired."

"Oh, no. You know how that goes. With a good night's sleep we might all wake up with enough foolish energy to try to keep hauling the stuff."

Back at our wagon, Rowland appeared at the tailgate with my spinning wheel.

"Rowland! I'll need that!"

"Not between here and the Willamette Valley."

But a spinning wheel wasn't a frivolous thing, like a clock shelf someone planned to nail on the wall in her new home or a lace-trimmed parasol, as if there'd be paved boulevards out west to stroll. A spinning wheel was a practical tool.

Rowland dropped it in the dust. "Takes up a lot of room too."

"But Pa wouldn't want me to leave this. Go ask him. I'm the best spinner in the family. He says so."

"Sorry, Lovisa."

Oh, Lord, I wasn't going to cry, was I? Not over a spinning wheel. Not with worse things happening—Meggie so sick right there inside. Blinking tears, I skirted the wagon to put the canvas between myself and Rowland and realized debates were in progress everywhere. Melinda Fuller watched her father set out her dead mother's rocker, a piece carried this far more for sentiment than practicality. Sol unloaded things as Annie directed. John was trying to comfort Susan over the abandonment of a little chest that had been a wedding gift from her mother.

Above it all, Mrs. Brown was yammering at Pa, saying his being on the idiotic Committee of Safety didn't give him the right to order her around about everything.

"We're pulling our own load," Mrs. Brown insisted. "We're not asking you Kings for help."

"You will if you break down."

"We will not!"

"Guess that remains to be seen," Pa said. "And since the rest of us wouldn't feel right about leaving you out here on your own, you're just going to have to go along with the rules."

Her whole body clenched in a spasm of anger. She climbed into her wagon and threw out a lovely little trunk, which sprang open on impact, spilling clothes. Stepping down after it, she began hurling the petticoats and shirts back into the wagon. When the trunk was empty, she flipped it closed, seized an ax, and brought it down with a crash through the blue-flower-patterned lid, leaving a splintered hole.

Wild-eyed, she looked up at all who'd found themselves interrupting their own unloading to watch hers.

"If I can't have it," she declared, "nobody can!"

Rowland had made a pile beside our wagon—a little trunk of Sally's that he'd emptied, a butter churn, a couple of flatirons. He was examining my spinning wheel.

"Change your mind?" I said bitterly.

He ignored my tone. "I think I could make you one of these when we get out there."

"Oh, Rowland." Sometimes he made it so hard to stay mad at him. "That's nice of you, but…" Who was I trying to fool, anyway? It wasn't really the wheel that distressed me. It was seeing Pa worried. "It just scares me," I admitted to Rowland, "because this isn't how we planned."

Rowland pressed the pedal, studying how it connected to the wheel.

"Plans aren't everything," he said.

At Fort Boise, five days down the trail, our men met with the leaders of several other companies who'd recently converged on the place, and afterwards Pa announced at our campfire that we'd been presented with an interesting proposition by a guide, Stephen Meek.

I knew of him. Rowland had pointed out Mr. Meek and his wife to us at Three Island Crossing where we had forded the Snake River. Meek was a wild-looking mountain man in buckskins, and even though he was over forty, his wife, folks said, was just eighteen. They'd met and married the very first week out on the prairie. Now they traveled free and wagonless, riding horseback side-by-side. To me, trudging in the dust, this seemed a rather exalted position, and I'd envied her, cantering by me, chin-strapped hat and long hair bouncing on her back.

"Meek's offering to take folks by a new route," Pa said. "Cuts 150 miles off the trip. Ten days."

Hope lit every female face. We were worried for our sick ones. Cutting ten days meant cutting ten days of suffering.

"Seems his piloting contract with Captain Welch's group only went to Fort Hall," Pa explained, "so he's looking to sign on new folks. Asking a dollar a wagon."

"Folks are talking about Indian trouble on the regular route," Arnold Fuller said. "Cayuse and the Walla Walla."

"Says he's trapped out there many a time," John said, "and he knows the trail. Says if he doesn't lead us straight through to The Dalles in thirty days we can kick his head all the way back to the States."

What a way to put it!

"I spoke with the manager at the fort," Rowland said. "Says, yes, he's heard of a trapper's trail out that way. We'll head west until we strike the Deschutes. Then we follow that river north to where it comes out near The Dalles. That means we'd be shut of the Blue Mountains."

An audible intake of breath met this revelation. Could it be true? The dread of that range had hung over us like a black cloud all the way west. A chance to somehow avoid the Blue Mountains now, when we were so tired, seemed nothing short of a miracle. Why, it was almost as if this Mr. Meek were standing here telling us railway tracks to the Willamette Valley had been laid real quick, and he'd be proud to hand out train tickets!

"The Greenwood Cutoff turned out fine," Pa reminded us, a conclusion no one had ever disputed.

"So everyone'll take the new trail then?" Ma asked.

Pa hesitated. "Some are, some aren't."

Ma's mouth went sideways. She was thinking the same thing that had suddenly occurred to me, I'll wager: If this route was so superior, why not? And why hadn't the wagons gone that way last year? Why wasn't it already the main route?

"Every man has to choose for himself," Pa said.

And choose for his wife and children too, I thought. After all, nobody was really asking us. The men in our family had decided to try this new road; we were simply being informed.

I looked around at the other women. Clearly I wasn't the only one with qualms. But at the same time, weren't we all wanting to believe in the shortcut?

Later I would think back and wonder. What if we'd dug in our heels and said No, we won't go. It's safer to stick to the regular route. Would they have listened to us?

Might things have gone differently?

CHAPTER 12

"MALHEUR?" I REPEATED WHEN ROWLAND
first told me the name of the stream. "What's that mean?" We were
a day's travel from Fort Boise and had just halted the wagons for
the night on the little river's bank.

Rowland jerked down one of the oxbows. "Never mind."

"What, you know but you won't tell?"

He sighed, exasperated. "They say it's French for 'evil hour.' All
right?"

"Oh." Odd name for such a pretty stream.

Bouncing Jimmy on my hip, I watched my brother-in-law lift the
heavy wooden yoke off the lead team.

He glanced toward the wagon. "And don't go telling Sally."

I flushed, turning my back. How stupid did he think I was? I'd
seen firsthand her habit of taking a name like Devil's Gate as an
omen. I wouldn't dream of giving her a chance to fret over the significance of evil hour.

She was probably too sick at the moment to pay any attention, anyway, having fallen to the fever even as Meggie improved.

"Pa?" Meggie said from the wagon seat. "Is this O'gen?"

"Well, yes, but not the good part. Not the part where we're going."

"But it won't be long now," I said, helping her down. "Right, Rowland?"

He looked to the west for a moment, hesitating. "Right."

After supper John Noble rode up.

"I probably won't see you for awhile," he told me, swinging down off his horse. "Our company's laying by a day here, let you get ahead of us."

I nodded, then glanced across the fire circle at Abbie, flashing mind-your-own-business eyes at her. I felt skittish enough when John came around without her forever watching, monitoring my every word. As soon as he was gone, I knew, she'd be telling me what I'd done wrong.

John took my hands.

I laughed, embarrassed.

"What?"

"Oh, just…my hands. They're awful." I'd never gone so long without my wool to spin. My dry, cracked fingertips sorely missed the lanolin.

"Feel fine to me," John lied gallantly.

I let my hands rest in his briefly, then eased them away.

"I'll probably see you at The Dalles," he said.

I nodded, scooping Jimmy up from the dirt, holding him between John and myself like a shield.

As soon as he rode off, I turned back to the basin of tin plates I was washing, pretending I didn't see Abbie coming for me.

"Honestly, that boy is devoted to you," she said, standing there with baby Charlie in her arms. "No matter how you treat him, he still likes you."

"What do you mean, how I treat him? Wasn't I nice?"

"You certainly don't act like you're as sweet on him as he is on you."

"Well, I'm not. How many times do I have to tell you that?"

"I thought this route was supposed to steer us clear of Indians," Mrs. Brown complained the next day when Natives were sighted in the distance.

Oh, why hadn't the Browns taken the fork to California, I thought, or stayed on the regular trail to The Dalles?

Soon, though, she wasn't the only one expressing skepticism.

"Wasn't this shortcut supposed to avoid mountains?" Annie said a couple of days on. "I could swear this is the rockiest stretch yet."

"Can't even call it a road," I admitted. "I don't see how the men even know where to go."

"I'm thirsty!" Meggie would whimper every time I walked near the wagon to check on her and Jimmy and Sally, who'd now broken out with the rash that seemed to go along with this fever.

"You just had a drink," I reminded Meggie.

"I want more. My tongue is dry." Demonstrating, she let it loll out.

I sighed. "Try to wait just a little longer, honey." How I hated not being able to answer a child's simple, reasonable plea. Glancing ahead to the other wagons, I wondered how Abbie was doing with Lexie. It seemed like another lifetime when we'd skipped along in the green prairie grass, chatting and gathering wildflowers. I looked back to our wagon. Meggie was still watching me. "We're almost to a new camping place," I told her.

She gave me the doubtful look I was coming to know so well.

"Really, Meggie. And the daddies will make sure there's a nice stream."

Poor child. Obviously she wanted to believe. Who didn't? I wished someone would lie to me. But somewhere along the way I had grown from a person whose ears were shielded from disturbing news to one called upon to join in whatever make-believe would help tease the little ones along.

"How's your mama doing in there?" I asked her, pretty sure I wouldn't like the answer. Sally seemed worse every day.

Meggie disappeared for a moment, then reappeared. "She's talkin' and I don't even know what she's talkin' 'bout."

"Well, don't worry, honey. It's just the fever."

So many had fallen to this illness now, and they were every last one of them going out of their heads. Walk next to just about any wagon and you'd hear some poor soul inside moaning in delirium. Between them and the bedridden who were well enough to keep up a loud, constant plea for the drivers to stop the bone-shaking bumping, we were a sorrowful sounding caravan indeed.

Our wagons were shaking apart.

Facing one particularly steep downhill grade, Rowland and I chained our back wheels. The two of us held ropes to brace the wagon too. But suddenly, the bony oxen caught the scent of water from a little creek in the draw and surged down toward it. The wagon lurched; the rope burned through my hands. Grasping tight again, I slid and stumbled uselessly after, my small weight doing nothing to hold us back. All around us, others suffered the same plight, as wagons and animals and people shifted downhill out of control. I could hear Sally's cry of alarm from the wagon, the yelling and cursing of the men, the bellowing of the animals, and the crashing of the wagons all sounded in a roar as we tumbled to the bottom in a cloud of dust.

But at least at the end of it, there was water.

The next morning we had to use up the coolest hours patching the wagons back together. Pa's rear axletree had snapped completely, one of the Fuller wagons popped two iron tires, and Annie's wheels had splintered spokes. By the time we pulled out, the worst heat of the day had already engulfed us.

Rocking along, I counted. Thirty days to The Dalles Stephen Meek had promised. Today made eight.

Somehow we had come to another fork of the Malheur, making camp in a hollow between steep hills that rose to a majestic crag of a rock.

Rowland stopped the wagon next to a couple of scraggly cedars and unhitched the oxen. I climbed inside. Whew. The trapped, stifling air stank of sickness. Sally lay in the hammock bed Rowland had rigged out of her quilt.

"Rowland?" Sally's eyes looked vacant as she scanned the wagon's interior.

"No, it's me, Sally. Lovisa. We're stopping now."

"Oh." Her voice came faintly. "Good."

"Here, let me help you. We'll get you all fixed up."

One at a time I unknotted the corners of the quilt. Rowland's contraption helped cut down on the hard bumping when the wagon was rolling, but I thought Sally would appreciate a chance to simply lie still, without swinging. Then I helped her with the chamber pot. As I climbed out to empty it, Rowland appeared.

"How is she?"

I just looked at him, wishing I could give an optimistic report.

He climbed in. I stood outside, listening to my sister's feeble mewlings, a running stream of apologies...sorry, sorry, sorry...

Sorry? For what? For being sick? For breaking down? For not being as strong as passage across this harsh land demanded? I couldn't bear Rowland's voice either, his anguish...

For heaven's sake, why was I listening, then? I hurried away with the chamber pot, and Sol pointed me to the camp's designated dump. A stinking place at every camp spot, here it was already worse than usual. Sally wasn't the only one sick. You could smell it; you could see it. People were throwing up. They had diarrhea.

I made a point not to listen as I passed back by our wagon and grabbed the water bucket from its hook. Taking a zigzag path through camp, I found my way to the gurgling river and swung up a bucket of fresh water. Returning to the wagon, I stood by the canvas flap, hesitating.

"Do you want some water for her?" I finally called through.

"Yes, come on up." Rowland took the bucket. When I climbed in he was sponging Sally's face. "I offered to carry her out but she doesn't want to."

"It might feel better," I said to Sally.

She made a face, shook her head. "Rowland?"

"Yes?"

"I don't want to be left out here."

"Nobody's leaving you."

"I mean, if I die…"

"You're not going to die," I said before Rowland even had a chance to react. "Stop talking like that. The worst is past, and by tomorrow you'll be up and out of the wagon."

Rowland turned and searched my face. Did I really believe this, his look asked? Gave me chills. Things are pretty bad, it struck me, when a grown man is looking to a seventeen-year-old girl for reassurance.

I took a deep, shuddery breath and started lying for all I was worth. "Tomorrow you'll be down at the river. It's…it's really pretty here. There's even a few trees. You'll have a nice wash and a good breakfast and then we'll move on."

"I want…" Sally lay there panting. "I want to see the babies."

I glanced at Rowland. We'd agreed it was best to keep them away, especially Jimmy, for fear of the fever catching. But now he nodded at me to fetch them, and I climbed out.

First I found Meggie at Ma's wagon where she'd been riding.

"How is she?" Ma said as I hoisted Meggie to my hip.

"Better," I lied again. Then I went to find Jimmy. Susan was nursing him.

"Oh, Susan, thank you for this." I watched for a moment, feeling inadequate, wishing I, too, were a nursing mother.

"She'd have done the same for me." As Jimmy pulled away and grinned at me, she buttoned her bodice. "How is she?"

I glanced at Meggie and shook my head the tiniest bit.

Back at the wagon, I lifted the children one at a time up to Rowland and climbed in after. No sooner had the little ones got a glimpse of their mother, though, than they were pushing to climb back out.

"No, no, now," Rowland was saying. "Let Mama look at you a minute."

But while I held Meggie, Jimmy struggled in Rowland's arms and kept trying to turn away. He would look at Sally, then lurch back, burying his face against Rowland's chest. Even this baby, I thought, knew a desperate state when he saw it. Meggie finally settled, finger in her mouth, staring with wide and solemn eyes.

"Margaret. James," Sally said, her hand lifting toward a caress she hadn't the strength to complete. Then it dropped back to pluck at her twisted chemise. "Who will—? Lovisa." Her eyes, infinitely large and sorrowful, fastened on me. "Take care of them. Promise you will."

"Sally! No, I won't promise any such thing! Because you'll be taking care of them."

"You will," Rowland said to Sally. "And I will."

Sally regarded the two of us sadly, as if she knew better but was too weak to argue. She closed her eyes. Her face relaxed a little, and for a moment she looked so peaceful, my breath caught. Was she—? Struck with the same fear, Rowland touched her cheek.

She opened her eyes briefly and smiled. He sighed, relieved. "Try to sleep now. Lovisa's right. The worst is over."

I took the children back to Ma's wagon. "She's resting a little easier," I told my mother, which seemed true enough.

I studied my mother's worn, sunburned face with its ever-deepening creases. There was so much we weren't saying. Ma already knew what it was like to watch a child die. She'd lost little Jimmy at three, and there'd been my older sisters Dulanny and Hannah, girls who'd been taken by some sort of sickness at the ages of eleven and nine before I was even born.

"I'll look in on her," Ma said.

Did it ever get any easier? I wondered, watching her go. Did mothers worry for their children just the same even when the children weren't children anymore?

My sisters and I went about the usual business of getting supper. Ma had returned, and I was rolling out biscuits on her wagon seat when Rowland came hurrying over.

"Lovisa, come here! She's wide awake! She's talking!"

Delighted, I passed the rolling pin to Lydia and hiked my skirts to step lively. What a relief! Only now could I admit to myself just how scared I'd been.

In the wagon Sally sat upright, bright and alert.

"Oh, good," she said, seeing me. "She knows where it is."

Rowland shrugged, a dazed little smile on his face. "Something about a blue dress she wants to wear."

I hesitated. "She doesn't have a blue dress."

"I didn't think so, either," he admitted. And then, with a hopeful note that somehow hurt my heart, "Maybe something she's tucked away?"

I thought. I shook my head. There was precious little left in this wagon and I knew every item.

"We still have your wedding suit," I said, picking up her hand. "But you wouldn't want to spoil that out here, would you?"

"That's fine then," she said, not quite making sense. "So we'll be there tomorrow."

I glanced at Rowland, back at her. "Or maybe the day after that," I said, humoring her. This seemed a disturbing turn, my sister somehow imagining we were but a day from the end of the journey. "Here," I said, fanning her with the brim of her threadbare sunbonnet. "Maybe this'll make you feel better."

"And you won't even have to be doing that anymore." Now she was looking at a place just beyond me, her eyes oddly glazed. "Dulanny," she said wonderingly. "Is that you?"

Dulanny? I lowered the sunbonnet fan. Oh, Lord—

"And Hannah! Oh! Ma always said—"

"Hannah?" Rowland said, glancing at me uneasily. "Isn't that—?"

I held up my hand, wanting to listen, afraid to hear. Together we watched Sally's face begin to glow.

Suddenly, a marvelous smile. Her eyes closed in pure yearning, then opened wide. "Oh, look!" she cried, lifting her arms, leaning forward, seeming to see right through me and Rowland to something beyond. "Look!" she said—and I will never as long as I live forget this—"Look! How green!"

For an instant she hovered. She was like a bird suspended in flight. Then she sank.

"Sally, no!"

Rowland and I lunged forward, catching her, trying to keep her from slipping away. But it was too late. She was gone.

We held her for a stunned moment. Then we eased her back.

I have no idea how long we knelt there like that on either side of her, but finally, Rowland passed his callused hand over those wide-with-wonder eyes, closing them forever.

NOTHING WAS THE SAME AFTER THAT.

And never would it be again. We had marked the vast continent's great divide at South Pass, but in my memory my sister's death would become the great divide of the journey. Beyond that, although I didn't know it as I watched Rowland stagger off alone toward the river, this dreadful hour would mark the before and after of my entire life.

No time to fashion a coffin, even the rudest sort. The boys went up the hillside that hot September evening to dig the grave while Melinda came over to help Ma and me lay Sally out in her plum silk wedding suit. We might have saved and treasured the dress, which was lovely and light, nothing to weigh down the wagon. It could have served some other sister. But for myself, I couldn't imagine one moment past this awful present, much less all the way to a time when one of us might once again care what we wore. It was just a stitching of silk, after all. Sally was our sister, Ma's favorite daughter, Pa's best birthday gift, Rowland's beloved wife, and mother of the two sweetest babies in the whole wagon train. As we washed as best we could her poor, worn-out body, I thought a decent burying dress was the least we could do, some small counter to this brutal haste, the horror of such a lonesome grave.

"How deep?" Ma asked the boys when they came back down from the hill.

Isaac and Amos looked at each other.

"Three, four feet," Amos said.

"It's got to be six."

"Well, Ma," Isaac said, "the ground's real rocky and hard."

"I promised her," Ma said. "She told me if she died this far out, she wanted to at least be buried deep."

This shocked me. The two of them had spoken of death? Admitted the possibility? Was I the only one fool enough to have imagined that death on the trail might happen, but never to us?

When Amos and Isaac still made no move, Ma grabbed one of their shovels and headed up the hill. The sun was almost down; her shadow fell long.

"It's a waste," Isaac said under his breath. "It's deep enough. Ma's got no call to use herself up on that."

"Isaac, she promised," I said, bitterly regretting I myself hadn't given Sally the promises that could have comforted her.

"But it doesn't make any sense."

As if any of this did. For an instant I felt as if I were floating away, watching us all from a distance. Such a sorry business. We wanted to be arguing with fate, or God, or Stephen Meek. Instead, we were bickering with each other over a couple of feet of dirt.

Melinda Fuller looked as torn up as any of us.

"Amos King," she said, "if you think I'd marry any man who'd let his own mother dig her daughter's grave…"

Amos looked at her standing there, fists clenched, eyes averted, a fierce flush across her cheeks.

"All right," he said. "Come on, Isaac. Ma!" he called. "Hold on."

The next morning, while the deeper hollows still lay in shadow, the sun's rising rays touched the hilltops as we Kings and the Fullers and a handful of others stood at my sister's grave. Little Meggie clutched a fistful of black-eyed Susans. At what seemed as good a moment as any, I prompted her to toss them in on top of her mother's quilt-wrapped form. Then our family members stepped back and let others take over the final, grim work of the shovel.

When the hole was filled, my brother John took the board on which Rowland had painstakingly hewn Sally's name and the date and shoved it into the ground at the head of the grave.

We stood there. Who would speak?

Reverend Moore had gone with another group of wagons, and no one had thought to bring a Bible up the hill. Maybe I should have said all the good things about Sally. How sweet she was. How she never said a bad word about anyone. How brave she'd been, really, when you thought about it, when you understood how much everything scared her. But I didn't. Everybody knew it all anyway. Everyone felt bad enough to lose her. In silence we stood in a circle around the raw plot. In the space of a few moments, the night's chill had dissipated, and the insects were beginning to buzz in the scrubby grass.

Finally, a voice. Susan spoke from memory:

The Lord is my shepherd; I shall not want.
He maketh me to lie down in green pastures.

Where? I thought bitterly. No green pastures out here. With one arm clasping Jimmy, my other hand resting on Meggie's head, I stared at the ground and I swear, my heart felt as hard as the rocks the boys had placed around the mound.

He leadeth me beside the still waters.
He restoreth my soul: He leadeth me in the paths of
righteousness for his name's sake.
Yea, though I walk through the valley of the
shadow of death...

Susan quavered on to a finish, the words, to me, a haunting mockery of our plight. This little boy's mother was dead. This little girl would never know Sally's tender guiding hand as she grew to be a woman herself. Show me one tiny bit of goodness and mercy in that.

A hot wind was already picking up, rattling the dried-out weeds. I couldn't bear to look at Rowland.

Eyes downcast, I noticed the scuffed boots of some not in our family shifting restlessly to go. Of course. They weren't heartbroken. Not over our Sally anyway. They only wanted to keep moving.

Just as I had, I remembered, at a grave or two before this.

But now it was us. Our family.

And I'd thought God was on our side! Oh, I saw it so plain now. I'd been assuming that for us Kings, things were always bound to go right. As if we were separate from other families. As if we were special, immune from misfortune. As if we would always make smart decisions that would keep bad things from happening.

Weren't we the family who so cheerfully boasted that for us there would be no girls left behind? Was this a punishment for our pride then, losing Sally, having to leave her out here?

I lifted my face, squinting against the wind's dust. I would remember this place. Such a strange, desolate beauty, as lonely as ever a grave could be. Above us, a rocky crag of a mountain for her headstone and below us, a river called the Malheur—evil hour indeed.

As we readied the wagons to go, Rowland stood at my side and spoke the first words I'd heard from him since the night before. "Will you go ahead and ride with my young ones, then?"

"Rowland." As if I'd abandon the three of them.

I did what I could to straighten out the wagon. We had buried Sally with the hammock quilt as her winding sheet, so I put the straw tick back on the platform bed. This would be my place now. I'd have to ride most of the time to make sure Jimmy didn't crawl over the tailgate and fall out.

As every creaking rotation took us farther from Sally that afternoon, I lay with him in my arms, heedless of my head banging against the wooden wagon side, unwilling to shift position and risk waking him.

Lord, how was I going to feed him? Susan was doing what she could, but with so little to drink herself, she hardly had enough milk for her own baby. The older sisters said I could wean Jimmy to a cup now, but poor Buttercup was so scrawny, she gave only a pitiful dribble.

It was hot in the wagon, the air thick and stifling. Above the buzz of flies, the low rumble of beast and the monotonous grind of the tar bucket swinging on its rusty hook, Meggie's voice sounded like chimes.

"Where's my mama?"

I opened my eyes. Had I dreamt that little voice?

"Auntie Lovisa?" Meggie's sticky little hand crept around my neck. "Why my mama's not in the wagon?"

Oh, I wasn't ready for this. Not ready at all. I took a breath.

"Remember up on that hill," I began, "when you threw the flowers?"

That had been my idea. The other sisters thought Meggie too young to remember any of this, but I knew Sally wouldn't have agreed. And maybe it would be a shred of comfort to Meggie someday, knowing she'd been there with a bouquet for her mother.

"But where's my mama at now?"

I stared up at the canvas. "Come here, lamb." I drew her down, shifting Jimmy, making a place for Meggie beside me. "Your mama's in heaven."

"I know," she conceded. "But where is that?"

Through the cinched end of the canvas wagon cover, I watched the rocking of the dull brown horizon. "Well, it's where God is."

That was honest, anyway. He sure didn't seem to be here with us.

Meggie contemplated this. "When she's coming back?"

I looked at the poor little thing—too young for these realities, I myself too young to be the one trying to explain them. Shouldn't it be Ma? Shouldn't Hope or one of the other older ones take over? No, everybody already had their own hands full and more. I ran my tongue over the deep stinging split in my lower lip.

"People can't come back from heaven, honey."

Meggie's flushed face puckered up. Two fat, miserable tears squeezed out.

Well, let her cry. Who wouldn't? It was good she could cry. I'd cry myself if everything in me didn't feel so completely dried up.

"Looks like I'll be taking care of you and Jimmy now."

Not that I felt up to it in the least. Folks were always saying God fit the back to the burden, but I'd never believed that for an instant. Look around! If it were true, why was the world so full of breaking backs? Still, that was probably no excuse not to try.

Meggie sniffled noisily for a few minutes and then: "Auntie Lovisa?"

"Yes, pet?" I wiped her smeary face with my apron.

"Is heaven like O'gen?"

Surprised, I smiled. "That's a nice thought." Then, after a moment: "Probably it is. And maybe if we're lucky, Oregon will be like heaven."

I was used to the men never agreeing among themselves exactly how things ought to be done. After all, we'd been listening to them argue since before we even left St. Joe four months ago.

But now, in these remote hills, the talk around the sagebrush fires at night had taken on a low, ominous tone that had me and my sisters trading anxious glances. The men weren't just weary and disgruntled, at odds over the best way to handle some small travel dilemma. No, this was worse, the way they sounded so frighteningly uncertain of everything.

I noticed Annie's look of alarm when we overheard Pa admitting he wasn't sure exactly which stream this was we were camped on. And Melinda's when Mr. Fuller wondered aloud why the trail of the companies ahead of us was leading us south instead of north to The Dalles as we'd expected. Mr. Herren, a member of the original Committee of Safety, kept insisting the mountains to the south must be the Cascades, but Rowland said everyone knew the Cascades were to the west.

"Maybe these maps are no good," Mr. Herren argued. "Or the compasses are broken."

"I'll tell you one thing looks clear to me," Melinda confided as she tugged a comb through Bitsy's matted curls, picking out lice as she went. "We're way past the time Mr. Meek said we'd strike the river running north."

Up until now, no matter how miserable the trail, how tiresome the travel, at least we'd known we were on the right road. I hadn't appreciated this feeling of confident purpose until it was replaced by its opposite—a dreadful hesitancy. Now, meandering through this vast territory, this arid, treeless tract, I began to fear we were simply moving ever deeper into a void. I had lost any sense that the turning wheels were actually shortening the distance between our wagons and some planned destination. I suspected we were traveling in circles.

Don't think about it, I warned myself constantly. Nobody was asking me. I had to concentrate on the problems I could do something about.

At a pastureless camp one night I ripped open the bedding tick, pulled out the straw and mixed it with a handful of flour. This I fed to the weary Buttercup along with extra buckets of water which I hauled right to her so she wouldn't have to expend any extra energy getting to the watering hole. The next morning she rewarded me with a half cup of milk, which I presented to Jimmy like a precious gift.

"Sure wish I was your own ma for real, sweetie," I said as I held the tin cup for him. "Be a lot easier than trying to get the cow to make your milk."

"He doesn't like it," Meggie observed, just the instant before Jimmy flung a hand, sending the cup and milk flying.

I sank back and sighed, then idly picked a louse out of a little crease in the baby's neck. I was crawling with them myself. God, it was awful. I'd have given anything for the water to boil and bleach every scrap of clothing and bedding we had, but all we could do was air them.

That and keep picking off the lice.

The sun beat down on our wagon's canvas cover. Beneath it I lay in the foul-smelling heat with the little ones, listlessly singing every song I could remember, repeating "Shenandoah" at Meggie's request more times than I could count. I paged through the handful of books Rowland apparently hadn't been able to bring himself to throw out, reading Longfellow aloud, anything to tease the children along: Let us then be up and doing, with a heart for any fate…Fine words. I wondered if Mr. Longfellow had ever ridden any distance at all in a springless wagon.

Every few yards a wheel would jam against a rock, stopping the wagon dead. I'd halt my patter and lie there, waiting for Rowland to dislodge it or make the oxen tug the wagon over. Then, with a lurch, a twisting of the wagon box that sounded as if the whole thing was set to splinter apart, we'd pull forward again. Mercy, walking every step had been exhausting, but this was worse, mentally pulling for the oxen and the wagon, thinking my way through every yard of progress—if it was progress. And on that I had grave doubts.

Fourteen days out of Fort Boise. But why keep count? Everyone seemed agreed Mr. Meek wasn't as clear in his own mind as he'd first sounded on exactly how long it would take.

As for the rest of us, we'd even lost track of the days of the week and traveled on the Sabbath without anyone complaining at being forced into such a sin. But then, would it make a lick of sense to stop for a service when most of us were probably praying for deliverance every moment, every weary step of the way?

Now, without the usual bang against a rock or thud into a rut, the wagon eased to a stop. I opened my eyes and stared dully at the sleeping baby, his black lashes on flushed cheeks. After a moment, I sat up. Why weren't we starting again? Climbing to the front, I squinted into the harsh sunlight.

My God. Rowland lay sprawled in the dirt. I scrambled down and hurried to him.

"Sol!" I called ahead to Annie's wagon. "Sol, help me!"

Halting his teams, Sol trotted back and the two of us hoisted Rowland to his feet.

"What?" Rowland said, dazed, half-collapsed between us.

"Oh, Sol, it's the fever."

Meggie watched, wide-eyed, as we pulled her father up into the wagon and stretched him on the pallet. I patted a few drops of water on his blazing face. I unbuttoned his shirt. The rash!

Sol and I looked at each other. He knew what it meant as well as I. Rowland had already been sick for days. Oh, Lord. This was too much.

I sat for a moment, then took a deep breath and tied on my faded sunbonnet. "Meggie, we both have to be big girls now. Give your pa a drink if he'll take it."

"But where you going?"

I put a hat on Jimmy, picked him up. "Somebody has to drive the oxen." Awkwardly, I climbed out, the baby under my arm.

Sol picked up the prod where Rowland had dropped it and handed it to me.

"It's not that hard," he said. "You can do it. It's gee for right, see, and haw for left and—"

"I know, Sol." Hadn't I been right there hearing those commands all day, every day, for four long months? I settled Jimmy on my hip and took a deep breath. Good land, I even heard those directions barked in my sleep. "Gee up, Star," I said tentatively. And then with more conviction, "Gee up!"

With a lurch and a creak and a groaning of wooden wheels and clanking parts, we were moving forward again.

Rowland taken sick. Why that should surprise me so, I don't know. The fever was felling young and old alike, the weak and the strong. Maybe I just never figured to see him in such a helpless state. In spite of the disdain I'd always made such a point of pretending, I'd secretly thought of him as so much older and wiser. He was a man who knew what was what. I had chafed at having him boss me; I never expected to have him depending on me.

In the days since Sally's death, the gap in our ages seemed like it had shrunk somehow. He didn't know everything, I saw now. He had never traveled the road to Oregon before either. He had never worried which route to take, or listened to his children cry for water. He had never before buried a young wife. These astonishing days of our lives were unfolding for him one at a time just as they were for me. And he, no more than I, knew what lay ahead of us down this road.

CHAPTER 14

THE SICKNESS SPREAD THROUGH OUR WAGON TRAIN.

"Looks like what we used to call camp fever," Pa told us. He'd served in the War of 1812 and knew first-hand. "Comes up and spreads whenever you've got folks crowded close, things not as clean as you'd like."

"Well, I hope to shout!" Ma said. "We're doing the best we can!" She yanked a quilt off a line where it had been hung for airing. "You want things washed nice, you find us some water!"

"Nobody's blaming you, Sarepta. We know you women have…" He hesitated, then started again. "We hadn't planned on…" Finally, in lame conclusion, "We know."

Each morning, each evening, we women gathered and took stock. Who was taken sick now? Who was improving? Anybody find anything that helped? Any reports from the other wagons?

"This fever just seems to hang on forever," Melinda said, weary from tending her sixteen-year-old brother Henry.

Annie and Hope glanced at each other. She doesn't know what forever means, I could imagine them thinking. Forever was a sick husband.

Ma turned to me. "How's Rowland doing?"

And right here—although I'm half-ashamed to admit it, seeing as how we were talking about folks being deathly ill—right here even as I was shaking my head to indicate the answer was "not so well," here is where I felt a strange little thrill. Rowland was mine to nurse, Ma seemed to be saying. Mine to report on. Which was just foolish and confusing anyway, seeing as how I was only doing my duty, doing what Pa'd made me. But I wondered if he ever pictured me sitting up all night with a man not my husband, taking his shirt off, trying to keep him washed, helping him with the bedpan.

It scared me to death when Jimmy started coughing and broke out with the rash. All night as he thrashed and fretted, I sat awake and watched over him and Rowland. If they dozed I stared at the flickering candle, remembering the day in Missouri when we'd molded these tapers, how I'd wondered where we'd be when each was lit to flame. I surely never pictured this—Sally dead and buried, Rowland helplessly ill, me fully in charge of the children and the oxen.

Is there anything longer and darker than a night in a desert where you're coaxing along each and every breath a baby takes? And Rowland...oh, God. This was a good man—gentle with his children, kind to his wife. He didn't deserve to die. And then I'd recall Sally sitting up those long sick nights with Meggie back on the Snake. Why didn't I think to relieve her, take on some of the nursing myself? I'd known she was worn down. Maybe if I'd helped, she wouldn't have fallen to the fever.

But I just didn't know! Oh, I wished I could tell my sister how sorry I was. But I'd still been just a girl then. Now I had to be a woman, and this is what women did—they sat up all night, watching, waiting, as if purely loving people could save them. And what a shock when, in my middle-of-the-night ruminations, it struck me—Sally had been younger than I was now, those summers she'd nursed me through the fevers. I'd thought she was so old and grown-up! I thought when you were seventeen you understood everything. Now I was seventeen and I understood nothing.

If the nights were long and cold, the days were even longer and mercilessly hot. We followed a bloody trail as the poor oxen's bruised hooves bled all along the way.

Passing one of the faithful beasts unloosed from the yoke to lie down beside the trail and gasp his last, I thought, This is it. We've descended into hell. Three weeks back, on the baking Snake River plain, I'd thought walking through a hot, suffocating cloud of dust was the worst it could get. I was wrong. All that was before. Now I understood: Our family could lose people too. We Kings were not all going to make it.

My cheeks were hot as stove lids. The children cried incessantly for water.

We stumbled past a broken-down wagon, the bravely painted "Oregon or Bust" slogan bleaching in the sun. Didn't seem one bit funny now. I cringed inside, remembering how I'd mocked the man who hadn't been able to buy a wagon as good as Pa's, how I'd smirked at what would prove some poor family's tragedy. Taking a last look, I aimed my bonnet forward. God probably had a special place in hell for people like me.

Human feet were bleeding too.

In the blistering glare of noon, I saw Mamie Brown picking her barefoot way along the rocky road, her foolish, fashionable boots no doubt long since gone to shreds. I looked away, wanting to ignore this. No use. I looked back. I couldn't forget I still had my second pair of boots in the wagon, completely unused, thanks to my Sioux moccasins.

Half-disgusted with myself, I stopped prodding the oxen and climbed into the wagon. I climbed past the children curled next to Rowland and pulled the boots from my cupboard. Jumping back out, catching up to Mamie, I thrust them at her.

"Here. Try these."

She blinked, dipped her head in thanks, and sat right down in the dirt to put them on.

Later Abbie asked me about it. "Lovisa! Why?"

I shrugged.

"It's her own fault! You'd have been the first to say so."

Yes, but that was before.

"I guess she can't help it," I said, "if her folks are idiots."

On the eighteenth day since leaving Fort Boise, we dragged the caravan thirty miles. We were desperate to stop but a dry camp wouldn't do for the livestock at this point. We had to reach water. It was two in the morning before word came back that a spring had been found up ahead. Pulling into the camp, finally coming to a halt, we all fell immediately into dirty, hungry, exhausted sleep.

First thing in the morning I went out to see what I could get in the way of milk from Buttercup. Found her dead. Poor thing. Gave all she could, then lay down and died. For a moment I just stood there with the empty bucket, staring at her bony carcass.

Finally I lifted my head and looked around. My God. Every wagon following Meek must be here—upwards of two hundred, scattered across this broad hollow.

The spring that had drawn us all to this spot turned out to be but a pitiful, seeping affair where I was soon spending a good deal of time in a line of other girls, waiting my turn to fill two green King buckets.

That first afternoon I met with Eliza Harris, one of my sister Lydia's friends from before the company divided.

"Lots of sick folks in your company?" she asked.

I nodded. "Yours?"

Her freckled face assumed a properly solemn expression, like she'd been imagining telling someone this story and maybe even practicing the words in her mind. "I'm sorry to say we had to bury a three-year-old boy. Little Elkanah Packwood." She darted a glance at the others in line, conscious of their attention. "With him it was whooping cough, though, not this camp fever like most folks." She sighed and shook her head. "He sure was everyone's favorite."

Well, of course. Weren't the favorites always the ones to die?

My turn had come. Stepping onto the board someone had laid across the mud, I pressed my buckets into the spring's mucky surface and watched the precious liquid begin trickling in. I wondered: Was God so cruel as to actually pick out the favorites? Were the ones like Sol or Lexie in particular danger? Or were we all just so poor at recognizing how special people were until they were gone? Did they have to die before we realized they were the favorites?

Our second day in the hollow, John Noble came looking for me. His group had just straggled in, he said. Half the people were sick, and he'd been anxious to hear about me.

"Everyone in your family well, then?" he asked.

"No," I said bluntly, annoyed somehow. "My sister died. Sally." It wasn't his fault he hadn't heard, I knew, but it hurt somehow, to find out people hadn't even remarked on our loss, hadn't hurried to quickly pass on the story of the beautiful, beloved girl from the King family.

"I'm sure sorry to hear that," John said. And to give the poor boy credit, he did look stricken.

Oh, why couldn't I be nicer to him? It's not like I enjoyed it, watching myself acting so cold and peckish. Sometimes I thought I must be trying to drive him away. Yet no matter how I endeavored to show him he wouldn't be happy with me, he kept coming around with that puppy-dog devotion in his eyes.

After what I guess he figured was the proper time to wait before following sad news with a topic more cheerful, he said, "I've been thinking. When we get to Oregon—"

"If we get to Oregon."

"Lovisa." He gave me a closer look. "That doesn't sound like you."

Well, I was different now. The girl I left behind was me.

"Lovisa, you're the one who's always said we have to keep looking forward. And I was just thinking that—"

"Sally? Is that you?" It was Rowland's voice, coming from inside the wagon. "Sally, can you give me hand?"

I jerked my head toward the canvas. "Got my brother-in-law in there, sick out of his head. Thinks I'm his wife."

I caught the flicker of John's surprise at this. He looked around like he hoped to reassure himself there was somebody else in on this with me.

"You're taking care of him all by yourself?"

"That's right," I said evenly, looking right at him. I knew what he was thinking.

"Shouldn't your ma or somebody help? At least do the part where…" He blushed. "You know."

"The part where he's naked?"

John turned away. Couldn't stand thinking what my maiden eyes had seen.

Oh, I'm sorry, I had no patience for this—that he should waste one moment in worrying about some old standards of keeping things nice. We just didn't have time for such trifles. We were trying to keep everybody alive.

He turned back to me. "I still think it'd help to make plans."

"I have a plan. I plan to get my sister's two babies to Oregon."

"Lovisa—"

"Right now that seems like enough."

Two days later, right outside our wagon, I heard a man from another company say the terrible word to Pa.

"King," he said. "Face facts. We're lost."

Lost. I froze, the word shooting a chill through me even inside the stifling wagon where I was sponging Jimmy down. I held still, letting the rag drip into the basin, straining to hear Pa deny it.

Only he didn't.

"We're lost," the other man said, "and that fool Meek refuses to admit it."

Pa, like the Good Book advises, gave the man's angry words a mild response. "I don't think he's trying to hide the fact the country doesn't look quite like he remembered it."

"But we should have struck that river he talked about days ago. And there's some saying this ain't no accident at all. He's plotted the whole thing with the Indians. Gonna drag us around out here until we're weak and starving, then the whole pack of 'em'll swoop down on us."

"Now why would he do that?" Pa sounded weary and annoyed at the same time.

"Well, who can say why a scoundrel does what he does? Other folks say he's being paid off by the goddamn Hudson's Bay Company to lose us out here. Or he was never planning to take us up to The Dalles at all. Some say a couple of fellows with a lot of cattle made him a secret deal to take us over the Cascades instead and that's why we're not on any route anybody can make any sense of. One way or another, we've been tricked and people won't stand for it, King. There's talk of a hanging."

"Now that's a real bright solution."

This was Rowland's voice now. He'd finally recovered enough to be out of the wagon. "Take the only man who's ever been through this country before and string him up. Oh, I'm sure we'll all be better off then."

"He's got to pay for this!" the other man insisted.

"Paying for it doesn't get us out of here," Pa countered.

"Or," Rowland added, "bring back the dead."

We'd called this place Stinking Hollow at first. It hardly helped to hear folks now had it as Lost Hollow. Men rode west each day, scouting for water and a way out.

"You sure you're well enough to go looking for water?" Ma asked Amos, who was still fighting his bout of fever.

"I'm sure as hell not well enough to lie here listening to these kids crying for it," was his answer.

Every time I'd watch them saddle up, I'd think how I'd gladly trade my own duties around camp for a day of solitary riding. Sounded easier than trying to come up with decent answers for fretful children.

"Why we aren't going?" Meggie asked.

"Well, we can't just yet."

"But I want to."

"I know, sweetheart. We all do. And we will. Soon."

Her black brows went together. "Are we lost?"

"No!" This perhaps a little too quickly to be convincing. "Who told you that?"

"That man, Auntie Lovisa. The one talking so mad outside the wagon?"

"Oh, him." I shouldn't have let Meggie hear that, but I'd been too caught up in listening myself. "Well, don't worry. We're not lost. The daddies just want to make sure they take us the best way."

Meggie refused to look reassured. I sighed. There was no fooling her now. No fooling anyone. You'd probably have to be a babe in arms not to realize we were all in a desperate situation.

"Is Jimmy going to die and go to heaven with Mama?"

"No! Absolutely not! Look, he's already better."

Lord, how exhausting, this business of trying to make optimistic predictions come true just by delivering them with sufficient conviction.

On the fourth day at Lost Hollow, Pa and Sol hauled the carcass of one of our skinny little heifers into camp.

Pa didn't say a word as Annie and I traded glances and sighed. We all knew what this meant. Those heifers were supposed to become the mothers of the new herds. Slaughtering them meant defeat.

It was like killing hope.

"I don't know what those idiots who led us out here expect us to eat," Mrs. Brown told the sky as I stood in line ahead of her at the spring.

I picked up my green buckets where I'd set them and shifted forward. She wasn't exaggerating about the lack of food supplies. Eating nothing but stringy beef didn't set well with folks. Everyone craved bread for energy, especially the little ones. But since I suspected she meant to include the King men among the idiots she blamed, I really didn't care to discuss it with her.

"I'll just have to feed Mamie and George on salted grass, although I hear it makes some folks sicker." Mrs. Brown peered around my drooping bonnet brim, determined to see into my eyes. "You folks trying it?"

I shook my head without looking at her.

"They say some are hoarding flour."

I pressed my cracked lips together. She knew perfectly well we must still have a bit. Hadn't she watched me lay down money for it at Fort Boise? Mocked me for paying what had seemed at the time an outlandish price?

My turn had finally come. I stepped out on the muddy board and stooped to the spring. Was it hoarding to have planned and provided? I could feel her squinty eyes on me. Go eat your money, I felt like saying. Try salting it. See how that goes down. The instant my buckets were full, I caught up the handles and hurried away.

Back at our wagons, everyone not sick in body seemed sick in spirit, just sitting around, weak and wasted, at a loss for anything useful to do. So hard for women, when we can't be busy. But there wasn't much to cook, and without water we couldn't wash. Water was so short, even the sick ones got only a rationed sip at a time.

I gave the children dippered drinks and told Ma about Mrs. Brown and the flour. "Plain as day, she was trying to get me to offer some."

Ma's face was hard. "They're not the only ones running short."

"And they're the ones I most don't want to share with," I said.

"Oh, well, then," Abbie said. "That explains why you went and gave your good boots to Mamie. Did you know she did that, Ma?"

Thanks, Abbie, I thought, figuring I'd catch it now. But I misjudged. Ma didn't have the energy to get mad.

"It feels different about the flour," I tried to explain. "They could have bought it at Fort Boise. She had the money. Bragged on it, even. And she was just so proud of herself, refusing to pay the price."

"Some people," Pa said, disgusted. "Should have sent that lot packing when they first showed up at St. Joe."

Nobody dared say, "Well, why didn't you?" but I caught Susan and Annie trading knowing glances, and I'll bet every one of us wanted to.

"You think I like seeing people's young ones sick with eating grass?" Ma said, as if someone had accused her of this. "If we start giving away our stores to all those doing without, pretty soon we won't have a crumb to give our own."

At that moment Mrs. Brown herself came sidling right into the middle of our camp and our debate, begging flour directly.

"My Georgie's real sick. He's just got to have some bread."

Ma's mouth made a thin line. She glanced at the rest of us, then reached past the lowered tailgate of her wagon and measured out a scoop of the precious white stuff.

Mrs. Brown opened the empty flour bag she carried so Ma could dump it in. As Ma put away the scoop and crossed her arms over her chest, Mrs. Brown held up the sack and shook it, frowning.

"Won't make much," she said. "But if that's all you can spare."

Astonished at the audacity, Ma dropped her arms and stared.

Annie stepped forward and spoke between her teeth. "You'd better take it and run, Mrs. Brown. Before we change our minds."

Mrs. Brown sniffed, spun, and marched off, chin in the air.

On the fourth night at Lost Hollow, the men held a meeting to shout out loud all the things that, up to now, they'd only been muttering. Honestly, we could hear them clear across the camp, and even if we couldn't, we already knew the debate by heart.

What on earth were we supposed to do? There was no turning back; we'd come too far off the regular trail. Going forward when no water had been found for as far as forty miles would be taking a terrifying chance. Two different groups had already risked it and been forced to return. Then again, how much longer could eight hundred fifty people and four thousand head of cattle, oxen, and goats survive here, what with the grass grazed to nothing, the spring overtaxed, and the entire hollow trampled into a giant cesspool?

Pa and Rowland returned from the meeting thoroughly disgusted. What a waste of brains—a bunch of men more interested in laying blame than in finding solutions. Tonight they'd gone so far, Pa said, as to prop three wagon tongues up into a tripod to form a gallows and insisted they'd lynch Mr. Meek the instant he again set foot in camp.

Luckily, when Meek showed up, he brought news good enough

to stall his own execution, and the more reasonable men were able to persuade the hotheads to back off.

Meek and a few others had climbed to the top of a butte we could see to the northwest. They'd spied bright green off to the north—the color you only find where there's water. Grass and willows. The plan now was to send the scouts out by moonlight in that direction. They would mark the trail. We were to wait for the signal to come ahead—three gunshots.

We waited all night. We waited all the next forenoon. Our ears were cocked for the gunshots but none came. All we heard was the moaning of the sick and the whining of the children.

"Water! Want more water!" Their poor lips were cracked and dry, their little tongues swollen.

Water. That's all I could think about. Please let them find it. Oh, if I ever got to a place where there was water cold and clear and I could gulp as much of it as I wanted, I feared I'd probably drink to bursting.

"Well, girls," Susan managed to say in the middle of all this, "I think we better be packing up here."

We all looked at her. Melinda looked at me. Had Susan heard something we'd missed? It seemed like there'd be more excitement if somebody'd got the word water had actually been found.

"I expect we'll be hearing those gunshots any minute now," Susan said, "and the men'll be wanting to move right out."

Ah, now I understood. Up and doing. Susan was acting more like a King than we Kings. Up and doing, and if there was nothing to do, do something anyway. Pretend! At the very least it would look reassuring to the children. And if the signal shots came, we'd be that much further ahead.

So we set about organizing our outfits in a tentative dance, tacit-ly conspiring in the trickiness of the steps. We must look optimistic enough to give the men heart and yet not so sprightly and efficient as to finish. It would only dismay them to find us ready and packed, idly awaiting their directions. They wouldn't appreciate having it made so plain, the fact that they still had no directions to give.

I was in the wagon with the children when it came, that hoarse and joyful cry.

"Water!"

Struggling over the crates and bags, I poked my head out from the canvas. Was it true? Had they heard the gunshots?

"Water! They've found it!"

The camp exploded to uproar. Lydia, who probably only a moment before had been languidly shaking out a quilt, now stuffed it in Ma's wagon and grabbed a water keg to fill. Isaac jumped up from his sick pallet as if Jesus himself had commanded him to rise and walk. He hustled off to saddle his horse. The little ones stood wide-eyed, watching us whip back and forth. Abbie and I hastily joined a long line at the spring, waiting to fill anything that would hold water from the slowly seeping puddle. Oh, if only the muddy liquid would come up faster.

In spite of our earlier preparations, it still took hours to get every-one's oxen yoked, the cattle rounded up, and the sick ones made as comfortable as possible in their soon-to-be bumping beds.

Finally, by the light of the full moon, we rolled out. Ahead, on the plain to the north, signal fires marked our way.

With Meggie and Jimmy tucked into their wagon beds, I walked all night beside the plodding oxen, the sagebrush catching at my skirt, trying to hold me back like so many sharp-nailed, clutching fingers. By daylight, I thought, this trail we were blazing would be plain enough to any following behind—they'd have only to follow the shreds of calico on the sage.

Just before dawn there came a roar like approaching thunder and, ahead of it, the warning shouts of the cattle drovers.

"To the wagons! Get to the wagons!"

In a quick double bound Rowland was at my side, grabbing my arm and pushing me unceremoniously up into the wagon, climbing after.

"What is it? What's happening?"

His answer was drowned by the thunder of cattle stampeding past us on both sides like a river dividing around rocks. Could these be our own, the footsore beasts that had previously been so hard to spur forward?

Once the herds passed, the oxen picked up pace.

"Couldn't hold 'em back," Amos called, riding up beside us. "Must smell it."

My heart jumped. He didn't even have to say the word.

Now the sun rose, revealing the most beautiful, most purely miraculous sight my eyes had ever beheld—a heavenly blue pool, the beginning of a river rising right up out of the sagebrush flats.

Water.

I burst into tears.

How foolish, I thought, but only for an instant. Because right away I heard the shouts of joy, the sobs coming from the other wagons. I wasn't the only one.

I turned to Rowland, and the two of us shared a look of naked relief. Maybe we'd make it. Maybe we weren't going to die out here in the desert after all.

CHAPTER 15

I LAY ON THE WAGON BED'S FILTHY TICK,
burning with fever.

The wagon lurched forward. It knocked side to side. It rocked
and creaked and groaned as if it must surely split apart. Down rocky
grades, up steep ones, zigzagging along creek beds, axles straining,
boards fairly screaming as they wrenched away from bolts. My head
ached; my mind skittered between memory and dream. Fluttering
scenes played before my closed eyes—the sweeping waters of a great
flood, the endless plains, a labyrinth of looming monoliths. Gee up!
Haw! And always the incessant pleadings of childish voices: More
water! I was following a mass of people enveloped in a great cloud of
dust. Then, ahead, I'd see a lovely little stream, clear water burbling
over rocks. I'd pick up my pace, hurrying forward, but somehow I
could never get to it. It would vanish into sand at my approach, and
again my throat would fill with choking dust.

"Lovisa?"

Coughing myself awake, I'd open my eyes to a face—Rowland's sometimes, then it would be Hope's or Susan's or Lydia's as they knelt there fanning me. I would hear the murmurs of concern, little Meggie's plaintive questions. A damp rag was being drawn across my brow. Helplessly, I surrendered my aching body into the tender hands of my sisters, who hovered over me like ministering angels. I felt their cool hands on my flanks as they helped me with the bedpan. Sometimes I thought the hands were Rowland's.

Meggie and Jimmy. Where were they? Who was looking after them? I tossed fitfully, dreaming they'd died. Voices assured me they hadn't, but I had to hear it again and again.

"Drink this," someone said, and I raised myself on a trembling elbow for a salty taste of beef tea. Falling back, exhausted with this feeble effort, I closed my eyes, again at the mercy of the flooding images, nightmarish, then heavenly. A long, pleasant dream of a dance—Sol and Bitsy together, Amos and Melinda, Abbie and Price. And me with John Noble, him pulling me into the warm shadows for a kiss. And I was kissing him back. Except then it wasn't John, it was—Oh, stop! The dream went hot and bad and wrong. Stop the beloved faces. Stop the people trying to tell me things I couldn't understand.

"What? What?" I'd cry, only to hear the hushing of real voices.

"Just rest, Lovisa." It was Ma.

My eyes flew open in alarm. God Almighty. I must be at death's door for sure if mine was the bedside Ma had chosen. She had so many to care for. I closed my eyes again, listening to them talking about me as if I weren't there. Somebody was crying.

So this was it, then. This was the valley of the shadow. Obviously it was an easier trail than I had ever imagined. The people walking along it didn't seem to be toiling at all. They moved effortlessly forward, all but floating. Up ahead I saw someone in the green grass. A girl. She turned. Sally! But after a flash of recognition, my sister's face went stern. She shook her head, and when I took a hesitant step forward, she stretched her arm forbiddingly, palm forward, as if to block my way.

"No?"

No, Sally mouthed soundlessly. And then suddenly little Tabitha was with her, and ahead of them both were others. Was that Sarah Fuller?

I stopped. I understood now. I was not to follow.

"Don't you dare," I heard Ma say from some distance. I felt her strong arms tighten around me. "Don't you dare" came that dear, fierce voice. "We've lost enough already."

This was true, I remember thinking in a calm, detached way, as if I were watching these events being enacted by others. This was reasonable. But the way Sally and Bitsy were going looked so pleasant, so inviting. Nobody understood how tired I was, and look! It would be so easy, skimming above that lovely green path...

"Lovisa! Listen to me!"

Oh, all right, I thought, half-annoyed. I suppose I ought to try to stay.

And for the rest of my life I would believe this: That my mother had bossed me back from the very brink of death.

The first time I felt well enough to get dressed and walk again, Rowland saw me lashing up my battered moccasins and said, "Wait."

After a bit of digging around in the wagon, he pulled out my worn pair of boots, now resoled and mended.

"Who did this?" I asked, admiring the repair job, obviously accomplished with salvaged materials and makeshift tools. I looked at Rowland. "You?"

He gave me a smile and a self-deprecating shrug.

"Rowland." I looked at him wonderingly. I wasn't surprised by his cleverness—I'd long since come to believe he could fix anything—it was that he'd set himself to the task in the first place. Imagine, while I was getting ready to give up and die, he'd managed to carry on, determined to believe I'd be up and walking soon. Needing these boots. Took grit, I thought, cinching the laces.

No, more than grit. Faith.

Turned out I was only one of many who'd fallen to the fever during this time. Dead were being buried at every camp spot—six just the night before.

Rowland ran through the names of the sick ones in our party and the others in the various companies who'd died. I listened, a bit dismayed, somehow, at how little I felt, even when I recognized the names.

"Then some little gal, Eliza…I forget the last name…"

"Eliza Harris?"

"That's it. Buried her back a ways."

"Oh, Rowland." To think a girl could be standing there in line for the spring, wistfully discussing the deaths of others, and then a couple of weeks later be dead herself.

"Lovisa? There's one more. This is the hardest—"

His tone. I felt my blood drain down.

"Tabitha Fuller."

"Bitsy?"

He nodded regretfully, then frowned, puzzled, cocking his head. "Somebody already told you?" I guess I didn't look that surprised.

I tried to remember but my brain felt so dull.

"Maybe someone did."

The Deschutes River turned out to be a surge of treacherous white water charging through an inaccessible canyon. Just like the Snake, I thought with disgust, the first time I stood on its high banks. Day after day we hauled the wagons of sick and dying along the upper rim, searching out a place to get the wagons down to cross.

The only good news was that at least our so-called guide, Stephen Meek, seemed to know where we were now—just fifty or sixty miles from The Dalles. Some Indians had pointed out the way. Rowland told me that while I'd been sick and delirious, a half-dozen young men from another company had ridden off hoping to reach the Methodist mission and bring back help.

Let them come fast, I prayed. Every day out here meant more people dying.

One evening I saw yet another knot of people up on a rise, all of them standing hunched and hatless against the skyline, Reverend Moore with his Bible open.

"Who is it now?" I asked Hope, instantly recognizing the scene for what it was, another hasty funeral.

Hope shrugged.

"Mrs. Hull," Sol told us.

Hope and I looked at each other. We had liked the woman well enough. We sighed. That was all: just a sigh.

Were we to be permanently hardened by all this? As the funerals increased in frequency, the time devoted to each grew shorter, and the numbers who stood at the graves diminished. It was the mothers who were dying, and even their own children were too weak and sick to pay their respects.

"I'll be damned," I heard Rowland mutter outside the wagon as we halted one night.

I climbed down, helping Meggie, lifting Jimmy to my hip. I looked around, saw that our wagons were clustered high over the river. I edged closer to the overlook where Rowland and my brothers had gathered. Just north the river formed a falls, with white water gushing through a narrow canyon.

The men regarded the river with grim consternation.

"Hard to believe," Amos said, "but the Indians swear this is it."

Suddenly understanding, my heart sank. The recommended crossing place. I stared at the roiling rapids. All I could picture was wagons and people and animals and supplies being tumbled away in the furious waves.

My God. We needed a Moses to part the waters. We needed a miracle.

It's never easy listening to children cry, but little ones will wail for such a range of reasons. Scream at small hurts, whimper from hunger or thirst. But they sometimes save their fiercest tantrums for such a trivial thing as a tug-o'-war over some tattered rag toy. More heartbreaking to me, then, were the tears of old men.

I saw one sitting on a wagon tongue as darkness fell that night, weeping in despair. This was a man who hadn't been as old as my father setting out, but now seemed to have aged twenty years in the crossing of the plains.

Rowland and I stood together next to the fire, apparently the last ones awake.

"I don't believe the Indians have steered us wrong yet," Rowland said. "They insist this is where they cross."

"But then, they're not usually hauling wagons, are they? And they all seem to be such good swimmers."

He hesitated a moment. "The men have been talking. We'll figure something out."

I rewrapped my shawl. The high desert sun blistered us in the daytime, but the nights had turned pinching cold. It was almost October after all.

The fire crackled.

I looked up at the sky full of sharp, unfriendly stars. I just couldn't believe we'd come all this way, crossed all those rivers, dragged the wagons up so many steep grades and tumbled down steeper ones, all these murderous miles, only to be stopped dead just a few days short of our goal.

In a nearby wagon Lexie wakened to cry. Susan made soothing sounds. Then came my brother John's voice, low and reassuring. I wondered what comforting thing he'd found to say. I wished I could hear it myself.

"Rowland," I said. "Do you pray?"

He stuck a branch of sage in the fire, lifted it out, watched it burn. "Kind of looks to me like God's not too interested in my opinion of how things ought to go."

Oh. Of course. Sally.

"She was one for praying," he said, knowing I'd understand who he meant.

I nodded.

"How 'bout you?"

I shrugged. Truth was, when folks were supposed to be praying, when the preacher had the Bible open or Ma was leading the evening prayer circle, my mind would just fly off, never stay on the words. I mostly found myself truly praying only as a last resort, when I couldn't think of a single thing to do on my own to help a situation that seemed hopeless.

This river looked hopeless enough, but what were we supposed to pray?

Dear God, please dry it up?

But then an amazing and miraculous thing happened: The sun rose and the men came to life.

In the clear morning light, that river seemed to look different to them. To me too. Why had we been so downhearted? Why did we have to take a simple geographical feature as God's punishment flung down before us? Mercy, it was obviously just a technical problem. And shouldn't every problem have a solution? Didn't our men have the God-given minds to sort it all out?

Men who'd slouched dazed and dispirited at Lost Hollow with

nothing to contribute but angry complaints now hustled about. A set of pulleys was found in the wagon of a man who'd planned, when he settled, to set up a ferry on some western river. Others contributed ropes.

They would rig an elaborate system designed to swing the dismantled wagons high above the churning white caldron below.

I stood at the rocky edge with the children later that afternoon, Jimmy in my arms, watching the proceedings in utter amazement and more than a little fear.

"Look at the daddies," I said, almost singing with cheerful bravado. "See what they're doing? Your pa says we're going to swing right over on those ropes! We're all going to ride in a wagon box and not even touch the water! Won't that be fun?"

Jimmy gave me his bright, expectant grin. Such a sweetheart, a child who always seemed to feel something good was just about to happen.

"Are those Innians down there?" Meggie said, pointing to a young brave swimming a horse across.

"Yes, they're helping us."

Meggie frowned. "Is that different?"

"Different from what?"

"He's not an Innian gonna hurt us?"

"No, he's nice to us, see?"

"Well, when are we gonna see the scary Innians?"

Good question.

"I don't know, honey. Maybe they just aren't so scary after all."

Not that folks ever stopped being scared and worried the whole way. If we'd known better, I thought, we'd have worried about not meeting up with Indians. How many meals of game and fish did we enjoy thanks to their trades? How many river crossings would have been our undoing without their guidance?

Now I noticed a burly figure down among the men. Could that

possibly be Arnold Fuller? Just yesterday Melinda was saying her father still couldn't get out of the wagon after being felled by fever and grief as he stood at Bitsy's grave. But now, there he was, lashing a rope around a boulder, shouting for an Indian on the other side to give it a testing tug. Where had he found this fresh strength? It lifted my heart. Look at them all, scrambling around down there, working together.

Suddenly, it struck me how shortsighted I'd been. Maybe this cleverness in a crisis, this summoning of strength and will to face an unforeseen challenge—maybe in the end these counted for more than meticulous planning and neatly ticked-off lists. Maybe figuring out how to patch a boot was more important than correctly judging how many brand-new pairs to pack in the first place.

Other women were watching the crossing contraption take shape too—Orlena Williams, for one.

She turned her bonnet brim toward me. "Do you really think that's going to be safe?" She, I noticed, had not discarded the slats of her bonnet. Bleached translucent by the sun, the frail fabric still stood guard over her most valuable asset, her beautiful face.

"Of course it'll be safe," I answered. "Don't you remember that Mr. Fuller and my own pa down there are the very ones in charge of the official Committee of Safety?" I smiled broadly at Orlena. "How could it not be safe?" Then I widened my eyes and jerked my head meaningfully toward Meggie.

"Ah," Orlena said, catching on, nodding.

I squeezed Meggie's hand. The men had thought of something to try. They had a plan. As far as I was concerned, nobody had any business admitting out loud the truth—that the whole thing looked perfectly terrifying.

Especially in front of these children. My children.

Orlena regarded the two of them dispassionately for a moment, then lifted her lovely dark eyes to me. "Sorry to hear about your sister."

I sighed.

"These are hers, I take it?"

I nodded. "That's their pa down there. The tall one."

Orlena smiled to herself. "Oh, don't worry. I know who he is."

As soon as the children and I started back to our wagon, Meggie spun around to walk backward in front of me.

"Auntie Lovisa?" she said. "Why does that pretty lady make you so frowny?"

I kept track of the construction progress as I repeatedly hiked the steep trail down to the river and back for water. That afternoon, I had just dipped up a bucket when a rider came stumbling his horse down the steep descent, a man from a company in the rear. He picked his way right up to Stephen Meek himself, who was sprawled against a powder box, half-dead with the fever but determined to help oversee the ferry's construction.

The man pointed in great agitation back the way he'd come, then in the opposite direction, northwest over the river toward The Dalles.

Meek staggered to his feet and yelled for his wife, who came running. A knot of men surrounded them, arguing, gesturing, looking over their shoulders to the bluff above. I saw that Rowland was among them.

"What's happening?" I asked Melinda, who was coming up from that direction, having delivered a meal to Amos and the others.

"Someone's gunning for Meek," she replied. "Said somebody in the train behind us just buried two of his boys, swears he'll kill the man to blame for it."

I stood there, transfixed by the little drama playing out before us. The pulley lines were ready, but the wagon bed had yet to be rigged. No time for it now. Men scrambled to help the Meeks into rope slings to swing them across. They had to get away. Nobody was exactly grateful to the man who'd got us lost in the wilderness, but

I guess folks figured we'd had enough dying without speeding the process by firing lead into each other.

Now they were helping Elizabeth Meek into the sling. Mercy! To think I'd envied her when I first saw her astride a sleek horse, riding beside her buckskin-clad husband at the Three Island Crossing. See how a girl has to take serious care who she signs on with? Because whatever trouble your husband gets into, you'll be in it with him. One day you're puffed with pride, wife of the man bragging he knows a shortcut to Oregon. A few weeks later you're dangling high over a river, skirts aflutter, folks chasing you with deadly intent. I most definitely did not envy her now.

On the far side, the couple scrambled to mount the wet horses the Indians had crossed for them. They were starting up the steep ridge when the distraught man from the train behind galloped to the bluff edge, swung off his mount and came stumbling down to the rocky shelf on foot, waving his gun.

Screaming with rage, he aimed. Then, apparently judging his target beyond range, he discharged his gun into the air. Weeping bitterly, he sank to the ground, probably just as glad, I somehow thought, to have the river there to stop him. He didn't really want to commit murder. He just wanted to blame somebody, like people always do. He just wanted God to see how he couldn't stand it, losing his two fine sons.

Only later that night when the tale was repeated complete with names and details did I figure it out: One of those fine sons, now dead, was John Noble.

"They're trying it," Sol came reporting the next morning, and no one had to ask what he meant. We all picked up the children and went to the bluff. At the pulleys, the suspended wagon bed had been loaded with the parts of a dismantled wagon. My brothers Amos and Isaac were helping man ropes on both sides of the chasm.

"Here she comes," someone yelled, and the bed swung out.

As the loaded wagon bed dangled over the white water, I stopped breathing. Would the ropes hold? The wagon was sliding, sliding… as waiting hands on the far side grasped the box, we all cheered. Abbie and I laughed and hugged each other with nervous relief.

The first wagon was already being put back together on the far side as the second load was sent swinging. The system was going to work. We would cross this river.

A line of wagons began inching down the steep incline, no sooner reaching the bottom than the owners were swarming over them, unloading, dismantling, piling up their belongings to be ready for their turn.

Now the first actual passengers climbed aboard. As the designated family rode out over the river, the children looked to their parents for reassurance. So this is how we go to Oregon, I could imagine them thinking, innocently trusting, still young enough to believe that whatever their ma and pa told them to do must be the right thing, the smart thing, the safe thing. Only later would they realize just how extraordinary it had all been, this journey across the plains, this detour through hell. Only when they told the story to their own children would they begin to understand what their parents must have felt, loading them into a wagon box to swing above a churning chasm of white water.

As the King and Fuller wagons took their places in the line inching down the grade to the improvised ferry two days later, the company that had been behind us on the trail pulled into the campground. John Noble's twelve-year-old sister, Mary, came looking for me.

"You might as well have this," she said, handing me John's broadbrimmed felt hat. "He always said your old bonnet wasn't doing you much good."

I took the hat, circling it in my hands, thinking of the boy who'd worried over me.

"Guess I better wear it, then." I gave her a sad smile and put it on.

Mary nodded. "He'd have liked that."

Then her eyes shifted past me, catching sight of the overhead ferry. Her mouth fell open. "That's how we have to go over?"

"Looks scary," I acknowledged. "But they've been doing this for two days solid, and nothing's gone wrong so far."

Still, she looked worried.

"Honestly. My brothers have been helping work it, so I'd have heard."

We watched a moment, the scene below reminding me of nothing so much as an anthill, all the workers in motion, each doing his bit, each carrying his share of the burden.

"It is some kind of clever," Mary allowed.

I nodded, experiencing an odd twinge of pride, remembering how beaten down we'd all been just a couple of days ago.

Mary and I watched a lone wagon start the grueling, four-mile climb to the top of the opposite ridge as, back down at the landing, the next one was being unloaded from the ferry for reassembly.

"Are they making another big camp when they get over the top of that?" Mary asked.

I shook my head. "Everybody's just heading for The Dalles. There's supposed to be some relief parties coming out to meet us." And I hoped to God that would prove true, for almost every wagon now carried someone near perishing, a weary soul for whom a bit of food might mean the difference between life and death.

As Rowland settled me and the children into the wagon-bed ferry with the others a couple of hours later, I tried to recall the words of reassurance I'd given Mary Noble. I tried telling myself this was perfectly safe.

I wrapped my arms tight around Meggie and Jimmy, and as the wagon bed dipped forward, so did my stomach. I shut my eyes against the dizzying white water below, and with a sickening swoop, we rolled out and across.

CHAPTER 16

THE LOST MEEKS—THAT'S WHAT THEY WERE

calling us. Our wagons were strung out in clusters all along the for-ty-mile stretch from the Deschutes crossing to The Dalles. Some were met by a relief party Stephen Meek had arranged, headed by a well-known guide called Black Harris. For many, though, the food supplies were too late. Graves were still being dug—four at the top of Tygh Ridge and another at Fifteen-Mile Creek, just a day short of The Dalles. There Captain Liggett's wife, a mother of seven, was laid to rest.

As our family's wagons pulled into the camp on the Columbia after dark on the night of October 13, we were met with lanterns lighting concerned faces. Folks from other companies who'd thought themselves worn out by the Blue Mountains seemed appalled at the sight of us and our terrible condition. Made them see just how much worse things could have been had they themselves taken the Trapper's Trail.

A woman offered us hot porridge.

"Appreciate it, but we're all right," Rowland assured her. "You might check these wagons right behind us, though. They've been on shorter rations than we have."

"Rowland!" I cried, aghast. I turned back to the woman. "We'd be so grateful to take a bit for the children. I don't suppose anyone has any milk?"

"Lovisa," Rowland admonished me.

"What," I said flatly, climbing past him into the wagon to fetch Meggie and Jimmy. I didn't care if I was speaking out of turn.

"We can make do."

It was dark; we had no fire.

"Rowland, that woman's got hot porridge right now. If it makes you feel better to sit here all confident and prideful, trying to look like you never need anyone else's help, you just go right ahead."

I jumped to the ground and lifted Meggie after me.

"I intend to see these babies fed."

I crawled out of the wagon the next morning feeling disgustingly filthy, and I would have made getting clean my top priority if only we hadn't all been so hungry. The previous night's porridge was a start, but we had way more than a bowl's worth of catching up to do when it came to filling our stomachs.

I looked around the windswept encampment: a shifting settlement on shifting sands, a temporary collection of wagons near the Methodist mission. And beyond the wagons…the Columbia. Finally. The mighty River of the West. It was blue, reflecting the sky, and looked like it ran clear, not muddy like the Missouri or sandy like the Platte. I regarded its beauty warily, knowing we were soon facing the navigation of that unimaginable volume of water. As the wind whipped the greasy hair about my face, I stood there a moment, gazing at the river. Halfway across the continent I'd walked to arrive at this sight—I reckoned I ought to give it a moment.

All right, now I'd seen it. I turned away. I was hungry. I was dirty. And so was everyone who was counting on me.

Since for the moment I seemed to be one of the least sickly, I settled Meggie and Jimmy with my sisters, smoothed my hair the best I could, and started the mile-and-a-half hike up to the mission to see what supplies could be had.

The prices! High at every fort along the way, the Methodist mission's were the worst of all. And then it turned out food stocks were rationed at that.

"This is all the flour I can buy?" I said to the man behind the makeshift, barrel-head counter. "Even if I'm willing to pay your price?"

"Eight quarts per family. That's the limit."

"But we have a really big family," I protested. "That doesn't seem right."

"We're not a supply depot, Miss. This is a mission. We came here to save heathen souls, not rescue travelers."

"But we were with Meek's group. The ones who were lost? We've been out there for weeks and people are near starving!"

His look was cold. "It's not our fault you tried a shortcut." He looked past me. "Who's next here?"

I stood dumbfounded. We buried over thirty people along the trail and this was his Christian response? The crowd bustled me aside.

Mrs. Brown stepped up, briskly counting out money. "My eight quarts, please."

Eight quarts for her family of four. Maybe she'd pay back what she "borrowed"? But no. Hoisting her bag, she sailed past me with a cool glance.

Mamie followed her, the heels of the boots that had been mine knocking smartly on the puncheon floor. I swear she made a point of not looking my way. That's when it struck me. Folks are so strange.

She'd never liked me before, and now that I'd seen her at her lowest, she hated me worse. She'd been barefoot, and I had boots to give her. She was never going to forgive me for that.

Well, I could hardly claim surprise. I'd seen it over and over. This journey had brought out the best in some, the worst in others. Whatever you had inside, the trail would test it, expose it for all the world to see.

And Mamie Brown wasn't the only one struggling with a painful mix of pride and shame. Honestly, Rowland just wore me out, the way he hated accepting help. Now that neither of us was going to die of camp fever, we were right back snapping at each other again.

I bought what they'd allow of the mission's precious flour, hauled it back to camp, then headed out to see what else could be found in the way of food.

By the shore, Indians were bartering for salmon, but our family hadn't much left to trade. Although the Natives seemed to love white-man's clothes, I doubted any self-respecting Indian would stoop to wearing the rags we were reduced to by now.

I picked my way upriver along the rocky shore, watching the Indians spearing fish from the wooden platforms they'd built out from the rocky ledges over the low falls. How easily they managed it, how gracefully. They seemed so at ease in this land. While they harvested an abundance of food, we pitiful Bostons, as they called us, had to scrabble for every bite. And then fight over it! We couldn't even seem to take care of our own.

People. Lord, I'd be glad when we got to the valley and found our own place. I wanted it to be just us Kings again, working together. I was so weary of butting heads on a daily basis with all these others, this great crowd of humanity that had so enchanted me in the beginning. I was sick of hearing men cursing and of being privy to other folks' shameful family fights. I didn't want to have to worry at night anymore, when the sound of some woman sobbing in her wagon reached my ears.

Looking down, I caught my breath. At my feet, a salmon flipped its tail in a shallow rock pool. Without a second thought I hurled myself at it, falling and plunging about in the knee-deep water, throwing my arms around the heaving hunk of muscle and energy, but I could no more hold the slippery thing in my grasp than I could catch rain in my hands.

"Give it up!" I commanded the fish through clenched teeth just before it flailed free. My only hope was that the creature might exhaust itself before I did. "Damn it!"

I stopped. I looked to the sky. When no heavenly thunderbolt struck me dead, I grabbed the fish again and let loose a string of all the cuss words I'd heard Rowland use against every broken spoke and splintered axle all the way from Missouri. What a wrestling match. Me against that fish. Over and over it slipped back to the water until I was left whimpering with frustration. And all that bad language didn't help me any more than it ever seemed to help Rowland.

That's when I heard a grunt, a word perhaps, but being an Indian word, only a sound to me. Staggering to my feet, I flung back my wet hair and looked up to find a young man. He wore nothing but a loincloth, and had I any sensibilities remaining, there's no doubt he would have put me to the blush with his well-formed and finely muscled body. His dark eyes locked on mine. With a jerk of his jaw, he ordered me out of the water.

Snagging my floating felt hat, I dragged my soaked skirts from the pool. The fish did belong to the Indians, I supposed. Belonged to the ones with the wit to catch them. Well, at least he hadn't laughed at me. That I couldn't have borne.

As I stood there dripping and humiliated, the Indian contemplated the salmon for a moment. Then, casually, with one fluid motion, he raised his double-pronged spear and deftly sent it through the fish. I sighed. So easy for him. He swung the spear bearing the flipping creature to the side, picked up a rock, and with one swift blow, dispatched it to stillness.

Then, suddenly, he was holding the spear with the silvery prize across the pool toward me.

I put a hand on my breast. For me? You're giving it to me?

He nodded sternly.

Why, he pitied me. Well, I deserved it. No, I needed it.

With a shake of the spear, he again urged the salmon on me, glancing over his shoulder, as if to say, Quick, take it, before anyone sees.

With a grateful sigh, I grabbed that fish.

This wind! It never stopped—howling up the gorge, blowing away anything in camp that wasn't heavy or tied down. And the way it snapped the dirty canvas wagon covers all day long, all night. Wap. Wap. Wap. Wap. I wanted to scream.

"Come on," I said to Meggie, knotting a shawl around her shoulders. "Let's go down by the creek."

At least for a little while we'd get away from the gloom that hung over the clustered wagons. Death seemed to be stalking us, punishing those who'd followed Stephen Meek. We'd had to bury Captain Parker's wife and newborn baby, and then it was Mrs. Terwilliger. And that Mr. Wilson—people were saying he was so famished, when he finally got some food, he sat down and actually ate himself to death. News coming back from downriver wasn't much better. Reverend Moore had drowned in the rapids.

With Jimmy on my hip and Meggie by the hand, I made my way to the little sheltered beach where a creek fanned into the river. Here the men were building the raft on which we'd float the Columbia.

Captain Barlow had taken wagons up to search out a route around Mount Hood, but you couldn't say the word shortcut to anybody in our family now without they'd blanch and shudder. Even if Barlow managed to get through, it didn't necessarily mean we could anyway. He'd set out in September. Now, in the middle of October, mountain snows could start any time. We were too late. And while we'd been languishing in the desert, the waiting list of families willing to pay for passage on the mission bateaux or in Indian canoes had grown too long.

Price Fuller and my brother Isaac set off driving what remained of our herd on a route that roughly paralleled the river. Supposedly it was a pack trail just wide enough for single-file cattle, but too steep and narrow for wagons. Fourteen days, they figured, for the drovers' route, and fourteen days to coax the exhausted oxen to drag the required logs down from the sparse patches of woods on the hills, build the raft, and descend the river. We'd meet below the rapids.

The rapids none of us even cared to discuss.

"Da!" Jimmy cried, spotting Rowland with the other men. Meggie edged down to the little beach to play with the youngest Fuller boys, and a girl my own age from another company joined me, perching on a rock to chat.

I was struck by her bright-blue calico dress and thought with a pang it might have been the very one Sally had raved about when she got so delirious. The girl introduced herself as Sarah Helmick.

"But they call me Sally."

Wouldn't you know? Well, it was a common enough name.

"Did you save that dress all the way?" I asked. "It looks so neat and fresh."

Sarah nodded, smiling prettily. "Since we're almost there, I thought I'd bring it out. It's nothing fancy, really, but I said when we started I did not want to arrive in Oregon wearing rags!"

Stung, I turned away and stared at the bubbling creek. My own dress, once rich maroon, was bleached a sickly pink. All of us King women had lost our rosy roundness. I was worn to nothing but bone and muscle and sinew. Altogether I felt like some Missouri corn-patch scarecrow, weathered to shreds by the elements.

"Oh, I'm sorry," Sarah said, realizing too late how her comment must have sounded. "I didn't mean—" But what could she say? We both understood my tattered condition was exactly what she'd hoped to avoid.

Jimmy fussed to be let down, wriggling, slipping himself free from my arms to go padding across the wet sand—pat pat pat—and for a few moments nothing more was said. Finally my new acquaintance seemed unable to contain a moment longer her delight at her own good fortune.

"Actually, I just got married in April and I have a whole trous-seau," she confessed. "Things much nicer than this. My mother and my aunts sewed it all. I haven't touched it the whole way. And my Henry is so sweet. When we had to leave things by the trail to light-en the wagon, he never once suggested leaving my trunk."

I sighed, purely sick with envy. Was it her kind and considerate new husband? The fact that she had a trunkful of pretty dresses? Maybe partly, but more, I think I envied her something harder to put into words. Sarah Helmick had made plans about this trip and they had come true. She'd been determined her arrival would be a certain way, and now, here she stood, a bit more freckled by the sun than she'd have liked maybe, but still, she was wearing a crisp new dress. She was buoyant, not—like me—broken.

We Kings made plans too. What good did it do? I felt like God Himself had slapped us down.

Jimmy fell back on his bottom, laughed, and gamely pushed him-self to his feet again.

"Your little boy's such a darling," Sarah Helmick said, a good-hearted attempt to steer away from the awkward comparison of wardrobes.

"He's not mine. He's my sister's. Same with the little girl over there." I pointed out Meggie, who had managed to work her way into the Fuller boys' digging project.

Sarah looked around. "Is your sister down with the fever then?"

I shook my head. "She's...we took Meek's cutoff."

Instant understanding clouded Sarah's face. "We heard about that." She watched Jimmy, all sympathy, and tactfully didn't require me to come right out and say it—that, like dozens of other children in our party, he was now motherless. "Poor little thing."

Jimmy didn't seem to feel like a poor little thing, though. Stooping to fling scoops of wet sand overhead, he appeared perfectly delighted with the world.

"He just took his first steps a couple of days ago," I said. "Now I'm chasing him all the time."

We watched him frolic for a few moments, then Sarah said, "I'm so glad we didn't go that route. My Henry just knew it would be bad. Even though we'd trusted Captain Parker right up until then, Henry said he wouldn't risk it, even if it meant signing on with a new captain."

"Did you hear about his wife and baby?"

"Captain Parker's? No, what?"

"They died."

"Little Ginny?"

"Well, yes, she died, too, but I meant the newborn."

"Oh, my Lord. Now you see, I'm sure that wouldn't have happened if they'd stayed with us. And then we all ended up getting here before you anyway."

I looked out over the river to the dry, tan hills beyond, trying hard not to hear the hint of recrimination in this.

"I reckon you must be kind of mad at your menfolk then," Sarah said. "That they dragged you out there the wrong way. Some say it's lucky you didn't all die."

People were saying that? In a sudden rush of love and loyalty, I said, "No, I'm not mad. It wasn't their fault."

Actually, right up to that moment, maybe I had been resenting what we'd been put through, but was that fair? The entire journey had been a series of choices, and up to the very last our King men had chosen right. They had good reasons for risking the cutoff. The fact that it turned out to be wrong didn't mean there was anything wrong with them. Why, I'd put up our bunch against anyone's.

I watched Rowland and Amos muscle a log into place on the raft.

"That's my brother Amos," I said, pointing him out. "He ran a ferry back on the Missouri, so he knows all about these things."

"That's lucky," Sarah allowed.

"Another of my brothers and a boy from the family we're with already set off on the cattle trail. We've got quite a fine herd—Spanish Durham. Didn't lose too many along the way."

Bragging, I know. But I couldn't resist pointing out something our family had managed properly, something that had turned out right. Because what if we had set out a bit puffed with pride? We'd paid for that, and more. And so what if all our plans hadn't worked out? That didn't make careful planning something to be ashamed of, did it?

"Who's the tall one?" Sarah asked.

"What? Oh, that's Rowland Chambers. My sister's husband." And there went my cheeks, getting all hot again. "Well, he was her husband. Before. He's this little fella's pa."

"Good looking, isn't he?"

"Yes, he is," I said, and then added quickly, "All our boys are."

The next morning I stood on the same spot and watched Sarah Helmick's party loading their two rafts. Honestly, one of the women looked so far past her time, it seemed she could have birthed her baby two months ago.

As their party untied the mooring lines, we Kings and Fullers stopped work to watch, a sign of respect, it seemed to me, for the bold and dangerous nature of this undertaking. As they pushed away, Sarah Helmick waved to me, then patted her little trunk as if to say, Here it is, the lovely trousseau I was describing to you!

I nodded and smiled, waving them off.

"Good luck to you!" Rowland called, and I saw Amos squinting at the rafts as they were caught by the currents, trying, as always, to learn what he could from those who were going before.

That evening I climbed into Susan's wagon, Abbie following.

"I'm hot," Lexie kept saying.

"Here's a drink of water, honey," Abbie said, glancing at me like she wanted to make sure I understood just how bad off Lexie was.

But by now I'd seen almost everyone in our family get sick and then get well. I wasn't overly worried.

"There, pet," I said, smoothing Lexie's matted curls. "What a good, brave girl you've been." Then I turned to Susan and made my voice cheerful. "Tomorrow's the day. Amos says the raft is ready and the weather looks fine. We're going to ride that river right on down."

"But I'm...I'm not ready to travel."

"Well, this hardly even counts for traveling!" I said. "You won't have to take one step! You'll just lie there like a princess, floating along."

She searched my face. "You don't think it'll be hard-going?"

"Oh, no, not at all," I said, and turned to Abbie. "That's what the boys are saying, isn't it?"

"Um...yes," Abbie said, as if she'd been so caught up in my play-acting, it took her a moment to think how to join in.

Poor Susan. There was no longer any such thing as too sick to travel, if there ever had been. For six months there'd been way too much stopping on account of scattered cattle, broken wagon wheels, lack of water ahead, or just plain not knowing which direction to go. Now, if the wagons, the ferries, the rope pulleys, the log rafts, or whatever current conveyance the men had rigged was ready, we had to be ready too. We could no longer afford to lay by—not for a person to leave this world or to come into it, much less for someone who was merely deathly ill.

"Besides, you're going to be better tomorrow," I said with as much conviction as I could muster. "You're not out of your head anymore, and once the rash starts fading, we know you're on your way to well. And you're strong! Look how long you've fought this off in the first place. Why, you fooled everybody. We thought you were frail!"

Susan moaned. "I know that's what your ma thinks. What she's always thought."

"She sure doesn't think that anymore. Just today she was saying how you turned out to have way more grit than she ever knew."

"Really?"

"Really. And she was telling the snake story again, wasn't she, Abbie?"

Abbie nodded.

Smiling faintly at the notion, Susan drifted back to sleep.

After we climbed out of the wagon and got a little ways away, Abbie whirled and blocked my path.

"The weather is not fine," she accused me.

I looked up at the cold, gray sky, then out to the whitecaps on the river's chopping waves. "It's as good as it's going to get."

"And you don't really think Susan's better."

"What! I do too!"

"You always think things are going to be fine," Abbie said. "You ever listen to yourself? You said the very same things to Sally. I heard you. And then look what happened. I think she knew all along she wasn't going to make it. And she was right! Sometimes things are not fine."

Well, she had me there. But so what?

"Let's see," I said. "Sally worried she wouldn't make it and she didn't. Does that make her the winner? For being right?" I pointed at Susan's wagon. "You want me to go in there and tell her I really don't think she's going to make it? Heaven knows I wouldn't want to be caught predicting wrong."

Abbie started sniffling. "You know I don't mean it that way. I'm just scared for them, that's all. And I'm scared about the river."

"I know." I sighed—a long, tired, almost-to-the-end-of-the-trail sigh. "Come on, then, don't cry. I'm sorry I sounded mean. The thing is, Abbie, I've just decided there's not much use in assuming the worst. If we'd started figuring we weren't any of us going to make it to Oregon the first time the going got rough, well, we could've sat right down in the dust and waited to die, right? Saved ourselves a thousand miles. And we would have! Died, I mean. Because I'll bet the quickest way to turn into folks who aren't going to make it is to start acting like folks who aren't going to make it."

Abbie gave that a grudging smile.

"We've got to have faith, Abbie."

"But it's so hard!"

"I know." I looked across the camp to my own weather-beaten wagon. "Almost as hard as not having faith."

CHAPTER 17

THE MEN TOOK THE KING AND FULLER WAGONS
apart and loaded them onto the raft, spacing them evenly, setting
each wagon box on its own four wheels laid flat. As soon as my brother John's wagon was in place, he carefully scooped Susan into his
arms and carried her onto the raft, tenderly settling her into the
wagon bed. Abbie followed with baby Charlie and Lexie. Next the
supplies were loaded and, finally, we women and girls brought the
last of the little ones aboard, including Little Lute, who was well
and feisty as ever. Nobody cared to keep that rambunctious child
quiet on the raft one minute longer than necessary.

Standing by our own wagon, having nestled Jimmy securely inside,
I gripped the front canvas bow as the men untied the raft and
pushed it off.

Other men on shore paused in their own raft-building labors,
straightened and turned our way. So did their women and children.
As one little girl waved, I lifted a hand in answering farewell.

"Everybody watching us," Meggie said.

I nodded, swinging her into the wagon box, wishing they weren't. Might've been easier to act brave if they all just kept working, pretending this was merely routine and not an undertaking shadowed by such grave risks.

But then, we'd done the same thing when others had departed. I guess a person just doesn't understand the ominous effect of this respectful witness until she's the one standing on the raft, floating away, watching all those figures on shore grow small as they recede into the distance.

Suddenly the raft teetered. I stumbled for balance. Water sloshed along the cracks between the logs under my patched boots. I looked to Rowland. Were we in trouble? Was it supposed to tilt like this?

He gave me a quick, reassuring nod. I started breathing again. Rowland I could trust. If he was calm, I could be calm too.

Big-eyed, Meggie stood framed by the cinched canvas at the end of the wagon box.

"See?" I said to her with forced cheer as the current caught the raft. "Here we go, down the river!" Looking across our craft, I realized Sol was manning one of the sweeps. Honestly, that boy simply refused to grasp the fact that he wasn't one of the grown men.

Abbie stood her post at brother John's wagon, inside of which Susan, Lexie, and little Charlie were bedded down.

"How are they?" I called over the rush of wind and water.

"Better, I think," she called back. Then, peering inside, she frowned. "Lute! You stop that!"

I faced forward into the wind as the dry, bare hills began to glide by. The watery air felt good on my face. Maybe this river passage wasn't going to be so bad after all. At least we weren't struggling over more mountains behind Captain Barlow. After hundreds upon hundreds of knock-about, bumping miles, this was almost pleasant.

The Columbia flowed north at first for a mile or two, then veered west, rounding a high-ridged point on the left. Almost immediately there appeared on the hillcrests and in the ravines dark green patches of timber.

Finally, after six months and two thousand miles: tall trees.

We made camp in a foreboding spot on the north shore that night, opposite an island the Indians called Memaloose, the resting place of their dead. I thought of Sally, how completely unnerved she would have been by this. At the north shore camp, when I went a little ways into the woods, I noticed an odd sound underfoot. I looked down. Bones. Human bones. I held my breath, shut my eyes, and backed out, wincing at each step. This wasn't just an ominous name. These were people. This was their sacred place, and we were trespassers here. I couldn't wait to get beyond it.

Late that night, when the other women and children had gone to bed, I overheard the men at the campfire debating yet another crucial choice. They spoke in low, earnest voices.

"I'm thinking maybe we should portage," Pa said. "I don't like the sound of the stories coming from down there."

"Down there" meant the dreaded rapids, I knew, but what had the men heard? I knew about Reverend Moore. Were there others who'd dashed their rafts on the rocks?

"But the time, Pa," Amos said. "To pack everything around on that road…"

"Not even a road, is it?" Rowland put in.

"Aren't some getting through?" Mr. Fuller asked.

"Some, yes," Rowland replied, "but did you hear that Hudson's Bay fellow? Churned to mud, axle-deep, he said. And now, with even more rain…" There was a pause. "I have to question whether we could get the wagons through at all."

"Not to mention the women and children," John added. "Well, some of them could do it, but the way Susan is right now, and the little ones…"

Rowland turned to my brother. "I thought they were better." And then he added, "Least that's what Lovisa said."

I shivered in the shadows. Just to hear him speak my name. Credit my opinion.

John sighed. "A little better, maybe, but Susan can't make any hard hike, that's for sure."

An owl hooted in the long, brooding silence as I imagined each man weighing the risks. No choice was free of them, not when time and weather were poised to take their own tolls. What was the use of playing it safe, avoiding the river, only to die of cold and sickness?

"I feel pretty good about the raft, Pa," Amos said finally. "She's not waterlogged like some."

That seemed to be it, then, the end of the discussion. It sounded to me as if they'd agreed on trying the river, the river all the way.

"So," Rowland said. "When?"

"Day after tomorrow, I figure," Amos said.

"Give you any clue what to watch for?"

Amos nodded, then laughed shortly, without humor. "Looks like a lake. Just when you think you're safe, see? That's when you're not."

When I crawled into the tent Abbie and I were sharing with Meggie and Jimmy, Abbie whispered that she had a secret to confess: She and Price were promised.

Now why did that news prick me like a knife point? After all, it came as no surprise. I sighed. I'd felt the same when Melinda and Amos had made their engagement official. Everyone was pairing up. It was getting harder, trying to pretend I didn't care. What was going to happen to me?

"He asked just before they started off with the cattle," Abbie said. "And you know what he said? He says, 'Abbie, I figured you were the one for me right from the start. Or at least for the last thousand miles.' He said he wanted to get my promise before, but it wasn't until now he felt he could. Because now we're almost there.'"

We were quiet a moment, perhaps at the solemn notion that the so-called Promised Land was at hand. It was hard to believe, for I could barely remember the time before, a time when we weren't on the road, when every day's main thought wasn't the struggle to drag the wagons a little farther west. And now, just as at the beginning, people would be going separate ways. Decisions had to be made.

"Think you'll marry right off?" I asked.

"I don't know. I hope so. But Lovisa, I'm so happy! Oh, I do wish you could be happy like this too."

I tucked a tattered blanket around Meggie. I could never be happy in the same way as Abbie, that was sure. Abbie's joy was so pure and uncomplicated. Her feelings were nothing like the mixed-up mess twisting inside me.

"Are you feeling bad about John Noble?" Abbie said. "Is that it?"

I hesitated. "I feel bad he died. I feel bad I couldn't even cry when I heard. It didn't make me think I should have wanted to marry him, though, if that's what you're imagining."

"No. I know."

And then, after a moment, "Lovisa? Sometimes I've wondered. Have you ever thought about—" Abbie dropped her voice to a whisper. "Rowland?"

In the darkness of the tent, a hot flush rushed from my center out to my scalp and down to my toes.

"What about him?" I whispered back—a desperate effort at not quite comprehending.

"You could marry him."

"Abbie!"

"Well, what? He likes you. Everyone knows it. I can't believe how pert you talk to him, and he doesn't even seem to mind."

191

"Well, what's he going to do? Tell me not to take care of these children? Stop washing his socks?"

"Oh, you know it's more than that! When you were sick he—"

"Abbie, stop it!" I whispered. "Not in front of—"

"Oh, pooh. She doesn't know what we're talking about."

"Talkin' 'bout my pa," Meggie muttered, but Abbie didn't even hear her.

"Rowland says this, Rowland says that," she mimicked. "You know you've always liked him."

"I have not! I didn't even want to be in his wagon. I told you that right from the first."

A long silence ensued. I thought maybe Abbie was ready to let it drop, but no.

"It's plain you don't think I'm too smart about these things," she finally ventured, "but I know you, Lovisa. I've watched you. Saying you don't care for a man to cover up how much you do care is not the same as truly not liking him."

Well. That fair took the wind out of me.

"In fact, I'd say it's more like the exact opposite."

What could I say? To think it should be my little sister who would nail it so neatly. Good thing it was dark. I didn't want her seeing my face.

"Abbie? Could we not talk about this anymore? At least not right now?"

Maybe she could talk about things like this in front of Lexie and get away with it, but Meggie was too smart. Poor little thing. She didn't need to hear talk about people marrying her father when her mother was hardly cold in the ground.

Lord, I'd die if anyone in the family even suspected I'd ever had such a thought! Me, thinking for one instant I could replace Sally? That was a good one. Sally was everything I was not—kind and patient, gentle-mannered, and I'll bet she never even had a bad thought about a person, never mind a bad word. No wonder Rowland adored her. And me so lacking in all those things, so completely the opposite, how could he ever feel anywhere near that way about me?

Out in the treetops, the owl hooted. Once again I felt surely I must be the last person in the whole camp still awake, staring into the darkness.

The mighty Columbia surged ever westward, and on it was borne our raft. Not the only craft navigating the waters that day, but it might as well have been for all I could see as we floated along, maneuvering the watery corridor one broad bend at a time.

The banks rose precipitously on either side now, forming majestic portals crowned with the tallest firs.

There had been so many gateways on this journey. We had traveled under the widest of skies, and now this final, breathtaking passage to the west had narrowed that sky to but a swath. I threw back my head. The mountains were so high, so magnificent. And at last, the forests. If I had felt small against the vastness of the plains, these towering palisades made me feel as if we were mere specks of humanity bobbing along.

At every turn, every bend, a new vista opened before us, and with each scene revealed, I'd wonder: Is this it?

I looked across the raft to Rowland, who stood braced at his sweep. I recalled the words Abbie had whispered in the dark. She was so right about how I felt about him. How I'd always felt, down deep. I'd been afraid to admit it even to myself, how much I admired my own sister's husband.

Finally the raft rounded a wooded point and…my breath stopped. The lake. The broad, flat water appeared to end at a distant shore straight ahead, where a low line of trees struck out across the river like a dam.

A glance at Rowland told me I'd guessed right. Something in his posture seemed newly alert. All the men had come to attention and looked to each other for affirmation. They traded grim nods. This was it. The married ones went to their wives. My heart gripped. Rowland had handed off the sweep to Amos and was coming to me. Well, to us, anyway.

"Ready, Meggie?" he said. "It might get bouncy."

Meggie nodded solemnly.

"Still thinking the same about being in the wagon bed?" I asked.

He looked at the wheelless wooden box, calculating. I could almost see him trying to imagine one more time how things might go wrong, which way the wagon might slide, how a tiny body might be crushed by some freakish upheaval. We had privately discussed earlier whether to lash the children to the wagon or to the raft itself, but the horrific notion of one of them being pulled under by the sinking raft still made me queasy every time I considered trying it that way.

"What do you think?" Rowland said.

Asking me. Oh, we were a good team. Suddenly I felt how desperately I did want to get through this. Wanted all of us to survive. Because if it was no sin, the way I felt, then at the end of this...

"Lovisa? What's best? In or out?"

I took a deep breath. No time to think about the end. Time to think about now.

"I guess I'll sit tight with them outside," I said. "You know, in case..."

He nodded. He didn't need me putting it into words: In case the raft smashes on the rocks and our only hope is jumping clear...

And now I heard a faint, distant roar.

"Rowland." I listened. "Is that...?"

"What? The wind?"

I shook my head. Now he heard it too. I saw something in his jaw work. The sound wasn't as loud as the roar of those falls in the Snake River, the ones we'd heard at such an amazing distance. But then, those weren't waters we were attempting to navigate. These were.

"It'll still take a little while to get there." Rowland tousled the children's heads.

"Get to what?" Meggie said, face upturned, looking to me, then Rowland.

Neither of us answered. We were looking at each other.

"We're going to be fine," he said. "You hear me?"

I nodded, pushing the wind-whipped hair from my face. We were alike in this—agreeing to try believing the best.

I watched him pick his way back over the slippery logs to take up one of the extra steering poles. I glanced around at the other women—Ma with Lydia and Rhoda, Annie having a quiet word with Sol, Hope struggling to hold little Wiley, who, at eighteen months most definitely did not want to be held, the younger Fuller boys under Melinda's wing. Something so helpless about all this. We were supposed to brace ourselves, but how? Left to our own instincts, we'd have gathered at the center of the raft and clung together for support. But we couldn't. We had to obey the men's instructions to keep to our assigned places. The weight of each wife, each beloved child, each bale of goods—all had been calculated and distributed in such a way as to keep the raft balanced.

I gave my mother and little sisters a brave, chin-up look, then turned to Meggie and Jimmy. "Well!" I said cheerfully, kneeling down to them. "Shall we just sit right here?"

"It's wet," Meggie pointed out.

"That won't hurt." I didn't appreciate the cold dampness either, but this would feel more secure, and if we got through this with nothing but damp skirts, we'd be doing fine. I sat down, my back against the wagon, and pulled the children close, one arm wrapping each.

"See?" I said. "We can brace our feet against these little logs the daddies tied on top. Then we won't be sliding around. Meggie? Has your pa ever ridden you fast on his horse?"

Meggie shook her head no.

"Well, then, I reckon this'll be the fastest ride you've ever had!"

Meggie, bless her heart, was too smart for this kind of talk. She bit her lip gravely, eyes widening in sick, inconsolable fear. She could see well enough nobody was getting ready for fun.

I sighed. "We'll be all right, honey."

At the next wagon Abbie looked frightened too. Susan, Lexie, and the baby, Charlie, lay inside. For them, there wasn't much choice. Wouldn't it be a blessing if they could just sleep through the whole thing?

Now a knickered leg swung over the back of their wagon.

"Lute!" Abbie said, blocking his way. "Don't! You heard your pa! You've got to stay inside!"

"Why?" he demanded. "I wanna see!"

"Stay in there!" his father John called from his post at the stern's roughly crafted rudder. "It's safer. You too, Abbie."

Abbie looked at me, shrugged, and climbed in.

Lord, I thought, staring after her. Even the men didn't agree what was best or safest. Well, this rafting of the rapids was not a thing with a lot of precedent, and as Pa had first pointed out way back in Carroll County, that's what pioneering was all about—being first, trying something new without any guarantees. How exhilarating that had sounded at the beginning! Now it sounded reckless. Foolish, even. We needed a better plan. A safer one. We needed people who'd done this before to give us advice.

But advice wasn't to be had. Not for this endeavor. As Rowland had confided to me, the best anyone could tell us about shooting the rapids could be summed up in two words: Try. And then, hope.

Oh, God.

The raft veered sharply to the left as we were pulled relentlessly toward that ominous roar. All the water of this wide river was being forced through a chasm at the southern side, a narrowing we would momentarily go crashing through. My eyes darted around. The raft had seemed so huge on shore, so sturdy, a veritable ark. Now it seemed painfully clear it was but a flimsy lashing of wet logs, a frail barrier between us and the churning white water.

No! The raft lurched forward. This isn't a good idea! We should have gone the new mountain road with Captain Barlow! This couldn't possibly be the safer route. Or we should have somehow portaged around this part. I could have walked. Mud was nothing to this.

But, too late. Our course was chosen. The raft rounded the bend, spun a complete and terrifying full turn, then plunged ahead.

One glimpse of the white water and I shut my eyes. Downward we crashed, bouncing in the waves. Under my arm, Meggie whimpered. Spray needled us. Through a space between the wagons, I could see Rowland, already soaking wet, struggling for footing. His face was set, his body braced, muscles tensed. Throwing every ounce of strength against it, he hoisted the sweep from its lock. There would be no steering now. Only a pushing away from the rocks. God help him. God help us all. Still, he didn't look panicky, merely resolute, as if he had expected this to be hard and nothing in it surprised him.

I looked down at the children and shouted, "Your daddy's a good rafter!"

Meggie had her face buried and wouldn't look up, but Jimmy crowed with delight as the spray hit him, the little darling. Made me want to laugh and cry at the same time. I loved his innocent fearlessness. I felt a hint of it too, the simultaneous joy and terror of racing ahead, the swift slide down a slope of water.

The tumbling rapids came in succession as the men struggled to aim the craft into the yawning jaws of each boiling cauldron.

Sometimes we'd hit a brief, calmer stretch, giving just enough time for us to stand, crane around, and get the all's-well signal from each other. We were wet and cold. We were scared. But still, we women clutched the children, and if the men could make no pretense of outright control, they mounted an energetic stance of defense against each rock outcropping, men who were for the most part learning the art of river piloting as they went.

"That way! Left! No, now right!" Shouting at each other, they were discovering the route as they went along, guessing their way, gambling they could choose against the deadliest of the rapids, pitting themselves against the river in a battle for everything they owned and every human being they loved.

Bucking and rocking, the raft careened downriver. My head knocked against the wagon. I shut my eyes, clenched my teeth, and hung on for dear life as random thoughts flickered through my brain. Abbie and the sick ones—what idiocy, imagining anyone might sleep through this! I clutched the babies tighter. Oh, Sally, I thought, look what you got to miss. Look down, see what's happening to us now. Be our angel.

The raft slammed against a rock, jarring bones, straining tethers. The log craft groaned ominously, creaking as the water rushed past.

"Push her off!" the men were yelling. "Look out!"

With a wrenching jerk the craft popped loose and dropped with a jaw-slamming thud into a pool below, spinning, hesitating, then hurtling downward again.

Jimmy was whimpering now, no longer amused. Even a one-year-old couldn't help the contagion of pure fear, the gut warning of danger. Four miles of rapids they'd said. The descent seemed endless. I opened my eyes in time to see Jimmy throw up.

"Oh, sweetie." I used the hem of his smock to wipe his mouth. "We're almost through," I murmured, noticing the light ahead where the river opened out.

But just then the raft hit something and stalled. Alarmingly, it began to tilt.

"Get her off!" the men were yelling. "Get her off!"

I jumped up. Ma and Melinda screamed. One corner of the raft dipped downward and, nightmarishly, barrels began tipping and rolling toward the white water that seemed ready to swallow the craft whole.

"Get down!" Rowland yelled. "Hang tight."

I obeyed, dropping to the uphill side of the wagon where we wouldn't be hit, I figured, if it slid, bracing my feet on the cross logs, gripping the screaming children. I heard a terrible groaning rasp and turned to see the rope holding John and Susan's wagon tighten, strain an instant, then snap.

The wagon lurched toward the water.

"Get out!" John shouted.

From the uphill canvas opening, Little Lute came tumbling, scrambling up the raft. Abbie climbed out right behind.

My sister and I locked eyes in split-second recognition. This wasn't a nightmare. This wasn't someone else's tragic story. This was us, our worst fear coming true.

What happened next was finished in a flash, but the horror of it seared a permanent scar in my mind, a clear and unforgettable picture that would be with me as long as I lived. I would always be grateful there'd been no glimpse of golden curls at the canvas flap. It was bad enough, just knowing Susan and the babies were inside.

The doomed wagon slid, rocked briefly on the edge, then flipped off.

"No!" John roared.

It was fast; it was simple. My brother's wife, his children were in the river. He was the father. He was in charge. He must save them. With a blind leap he threw himself after them. He must save them or die trying.

Just as he, too, disappeared beneath the waves, the raft popped free, righted itself and shot down the last hundred yards of the rapids to a landing.

As fast as they could, the men brought the craft to rest at the point of land around the right of the chute, and we all clambered ashore, crying and screaming, staggering up and down the rocky beach, the men yelling at each other as if there was something they ought to do to save the lost ones, and do it fast.

But there was nothing. Just like that, it was over.

"Oh, my God!" Abbie cried, hands to her face. "Oh, my God!"

I thought I saw something white go by in the green water, but nothing more.

John, Susan, Lexie, and baby Charlie. Two thousand miles they'd come, only to be swallowed up and carried away by the River of the West.

CHAPTER 18

STUNNED, WE SPRAWLED AROUND A MAKESHIFT
camp like shipwreck survivors. No one could grasp what had happened.

Orphaned in an instant, even Little Lute, for once, seemed shocked to silence. He lay with his head on Ma's lap, staring blankly at the river.

Next to them, Pa slouched on a log, elbows on his knees, hands dangling uselessly between. I watched Rowland walk over and place a hand on my father's shoulder. Pa startled, as if ashamed to be caught like this, dead-still in defeat. He looked around. There must be something he should be doing. But what?

Only Sol was up and about, trying mightily to coax a fire from nothing but the wettest of wood. The rest of us just sat, benumbed, waiting until we could somehow regain the will to rise and move forward again.

At my feet, Jimmy played in the gravel. Into the narrow range of my vision moved a girl's boot, and, above it, the hem of a familiar blue dress. I looked up. Sarah Helmick.

Apparently we weren't the only ones cast up and stalled on this spot, severely chastened for the notion we might dare defy nature. Sarah's formerly crisp dress was now torn and drooping. Her hair hung loose over her shoulders.

"Sorry for your loss," she said. "Henry saw the whole thing." She sat down beside me. "I guess it was worse than everybody thought."

I nodded. She meant the rapids, I knew; I was thinking of the entire journey.

"Your folks all got through, though?" I asked.

"Yes. But we did lose a whole raft of goods. My trunk."

I lifted my head. "Your trousseau? The whole thing?"

"Every stitch."

"Oh, that's too bad." What a waste, their poor oxen hauling that trunk up all those steep passages. And the beautiful, lovingly sewn clothes, soaked in mud, probably tumbling along the bottom of the Columbia's channel somewhere.

Sarah shrugged. "It's nothing compared to what happened to you."

True. Still. I guess she had a right to feel bad too. Just because somebody else had it worse wasn't going to make her feel better, was it? Somebody always has it worse. I thought about how I'd envied her when it seemed like everything had gone so well for her and always would. But now I understood: we none of us know what's going to happen next in the stories of our lives. Envy's just a pure waste of feelings.

Meggie came picking her barefoot way across the rocks to nestle in my lap. She pulled a finger out of her mouth and tipped her head back against my shoulder. "Lexie's in the river."

I shut my eyes.

"Is that one of your sisters lying down over there?" Sarah asked, tilting her head toward Abbie.

I nodded, stroking Meggie's hair. Thank goodness Price and Isaac were here, already come through with the cattle. Price was sticking right by Abbie's side now.

"That's Abbie. She was with their wagon. The one that fell off."

Sarah's lips parted in surprise. "She was in it when it went off the raft?"

"No, she got out in time. I meant, she was with them. Their helper. You know, just like Pa put me in to help with these two."

"Ah," she said with such sympathy it was clear she instantly understood about Abbie and why this would be especially devastating to her. We watched my poor sister lying there a moment, then Sarah said, "I suppose it'll feel strange to have a burying when you don't... well, when you can't find them."

I tightened my arms around Meggie. I hadn't thought of a funeral at all. I doubted any of us had. What a long way we'd fallen, from a huge company where everyone paid respects at Sarah Fuller's grave to these last sad remnants, where no one even thought to bring out the Bible. But nobody could quite believe yet what had happened, that we'd lost almost an entire family.

"Did you hear about Mrs. Crabtree?" Sarah asked finally.

"Who?"

"The woman in our party so close to her time? Gave birth right on the raft! The men couldn't even pull it over."

"Oh, my goodness!"

"And she had twins!"

Well, I had to smile into Meggie's hair at that. Life would go on. Babies would keep getting born. Even if they had to do it shooting right down the rapids! I nuzzled the little girl in my arms. Folks dying. Folks getting born. God sure had some startling plans for how it all ought to unfold.

The overcast had lifted and the sun seemed to drop right into the river at the far horizon, aiming golden rays back at us. The clouds went red, and now, against the ruddy sky, the sun's last light struck something white—sails. On a ship.

I stood, shading my eyes, then picked up Jimmy and walked to Rowland, who was also watching to the west. He and Amos traded a nod.

Rowland tilted his head toward me. "Should be the sloop from the Hudson's Bay Company."

It seemed a strange sight, this evidence of civilization so far out here.

"They're coming to help us," Rowland added.

"They are?" I turned to him. "Why? I thought they didn't want us here."

Rowland shook his head wonderingly. "John McLoughlin, their chief factor. He's just a good man, they say. A good Christian. Refuses to stand by and watch folks starve. Trappers say they're sending up every boat they've got. Help us get you women and children down to Fort Vancouver."

Holding Jimmy up to see, I pointed out to him that beautiful boat, those shining sails of deliverance.

And isn't it strange? After all I'd been through and stayed dry-eyed, it was this that finally set free the tears:

Someone was coming to help us.

CHAPTER 19

"ARE YOU GOING TO EAT THAT APPLE,"

Rowland asked me, "or just sit there admiring it?"

I laughed and took a bite of the juicy thing. Truly, this sweetness in the wilderness seemed a small miracle.

In the field between Fort Vancouver and the river, Dr. McLoughlin had ordered a big tent set up, inside of which the sympathetic Indian wives of the Hudson's Bay employees were serving us hot beef-and-barley soup and platters of buttered bread. This had become a daily ritual for them apparently, ministering to the needs of rescued emigrants. Today, the twenty-ninth of October 1845, the weary, grateful batch included us, the families of Arnold Fuller and Nahum King.

Food had never tasted better. And everyone at the fort was so kind. Dr. McLoughlin refused to take a penny for anyone's rescue passage on company craft, or for this banquet, or for treatment at the fort's little hospital. Half-ashamed, that's how I felt, seeing as none of us had spoken a good word about the Indians or the British the entire trip. Who'd have expected they'd turn out to be God's own agents in answering prayers?

"Looks like these grow good out here," Rowland said, cutting the peel away from a bit of apple for Jimmy to taste. "We'll have to plant some of our own soon as we can."

I nodded. That word: we. We, the Kings? We, you and I?

I glanced up and noticed Annie and Sol watching me and Rowland with little smiles.

Regrouped with all members and cattle herds, we reached the landing at Linnton on the Willamette the first of November. From there, our reassembled wagons threaded a twisting road up through a cut in the forested ridge. All during the muddy, uphill slog we got a miserable soaking from the far-famed northwest rains. Finally we came out into a clearing on the other side. Here, I expect, there might have been some glorious view had we not been so hopelessly enshrouded in clouds.

Below, in the mists, were the Tualatin Plains, watered by the first major tributary of the Willamette. We descended and then traversed these plains to the foothills of the Coast Range, where we found an enterprising settler by the name of Joseph Gale who offered us the use of an abandoned trapper's cabin.

We were glad to get it. Most of the folks from the summer's crossing were spreading out right around here, and we were like an invasion, instantly outnumbering the earlier settlers. I doubt there's ever been a case of so many being forced to rely on the charity of so few, and every vacant shed and smokehouse was quickly taken up. In our cabin by the creek, with supplies bought on credit at Fort Vancouver, we planned to hunker down until suitable land could be found.

The winter days were dreary. Sometimes I'd stand at the open door, looking up, hoping for some break in the weather. Mercy, when folks talked of the trees out here pushing up into the clouds, they usually weren't pointing out how blamed low to the ground those clouds might actually be hanging! Would they ever part? Here I was in Oregon, and I still had yet to lay eyes on a single one of those long-imagined scenes of sunlit green and gold. Jimmy would toddle over to cling to my knees, and eventually, someone would complain that I was letting in a draft. So I'd have to shut the door, go back to breathing the stale, smoky air of the tiny shack where, as Annie was always saying, we were packed in so tight you could stir us with a stick.

With the rain forever pounding on the leaky roof and dripping through it, too, it seemed plain on every face: Oregon was a disappointment. In every tired sigh or cough you could hear it, the feeling that this new place was not all we'd hoped, and certainly hadn't been worth the cost in the lives of those we'd lost.

With no more call to hurry, hurry, keep moving, the grief we'd almost seemed to outrun had at last caught up with us. We never spoke of it, but more than once I wandered away from the cabin to be alone and rid myself of the tears I'd never been able to shed back on the trail.

I tried to keep busy with a project, cutting out pieces of my wool blanket to sew into little coats for Meggie and Jimmy. Still, I had too much time to think.

Amos and Melinda announced their wedding date, only a few weeks off, and I'm ashamed how it bothered me, being reminded I had no certain place and other folks did. I knew I could go with Pa and Ma on their claim, but what about Meggie and Jimmy? I couldn't bear to be separated from them, but my folks wouldn't likely want to take on more little ones; they already had poor Little Lute to deal with. And Rowland wouldn't want to be apart from his children on any account.

He and Pa and my brothers rode out every chance they got, not only to find our land, but also, I'm sure, to get away from us. Who'd want to stay shut up in a shack packed with moody women, fussy children, and a line of steaming diapers that was forever strung across the room, slapping a hapless man in the face whenever he tried making his way to the fireplace pot, which never contained anything but plain boiled wheat anyway? Lord. I'd have got out too, given the chance. I couldn't help wondering if the general unpleasantness had actually helped Lucius and Stephen recover. Riding out with the other men must have looked a sight better than lying sick, stuck with this lot.

How eagerly we'd throw open the leather-hinged door at the sound of approaching horses on their return. Had they found the land? Could we finally get out of here?

But every single time the men would come back discouraged. A lot of the best claims, they reported, had already been taken up.

"Pa always complains I think too much," Isaac muttered one time, "but he's the picky one now. Made us pass up a fine section today."

"Now, look," Pa said. "We didn't drag ourselves two thousand miles just to start plowing land that's bound to go under water again!"

"But how can you tell it will?" I asked.

"Fence railings stuck in the trees kind of give you the idea," Rowland said dryly. "Your father's right, Lovisa. No more farms in the floodplain."

I picked up my sewing, sank back to my stool, and took up again the pastime in which, over this last year, I'd had far too much practice: Waiting.

Then, on a February day that seemed very like spring, the men rode up to the cabin, dismounted, and came bounding across the mud-packed yard.

"We found it," Rowland announced.

Well, if it's possible, my heart simultaneously jumped and sank. At last we had the prize, a tract of unspoiled, unsettled acreage some sixty miles up the valley, and for that my spirit soared. On the other hand, if the claims were taken up, things were going to be decided. Important things. And I feared which way they might go.

We weren't the only family astir. That very afternoon the Williams family stopped with us on their way south. They'd been camped under a huge fir tree all winter and now were headed down to claims not far from where we'd be settling.

"You mean to tell me that handsome brother-in-law of yours doesn't have a new wife yet?" Orlena said. We were standing in the yard, watching the men unhitch the horses. "Well. I thought sure he would by now."

I wrapped my arms around my middle. "Don't forget, my sister just died in September."

Orlena blinked her black eyelashes. "But way back on the trail, right? That was a long time ago. Folks have to get on with it."

Easy for her to say, I thought. Their family hadn't lost a single member.

We watched the reunion of her brother Jont and our Lydia, who gave each other shy, fond greetings, then walked away together toward the creek, swinging their joined hands between them.

"Don't people usually go through a year of mourning or something?" I offered, still thinking of Rowland.

Orlena waved that off. "I doubt you'll see folks sticking to any of that out here. People need partners. A man needs a wife." She looked across the yard at Rowland. "We need husbands."

I glanced at Annie in alarm. Bless her heart, I think she knew how I felt at that moment better than I did myself.

"Orlena," she said, "Rowland doesn't have a nickel." Because we'd all figured Orlena would be saving her beautiful self for the man with the best prospects. But Orlena merely shrugged. "No one does out here, haven't you noticed? But I figure I'm as good as the next girl at guessing who's most likely to have money soon."

"And you think Rowland will?" Annie glanced at me, conscious of my reaction to all this.

"Well, surely! For heaven's sake, look at him! Anyone can see he's a man who knows what he's about." Then she stopped and sighed. "Of course, personally, I'd rather not be taking on another woman's young ones right off."

Well! My eyes popped wide as I clamped my teeth down hard. Those children she didn't want were Meggie and Jimmy! She was saying all this like it was up to her to choose. She was saying it right in front of me, like it never occurred to her for one instant that Rowland might…oh, I just couldn't stand it.

Between knowing Orlena Williams was asleep right over there on the floor and the news about the claims, I lay awake in a dreadful fret all night. I wanted Orlena Williams out on the road again. I didn't want her having one more chance to flash her flirty smile at Rowland. And furthermore, I had gone on just about as long as I could stand with everything in an upheaval. I wanted things settled!

The Williams' wagons rolled out early, and it wasn't but midmorning when I found myself leaning in the doorway, watching Rowland and the others saddling up for Oregon City. They had to file on the land and buy supplies for the trek to the new claims.

I watched Rowland mount his mare. Look back, I willed him as they started off. This wasn't about Sally any more. Like Orlena said, life had to go on. It didn't matter how much Rowland had loved my sister. Sally was no longer one of his choices. But Orlena Williams might be, and the thought of that girl taking over as Meggie and Jimmy's mother…Well, I wasn't going to lay down in the dirt and let that happen without a scrappy scuffle!

My heart thudded in my throat as I watched Rowland trot off

behind Pa and my brothers. Go after him, I berated myself. Now! Quick! Or you'll miss this chance.

Just as he was about to disappear at the place where the trail curved behind the trees, he glanced back.

This was it.

"Rowland!" Hitching my skirts, I bolted after him.

He wheeled the horse and danced the creature in place as I flew across the yard, ran up and lurched to a halt.

"Rowland," I said, breathing hard. "I was just thinking. Aren't you…well, I was wondering…aren't you going to need help on your claim?"

He paused. "That's the advice folks give me."

I waited. "Well?"

He cocked his head, narrowing his eyes quizzically. Then he stood in his stirrups and signaled my brothers to head out, he'd catch up, and swung down off the horse.

"What did you have in mind?"

I looked off toward the creek. "What do you think?"

"Beats me."

"Rowland!" My face must have been a miserable red. I was in deep now. Obviously he'd never thought along these lines, and I was making a total fool of myself. "I thought," I began again. "Well, Meggie and Jimmy need a ma. Maybe the decent thing would be… well, I could marry you."

He rocked back a step. "Well. That's a handsome offer." His brow furrowed. "But I couldn't ask you to do that."

"Why not?"

He squinted up at the sky with a little half smile, then turned back to me. "You have kind of put it out there to everyone you don't much like me."

I hung my head. It's true, I'd made that complaint often enough. Foolish of me not to realize it would have got back to him.

"See here, Lovisa, we got the wagon and the kids to Oregon. I don't think your pa meant to obligate you beyond that."

"Oh, Rowland." My voice came out husky. "You know I like you fine." I stabbed the toe of my boot in the mud, one of the very boots Rowland had mended for me. "More than fine. I...that other was just...little-girl talk. Sister-in-law talk."

He didn't answer, just kept looking at me like he was waiting for more.

"Maybe it scared me how much I really did like you," I said, looking up now, meeting his eyes. "You were Sally's. I wasn't supposed to."

"Lovisa." He looked away. Looked back.

"And I know I'm not like Sally."

He scrunched up his mouth. "Sally was Sally. You're you. And Lovisa, you've already done way more than I had any right to ask."

"You did for me, too," I protested. "Didn't we kind of...take care of each other? Don't you think we make a good team?"

"Well." He cocked his head. "We got here."

And nobody but the two of us would ever know exactly what that meant. Or all that we'd been through together.

"I don't want a wife who's feeling beholden."

"Beholden! Oh, Rowland..."

"Look around, Lovisa. Not a whole lot of young, marrying-age women out here yet. You girls are like gold." Now his voice went soft. "And you, Lovisa, a girl like you could have her pick."

"I could?"

He grinned. "You don't see that, do you?"

"Well, Rowland, if that's true, it's simple then. If I get my pick, I pick you."

He laughed and ran his hand through his hair. "All right, then." He laughed again like he wasn't quite believing this. "And here I'd been thinking this was such a big day already, going in to file those claims."

I smiled back at him. This was a big day.

"Well," he said finally after we'd stood there looking at each other long enough. "Well."

And then he leaned down and kissed me.

Now this was a first kiss. It had nothing to do with the rush of spring, nothing to do with the thrill of finally finding our land. It had everything to do with the fact that, at last, this was Rowland Chambers kissing me, Lovisa King.

And yes, I kissed him right back!

Took it as an excellent omen, too, when he made it plain this was perfectly fine with him.

We were still grinning like fools as he remounted his horse, both of us somehow surprised, I think, at this quick settling of things and, at the same time, ridiculously pleased with ourselves. As he cantered off to catch up with the others, I spun on my heel and spied several female heads pulling back inside the doorway. Busybodies! But I was far too happy to be truly annoyed.

Marching in, I found everyone watching me, waiting expectantly.

"I have some news," I said. "I'm to marry Rowland."

My sisters burst out laughing.

"What?" I said, baffled. "What's funny?"

"The way you said it," Annie told me, "as if you'd just now figured it out."

I blinked. "Well, I did."

"Oh, mercy," Hope said as I unpeeled Jimmy's arms from around my legs and picked him up.

Abbie grinned. "We've all known it for ages."

"What!"

"Isn't it lucky," Lydia added, "that the two of them finally caught on?"

Go ahead and laugh, I thought, bouncing Jimmy. It's not always so easy to figure out how things ought to go or what you ought to do. I was just grateful to have made up my mind now and have such a surefooted feeling about my decision. This was a road I could start down and know, with each step, I was headed in the right direction. This was a fate to which I could gladly give my heart.

I'd seen it all out there on the trail. Rowland Chambers was the finest man I'd ever known, and I was going to be proud to be his wife.

I figured that's about all there was to it.

CHAPTER 20

AND SO IT CAME THAT WHEN I FIRST LAID
eyes on the land that would be known ever after as Kings Valley, I
was seeing it as Rowland's new bride, sitting right up there beside
him on the seat of the same old wagon that had carried us all the
way from Carroll County, Missouri, the wagon in which I had most
vehemently wished not to ride. I had to smile at myself, remembering. Good thing I didn't get my way.

Once more we'd packed our goods, hitching up not oxen this time
but horses, and set off on the final leg of our journey. Following an
old Hudson's Bay Company trail, we skirted the western perimeter
of the Willamette Valley and, after fording a small stream, forked
off on a less-traveled path running through the gentle swells of the
first of the Coast Range foothills.

I will never forget the moment we crested the rough trail's rise
and I saw spread before me our little valley. The sun was lowering,
sending slanted gold rays across the landscape. Not another settler

in sight. Just a beautiful broad sweep of green grass running up to thickly timbered hills.

Rowland pointed to the west. "The river runs along there."

"Where the trees are?"

He nodded. "They call it the Luckiamute."

Beyond the near ridges to the southwest rose the pale blue of a high and gracefully sloped mountain. Such a fair prospect. I loved the look of those layered ridges against the sky, and honestly, right then I didn't care if I never again in my life gazed out at a flat horizon.

Rowland was watching me. "Like it?"

Turning to him with brimming eyes, I nodded.

Pa and Rowland and my brothers had already laid out the various claims on their first trip. Now Pa suggested drawing straws for first choice.

"Fair enough," Rowland said, "but if you let me choose first, I'll take the section with the little fall in the river and build a gristmill there. You'll have my word on it."

Rowland looked at Pa. Pa looked at his own sons. Everyone nodded. They knew if Rowland Chambers said he would build a mill, he would do it. That's exactly what this new land needed—people with plans, people you could count on to see those plans through.

Carrying Meggie and Jimmy, Rowland and I walked out into the grass of our claim—640 beautiful acres.

"Look here," Rowland said, leading me through a grove of alders. "I thought you'd like this."

Our own little stream, a branch of clean, clear water rushing over stones down to the river.

"It's exactly like I pictured!" I cried, setting Meggie on her feet, picking up my skirts to hurry along the gravelly bank. "I saw this, Rowland," I called back over my shoulder, then whirled to face him again. "I saw it in my mind all those days on the desert!"

And here it had been all along.

Here was the green grass, here was the clear, pure water. Here was the soil that Rowland scooped up from between the grass roots and regarded with deep satisfaction.

But as we strolled the fields on that first and ever-to-be-remembered day, when we were young and fresh and life once again seemed full of every good possibility, I was seeing not just what lay before us now, but what would be in the years to come—the snug log house with a stone chimney, the gated garden full of every fruit and vegetable promised to grow in abundance here, the woolly lambs that would someday frolic in the meadows.

I saw our children, Meggie and Jimmy, the other babies yet to come, the children who would grow up with the country.

Meggie tugged on my skirt, her face turned up brightly. "This is really Oregon now, isn't it, Mama?"

Rowland and I shared a quick flash of delight. And then for a moment we just looked at each other. We had come so far together already, and perhaps all those trials weren't the worst way for love to begin. Now, God willing, we had many good years ahead of us to make all these visions of ours come true.

Meggie tugged again for attention. "Is it?"

"Yes, sweetheart," I said, smiling, scooping up our little girl and holding her so she could see all the way across the green valley.

"This is Oregon."

THE YEARS BEYOND

NAHUM AND SAREPTA KING SAW THEIR DREAM

come true; their remaining children settled on good Oregon land.

That first summer, Abigail married Price Fuller. They settled on a claim next to his father's in the neighboring Soap Creek Valley. They had two daughters and a son.

Arnold Fuller, who buried his first wife at the beginning of the trail, eventually remarried. He donated land for the one-room Soap Creek School, which still stands north of Corvallis. His tombstone in nearby Locke Cemetery bears the proud inscription "A pioneer of 1845."

Hopestill and Lucius Norton took up the claim adjacent to Rowland and Lovisa's and settled down to farm, producing eight more children, including a set of triplets. When Lucius died in 1859 at the age of forty, Hopestill packed up the children and moved to the nearby upper Yaquina Valley where she operated a way station for travelers.

Amos and Melinda Fuller married and, in 1849, bought up the 535-acre claim of two men who were joining the gold rush to California. There, for a while, they ran a tannery. The land, which encompassed a good deal of what is now downtown Portland, made the family wealthy as it was slowly sold off in city lots. The Kings were considered highly public-spirited when they sold forty prime acres to the city at a fraction of its actual value for the establishment of Washington Park, the section in which the statue of Sacagawea stands today. The Kings Heights district is named for them, as is the street called Melinda.

Isaac married a girl who came to Oregon in the emigration of 1846. They held a large claim in the Wren area, near Kings Valley, and had several children. Isaac was killed by a gunshot in his own barn on his forty-seventh birthday. Whether it was an accident, suicide, or murder has never been determined, but oral histories of Kings Valley include stories of a ghost haunting the barn where he died.

Lydia married Jonathan "Jont" Williams in 1847, when she was sixteen.

Annie had a baby a few years after arriving in Oregon, but her husband, Stephen King, died not long after. Annie was a thirty-one-year-old widow when Solomon, now twenty, married her. They had several children and eventually settled their family on a prosperous spread encompassing the present-day Kings Boulevard area in Corvallis. A popular man, Sol served five consecutive terms as sheriff of Benton County in the 1880s. Family legend has it that until the day death parted them, Sol referred to his wife as "Miss Annie."

Some say it was Solomon King who rode back later and located his older sister Sally's lonely grave in order to place a carved stone on it. The resting place of Sarah King Chambers is located north of Beulah Reservoir, at the foot of Castle Rock on the north fork of the Malheur River, and of the thousands who died on the overland trail between 1841 and 1869, hers remains today one of only a handful that is marked.

Rowland Chambers became the family's patriarch in Kings Valley and built the grist mill as promised. The grinding stone was imported from France, shipped around the Horn and hauled to Kings Valley from Portland in the very wagon that had brought the family west from Missouri. According to the family, Lovisa was in labor the afternoon the wheel, with great difficulty, was being installed. After a day of such ordeals, they jokingly named their new baby daughter "Ordelia." The mill, the first in the area, ground flour for fifty years and is now mounted for display in the rose garden at Avery Park in Corvallis.

The two of them had fourteen children together, the first of whom they named Sarah, after Sally. When Willamette University opened, the first institution of higher learning in the state, Rowland and Lovisa's children were among the earliest students. Little Jimmy grew up to serve as president of Philomath College.

When Nahum King died, the widowed Sarepta came to live with her daughter Lovisa. Sarepta died in 1863 and Rowland died in 1870, leaving Lovisa the forty-two-year-old matriarch of the Kings Valley clan. As of this writing, there are approximately 450 living descendants of Lovisa, Rowland, Margaret, and James Chambers.

In 1888, the year before Lovisa died, she and Hopestill held the first family reunion, and the annual event has been a tradition ever since. Each June, some of the hundreds of King descendants gather in Kings Valley to celebrate the family's proud pioneer heritage.

Lovisa, in her best white apron, gathers the clan for Thanksgiving in Kings Valley in 1887.

THE KING FAMILY
IN OREGON

LOVISA KING WAS A REAL PERSON.

She and her family endured the gravest of hardships on their journey west, but despite many obstacles, they managed to prosper in their new life in Oregon. New generations were born in the new land, and a King legacy was left behind throughout Oregon. The United States was so young when the Kings left for their destiny in 1845—a mere sixty-nine years old—that some of those who made the journey had actually been alive during the birth of our nation. As America matured, so did the Kings, each generation adapting to—and participating in—change.

Lovisa was wed on February 22, 1846, in Washington County, Oregon Territory, to her brother-in-law, Rowland Chambers, a widower following the death of Lovisa's sister, Sarah "Sally" King Chambers. Members of the King family spent their first winter south of Portland on the Tuality Plains. The men went out on horseback during that winter to locate land claims. Each claim was approximately 640 acres along the Luckiamute River, in the northern Benton County valley that now bears the family's name, Kings Valley. The valley, about six miles long and two miles wide, offered quality, fertile land for growing crops and raising livestock.

Moving to the new land in the spring of 1846 posed many hardships. The first orders of business were to build homes, to till the land for planting crops, and to establish

The grist mill that Rowland Chambers built at Kings Valley, Oregon, about 1854 or 1856.

The extended family of David and Mary King gathered in front of their home near Philomath in the 1890s.

lines of good livestock. King family members were to draw lots from a hat for the land claims. Rowland volunteered to build a gristmill for the area, in return for a particular claim along the Luckiamute, where he had noted an outcropping of rocks that produced a natural four-foot waterfall. Everyone agreed to let him have the land, and he kept his promise, building the gristmill in 1852 with the help of A.H. Reynolds and Lovisa's brother, Stephen. According to the account book kept by Reynolds, the cost was at least $7520.13, a staggering amount of money at the time. However, it paid off. The mill was in use for over sixty years, grinding out high-quality flour from locally grown wheat.

Rowland and Lovisa's first home was essentially a log cabin. Later on, they built a larger house, with high ceilings, numerous bedrooms, large halls, a parlor, a kitchen, a dining room, and even a pie room where mincemeat pies were set on shelves to freeze in the winter. Lovisa may have had the first house in Kings Valley to contain a stove. Fire nearly destroyed this house, and the house that replaced it can still be seen along the Kings Valley highway.

Lovisa and Rowland's greatest legacy is not, however, the buildings they left behind; it is their fourteen children, seven boys and seven girls, and the generations that followed them. Sadly, only twelve of their children reached adulthood. In 1879, two of their daughters, Annie and Alice, died tragically during a diphtheria outbreak. A stroll through the Kings Valley cemetery where these two girls are buried together reveals a staggering number of people who died during this same period, a testament to the threat this disease posed at the time.

The twelve children who survived all went on to marry and have children of their own. The first of the Chambers children, Sarah, married William Watson of Kings Valley and bore him eight children. They lived in Lewiston, Idaho. William Chambers married Minnie Fairchild and resided in Portland. Jackson (Jack) Chambers married Martha Culp and had two children, staying in Canyon City, Oregon. John Chambers married Mary Burgett and fathered three sons. Franklin (Jake) Chambers married Emma Maxfield. He and John both stayed in Kings Valley. Henry Chambers and his wife, Barbara, had one son and lived in Whitcom County, Washington, before moving to Portland. Ordelia (Delia) Chambers married Henry David Randall, a schoolteacher in Kings Valley, and they raised eleven children in Olex, Washington, before settling in Portland in later years. Samuel Chambers raised two sons in Newport, Oregon. Lydia Chambers married Hiram (Tip) Maxfield and bore eleven children in Kings Valley. Rebecca Chambers married Asa B. Alexander, raising three daughters in Benton County. Julia Chambers and Larkin Price married and had five children, living in Corvallis, Oregon. Lincoln (Link) Chambers wed Cora Garrison and raised three children, also living in Corvallis.

When she married Rowland, Lovisa became the stepmother of Margaret and James, Rowland's children from his first marriage. Margaret grew up, married Orthellow Bagley, and had five children. She died in 1882 and is buried in Portland. James married Clarinda Kisor, and they had five children as well. James died in 1883, at the age of thirty-eight, and is buried in Kings Valley cemetery. He had become a teacher in Kings Valley, and went on to become President of Philomath College. Margaret and James's mother, Sarah, died at the age of twenty-two, but her legacy has survived, in part because of her sister, Lovisa. Sarah's grave is of historical interest, as it is believed to be the only marked grave along the Meek Cutoff, the treacherous shortcut followed by the King family. Sarah was buried on a sage-covered hillside above the North Fork of the Malheur River near present day Beulah Reservoir, under the watchful eye of Castle Rock in Eastern Oregon. On September 3, 1995, exactly one hundred and fifty years after she died, King family descendants met for a commemoration of the event. Present were Warren King,

Charles William "Bill" King, James King, Patricia Holler, Carole Putman, and David Trask, representing descendants from Sarah's brothers, Sol and Isaac, and sister, Hopestill, ancestors who had stood at that very spot a century and a half earlier.

Much of what we know about early life in the new settlement comes from interviews conducted by Mark Phinney during the Depression as part of the Historic Records Survey of Benton County. During this survey, Mark interviewed two of Lovisa and Rowland's last three surviving children, Julia Price, who died in 1945, and Rebecca Alexander, who passed away in 1951. Julia described the importance of compassion in her family. When her grandfather, Nahum King, decided to take the family to Oregon, Julia's father Rowland was originally going to stay behind in Missouri because he couldn't afford the trip. Nahum, however, insisted on funding the trip for Rowland and his wife Sarah. Whether it was an advance or a gift, Nahum's gesture showed that keeping the family together was of the utmost importance to the Kings. This instilled a strong sense of values in the family, which Rowland and Lovisa passed on to their children and to subsequent generations, and which can be seen even today in their living descendants.

Rowland and Lovisa considered their children's education a high priority. Julia stated during her interview that she and her siblings first attended school in the Chambers' house. Even though Rowland was not at all wealthy during those early years, he hired a teacher for his children because "the roads were bad and the school terms too short," said Julia. Rowland did not want his children walking to and from school in bad weather. Soon, Julia and the other children attended the "Little Red Schoolhouse," located about two miles south of the present day Kings Valley store. This is where her half-brother James taught initially. "We studied the three Rs and geography. There was a class in algebra for the older boys." Some of Julia's brothers and sisters went on to attend a school in Salem, which later became Willamette University. Many of the Chambers, as well as other King descendants, graduated with degrees from schools that are now Western State University and Oregon State University. The early emphasis was on learning the agricultural trade, but as time passed, King descendants became educated and received degrees in other fields.

A strong work ethic was a must in order to survive the new life out west. Great effort went into farming and raising livestock in order to make the settlement self-sufficient. Initially, the land had to be tilled by hand with the help of oxen. In time, tractors and combines became available and helped to raise and harvest the crops. Despite the modern equipment, the work remained difficult.

Lovisa and Rowland took pride in their work and in their children. They wanted their children dressed well, and dressing them well required a lot of manual work. Rebecca said, "When my folks first came to Oregon, they spun and wove the wool of their own sheep to make all their clothing. Mother would spin and my sisters would weave. After there came to be carding mills in the country, they would buy the rolls already carded. I used to hate my home-spun dress and wished for a nicer one, but I was quite a good-sized girl before I got one. Mother would dye the wool with peach leaves and different kinds of bark." This process required a good deal of hard work for all, and demonstrated a desire to provide nice things for loved ones, as well as a sense of confidence that it could be done. All the hard work the Kings and Chambers put into building a new life ultimately paid off; Rowland amassed a wealth of property during his lifetime, an investment that would benefit his children in the years to come.

In their interviews, both Julia and Rebecca told of strong church and community values that were a part of their upbringing. Attending church services was an important part of life for the King family. In the beginning, church was held once a month, but it became a

Part of the extended King family pose together in the 1930s.

weekly event after 1873. Dancing was prohibited in Kings Valley in the early years. The children would engage in innocent, dance-like games, though, and enjoyed singing and participating in community and church activities, such as the annual May Day picnic. Another tradition was the family reunion, usually consisting of Chambers and other King descendants. We know that these were held before Lovisa died in 1889 and usually included a large dinner for the many attendees. Over the years, reunions have continued to be held annually. Since the 1930s, the yearly event has been referred to as the King-Chambers-Norton reunion, and is now held on the third Saturday in June.

The reunion attendees, of course, changed over time. Death was all too common in the early days and had to be contended with often and sometimes unexpectedly. Julia and Rebecca recounted when their sisters, eleven-year-old Alice and fourteen-year-old Annie, died May 25 and May 27, 1879, respectively, of diphtheria. Rebecca and her husband's own two-year-old daughter Minnie had fallen ill with

Lovisa and Rowland's descendants erected this obelisk in their honor in the Kings Valley Cemetery. Lovisa's original headstone is propped at its base.

the same horrible disease just two weeks prior. Julia was afflicted with diphtheria at the same time as her sisters. Although larger families were common in those days, it was no less painful for family members to lose a loved one than it is for today's comparatively smaller families. Death affected siblings and parents for many years. Rowland had already passed away before the deaths of his two daughters, but Lovisa and her other children never forgot the tragic loss of these two girls, as evidenced during the interview with Julia and Rebecca nearly fifty years later. Both recalled that Alice and Annie were buried together in Kings Valley cemetery wearing their new dresses, which had been made for them just weeks before to celebrate the annual May Day picnic. Later generations would often recall stories of such sad events affecting family members for many years after.

Military service is another proud legacy left by King descendants, and many have proudly worn the uniforms of our national armed forces over the years. King descendants have served bravely in every major war during the twentieth century. Some even gave their lives during World War I, World War II, Korea and Vietnam and are buried in national cemeteries including Portland, Eagle Point, Oregon, and San Francisco. There are currently King descendants serving in the War on Terror.

Rowland died in 1870; Lovisa in 1889. Perhaps the greatest legacy they left behind is summarized by Charlotte Price Wirfs, their great-great-granddaughter.

> "Lovisa's children were infused with self-confidence and a desire to do better, not only for themselves, but for their family members and for the community. Julia ends her interview saying 'I have had a good time, but would like to live it all over again. I think I could do a lot better.' I [Charlotte] never knew Julia, my great-grandmother, but I did know that Julia was respected, valued,

appreciated, and well loved. She is remembered that way because her mother, Lovisa, was a nurturing individual and passed on those traits to Julia, who in turn passed them on to my grandfather, and my father, and then to me. Through me, those traits are being passed on to my son and daughter and to their children. I would have told Julia that she and her siblings did good enough and there was little left to improve."

As a cousin to Charlotte through our mutual ancestor Isaac King, Lovisa's brother, I could not agree any more with what Charlotte said. The values of which she spoke extend through Isaac and all of his descendants, as well as the descendants of Lovisa's other siblings, many of whom attend the Kings-Chambers-Norton Family reunions. Lovisa's legacy of love and strength runs throughout all of the branches of the King family tree and will likely manifest itself in the generations to come.

David M. Trask
King Family Historian
July 1989–present

Haley Thompson, eighth-generation descendant of Lovisa's elder sister Hopestill, in Benton County, Oregon.

AUTHOR'S NOTE

In researching the history of the Oregon Trail to better imagine what the trek of 1845 might have been like for the King family, I have relied heavily on original trail journals kept by the pioneers. Although I read many reminiscences recorded in later years as well, these must always be put in the perspective of hindsight, particularly as regards the treatment of Indian encounters. Some pioneers, swapping stories decades later, seem to have felt the need to maximize the Indian threat. Maybe they simply wanted to tell a more dramatic story. Or perhaps so much energy was expended fearing the Natives, they honestly felt they had survived an Indian ordeal, conveniently forgetting that in so many cases relatively little actually came of those fears. In imagining the crossing of the King family in 1845, I have tried to fairly portray the actual reported encounters with Native Americans—which is to say, horse thievery was an annoyance—but in far more instances, Indians helped the overlanders. All of the instances of aid are based on journal entries, including the spearing of a salmon from a shallow pool.

Much has been written about the overland trail experience, and I thought I'd already covered the majority of it when a costumed guide at Fort Laramie, Mike McKinley, recommended *The Plains Across* by John Unruh. Written as a doctoral thesis, this book turned out to be the most comprehensive analysis of the trail's history I encountered. While many studies purport to present the "typical" covered wagon journey, Unruh shows how the experience traveling the road to Oregon changed over time. A trip in 1845 was thus very different from one taken in 1860. Even year to year there were great variances. The composition of the trains of the Gold Rush years of 1849 and 1850 were quite different from any other years, for example, and 1852 stands out for the high numbers of emigrants who succumbed to the scourge of cholera, a disease felling emigrants mainly between 1849 and 1854 but often not encountered at all by those traveling in other years. In general we can note that in the roughly three decades the trail was heavily traveled, the logistics of travel itself became easier. At first even the smallest creek was without a bridge, and there were only a handful of supply posts. Twenty-five years later, the road had been transformed. Bridges, ferries, trading posts, and even towns marked the entire route. On the other hand, difficulties with Indian encounters increased.

Only recently have efforts been made to fully document deaths resulting from emigrant and Indian interactions. As it turns out, far more Indians died at the hands of whites than the other way around, and all told, the number of overlanders killed by Indians is certainly small when compared with the typical Hollywood depiction. Most of the conflicts occurred after the Indians began to realize how deadly the threat of the vast emigration of whites would be to the survival of their culture. As documented by the earliest settlers, helpful encounters with Natives far outnumbered the negative, although sometimes it seemed the journalists themselves didn't realize this. I was particularly struck by one woman who almost daily wrote of being helped across rivers by Indians or of the beneficial trades they offered, and then would faithfully note that the truly dangerous and threatening Indians were reported to be lying in wait, just ahead. As she traveled the trail, she refused to notice that her worst fears simply were not materializing, and, to the final entry, her opinion of Native Americans never seemed to be influenced in the slightest by her actual experience.

I am indebted to Donna Wojcik Montgomery for *The Brazen Overlanders of 1845*, a massive collection of what must surely be every single fact documented regarding the pioneers of that year. Likewise to Keith Clark and Lowell Tiller for *Terrible Trail: The Meek Cutoff, 1845*, which does a wonderful job of narrowing the focus to the probable route of those who took the "shortcut." Irene Paden's

1938 work, *In the Wake of the Prairie Schooners*, provides a detailed description of the trail itself both as it was in the pioneer years and in the 1930s, when she and her family spent a decade exploring the route by automobile.

If anyone in the King family kept a journal of the trip, no one seems aware of its existence, so I was unable to document with accuracy exactly where the family was each day or, since the larger company divided and reorganized several times, who they were traveling with on any particular segment of the trail. Several journals kept by others do document the ill-fated journey into the cut-off country, and these have been painstakingly studied by many before me in order to map the probable route.

It certainly seems that the great interest in discovering the old route of Meek's Cut-off (some have spent several summers driving every mile of the ruts in eastern and central Oregon) stems in large part from the perpetuation of the legend of the Blue Bucket Mine. The story has it that children on the trek had brought yellow nuggets from a stream into camp in a blue bucket, but no one at the time truly registered that it was, in fact, gold. Hopeful prospectors have been searching for it ever since.

To many, the notion of gold in eastern Oregon must be the most intriguing aspect of this entire story, and perhaps they would be surprised that I make no mention of it in *A Heart for Any Fate*. It seems clear to me, however, that to my characters, lost in the desert, desperate and dying, gold would have been of relatively little concern.

In later accounts of this story, mention is sometimes made of Stephen Meek's plans to lead the wagon trains through the Cascade Mountains and directly into the Willamette Valley. I never found any hint of this in contemporary journal accounts, however, and chose to depict the planned route as it made sense to me. Wagons had never been taken through the Cascades before, and it was only in September of this year—1845—that Sam Barlow hacked through, for the first time, what would become the Barlow Pass around Mount Hood. I couldn't imagine even an overconfident Stephen Meek thinking he might attempt to bring hundreds of wagons over a trackless, heavily forested mountain range, or the King family and others agreeing to go along.

On the face of it, the "Trapper's Trail," as some called it, might have made perfect sense as a shortcut, and in a different year, the story's outcome itself might have been quite different. The year 1845 was exceptionally dry, and apparently the shallow lakes Meek remembered from earlier treks had completely evaporated. How uneasy he must have felt as it dawned on him the country did not look at all as he recalled. How horrified he must have been to realize he had led hundreds of people into a desert only to find that the water he had counted on was gone.

Readers may be interested to learn where the line between fact and fiction has been drawn in this novel. While births, deaths, and marriages are documented, the actual personalities of the King and Fuller family members are, for the most part, the product of my imagination, the only clues coming from a few recorded facts of their later lives. In only one instance did I claim poetic license and knowingly contradict the historical record regarding the Kings. The family apparently did not approve of dancing, but I couldn't bear to let my characters miss out on the trail dances that seemed to loom large in the memories of many pioneers.

The vast majority of incidents described in the novel were inspired by anecdotes from trail diaries. For the record, the "camp fever" that felled so many was probably a form of typhus spread by body lice. The trees referred to in diaries as "scrubby cedars" were juniper.

Almost all of the people named are real, and their fates were as depicted. John Noble (I wouldn't dare make up that name!) was a real person who died of camp fever as described, to the great anguish of his father, who did, indeed, blame Meek and threaten to kill him. Whether John and Lovisa ever actually knew each other is pure speculation on my part, but there's certainly no reason to think they wouldn't have met somewhere along the way.

Likewise, Sarah Helmick was a real girl who did lose her wedding trousseau in the Columbia about the same time the Kings were descending the rapids themselves. Sarah lived a long and fruitful life in Oregon and generously gave part of her land donation claim for what is now Sarah Helmick State Park in Polk County.

Orlena Williams was the belle of the company as described, impressing a lieutenant with the dragoons enough that he noted in his journal she was sure to cause a sensation among the young men upon her arrival in the Willamette Valley. She married a man of thirty-one, Isaac Staats, that first spring in Oregon. Interestingly, the husbands of Orlena and Sarah Helmick were, like Rowland Chambers, the first to set up grist mills in their respective areas.

The exceptions to named characters being real are the Browns. According to accounts, it seems every overland company was plagued by at least one truly difficult, quarrelsome, or annoying family. I gave mine a fictitious name because descendants of trail pioneers treasure their heritage and the memories of their ancestors, and to assign petty foibles to names drawn randomly from a trail roster simply for the sake of using a real name hardly seemed fair.

My own great-great-grandmother, Minerva Strawser, traveled the Oregon Trail in the 1860s. I'm proud of that, but I know nothing more of her story, and a name and family connection are not enough on which to base a novel. So it's been a pleasure and a privilege to share the rich family history of the Kings and all the others who did leave records of their westward journeys. I have loved imagining Lovisa's story.

Linda Crew
Corvallis, Oregon

ACKNOWLEDGMENTS

I am grateful to the staff at Ooligan Press for their enthusiasm in choosing to reprint *A Heart for Any Fate* after the original publisher, Oregon Historical Society Press, was forced to cease operations.

I remain grateful to all those who helped me with the original research and writing of the book. These include Mary Gallagher at the Benton County Historical Museum; Eugene and Lillie Audsley of the Carroll County (Missouri) Genealogical Society Association; Mimi Stang, for King family contacts and for continuing to promote the book; Robin Metzger, for spinning wheel advice; Jeff Hieb, for advice on oxen; Gail Carbiener, for graveside maps; Ann Dickerson, for guiding me to the covered wagon paintings at the Benton County Courthouse; and Joe Mardis, for help in pinning down original land claims.

Thanks to the King family descendants who shared research materials and family stories, including Daniel Frommherz, Earle Greig, Norm Chambers, Charlotte Wirfs, James H. King, Charlotte Murphy, Thia Bell, Maxine Bell, Pat Bearden, Fred Raw, Lou Raw Baxter, and David Trask.

A special thanks to Jay Ungar and Molly Mason, as well as to the members of our own beloved Trail Band, for the unending inspiration I found in their music. I listened to their CDs literally thousands of times during my research and writing and while driving the trail itself. I have always loved the song "Shenandoah." Their versions are my favorites.

Thanks to those friends and relatives who read and offered suggestions on my manuscript: Mike Kinch, Molly Gloss, Margaret Anderson, Mary Crew, Bob Welch, Sally Welch, Margaret Chang, and Clara Hadjimarkos. Special thanks to the two readers and friends I've come to think of as my angels on this particular book and in my life—Nancy Ashby and Theresa Nelson. They know why.

As always, I remain grateful for the support of my family, especially my husband and best friend, Herb.

ILLUSTRATIONS

"Grass Helm Waving in the Breeze Green Stormy Field." *Courtesy of Image*After.com, 2008.*

"Cumulus Clouds over Yellow Prairie2." *Courtesy of Wing-Chi Poon via Wikimedia Commons Creative Commons Attribution ShareAlike 2.5 license, 2006.*

Thanksgiving dinner, Kings Valley, November 25, 1887. Lovisa Chambers (in white apron) and Hopestill King Norton (seated second to the right of Lovisa) are posed, along with 29 members of their families, in front of the Kings Valley Store. *Courtesy of Benton County Historical Society & Museum 2003-062.00010.*

The grist mill that Rowland Chambers built at Kings Valley, Oregon, about 1854 or 1856. *Courtesy of Benton County Historical Society & Museum 1994-038.0231.*

The extended family of David and Mary King gathered in front of their home near Philomath in the 1890s. Photograph by S.B. Graham. *Courtesy of Benton County Historical Society & Museum 1989-049.0006.*

Part of the extended King family pose together in the 1930s. *Courtesy of Benton County Historical Society & Museum 2000-026.0062.*

Lovisa and Rowland's descendants erected this obelisk in their honor in the Kings Valley Cemetery. Lovisa's original headstone is propped at its base. *Courtesy of Linda Crew, photographer, 2004.*

Haley Thompson, eighth-generation descendant of Lovisa's elder sister Hopestill, in Benton County, Oregon. *Courtesy of Linda Crew, photographer, 2004.*

ABOUT THE AUTHOR

Linda enjoys exploring stories she feels uniquely situated to research. In preparation for writing A Heart for Any Fate, she and her husband retraced the Oregon Trail by car from Missouri to their home at Wake Robin Farm in the Willamette Valley—the end of the trail for so many pioneers. Linda's choice of the Kings as the main characters came from her attachment to Kings Valley in her native Benton County. Recently, Linda and her husband were able to fulfill a dream by acquiring forested property adjacent to some of the original King family land donation claims, where they farm trees. Linda looks forward to many happy days of working in Kings Valley.

ABOUT OOLIGAN PRESS

Ooligan Press is a general trade press at Portland State University. In addition to publishing books that honor cultural and natural diversity, it is dedicated to teaching the art and craft of publishing.

As a teaching press, Ooligan makes as little distinction as possible between the press and the classroom. Under the direction of professional faculty and staff, the work of the Press is done by students enrolled in the Book Publishing graduate program at PSU. Publishing profitable books in real markets provides projects in which students combine theory with practice.

Ooligan Press offers the school and general community a full range of publishing services, from consulting and planning to design and production. Ooligan Press students, having already received important "real world" training while at the university and in various internship positions in the greater Portland area, are ideal candidates for jobs in the country's growing community of independent publishers.

This edition of *A Heart for Any Fate* was produced by the following students on behalf of Ooligan Press:

Acquisitions Editors
Twig Delugé
Kylin Larsson
Megan Wellman

Copyeditors
Scott Parker
Leah Sims
Ian VanWyhe

Cover Designer
Rachel S. Tobie

Interior Designer
Kari Smit

Project Managers
Carly Cohen
Twig Delugé
Bradi Grebien-Samkow
Megan Petersen-Kindem
Whitney Quon
Emmalisa Sparrow
Amanda Taylor
Megan Wellman

Proofreaders
Daniel Chabon
Heather Frazier
Sarah Peters
Matt Schrunk

COLOPHON

Interior set in ITC New Baskerville Std, Bodini Std, Mesquite Std, and Rosewood Std.

Cover set in Adobe Garamond and Old Claude LP.